SEDUCING
THE WIDOW

Praise for Jane Walsh

The Inconvenient Heiress

"Reading a Jane Walsh novel is a dream with every page. It's a reminder that we have always been here, that we have always been finding community and finding love, that we have always risked it all and been rewarded for our bravery, that queer love is about the quiet moments as well as the loud ones, that we deserve to wear flowy gowns and make our art and find our future, that we deserve to have our love and care returned to us in spades, that we deserve and deserve and deserve."—*The Lesbrary*

"I enjoyed every moment of this. Those forbidden feelings and moments Arabella and Caroline shared were magical, but when everything changed for Caroline and she had to contemplate marriage, my heart broke for them both. I was completely invested in them being together and so being on that emotional roller coaster with them, especially Arabella. I could only hope they might get their chance…[Jane] has a real talent for delivering exciting regency romances that are rich, loving, and deeply sentimental."—*LESBIreviewed*

Her Duchess to Desire

"One of Walsh's strongest points is her ability to build a strong, positive queer community in a time period that is known to have sometimes been hostile to them…I love an Ice Queen heroine who melts in the hands of the right person, and Anne is a great personification of that."—*Courtney Reads Romance*

"What a fantastic story. Not like anything I have read before, so it was exciting and new and captured my imagination right from the start. Everything is so regal, from the characters, to the lifestyle, to the exquisite designs that Letitia draws up and produces. I just closed my eyes and could picture it all perfectly. It was the element of forbidden romance between Anne and Letitia that had me hooked because it was delicious, came with risks, and none of us knew what the consequences would be."—*LESBIreviewed*

Her Countess to Cherish

"This book was a nice surprise to me in its portrayal of gender fluidity, along with a delightful romance between two sympathetic characters. If you love queer historical romance, you should absolutely check this out."—*Courtney Reads Romance*

Her Lady to Love

"If you are looking for a sweet, cozy romance with grounded leads, this is for you. The author's dedication to the little cultural details do help flesh out the setting so much more. I also loved how buttery smooth everything tied together. Nothing seemed to be out of place, and the romance had some stakes...Highly recommended."
—*Colleen Corgel, Librarian, Queens Public Library*

"Walsh debuts with a charming if flawed Regency romance... Though Honora's shift from shy curiosity to boldly stated interest feels a bit abrupt, her relationship with Jacquie is sweet, sensual, and believable. Subplots about a group of bluestockings and a society of LGBTQ Londoners add depth."—*Publishers Weekly*

"What a delightful queer Regency era romance...*Her Lady to Love* was a beautiful addition to the romance genre, and a much appreciated queer involvement. I'll definitely be looking into more of Walsh's works!"—*Dylan Miller, Librarian, Baltimore County Public Library*

"[I]t's the perfect novel to read over the holidays if you love gorgeous writing, beautiful settings, and literal bodice ripping! I had such a brilliant time with this book. Walsh's novel has such an excellent sense of the time period she's writing in, and her specificity and interest in the historical aspects of her plot really allow the characters to shine. The inclusion of details, specifically related to women's behaviour or dress, made for a vivid and exciting setting. This novel reminded me a lot of something like *Vanity Fair* (1847) (but with lesbians!) because of its gorgeous setting and intriguing plot."
—*The Lesbrary*

By the Author

Her Lady to Love

Her Countess to Cherish

Her Duchess to Desire

Seducing the Widow

THE SPINSTERS OF INVERLEY:

The Inconvenient Heiress

The Accidental Bride

The Secret Duchess

Visit us at www.boldstrokesbooks.com

SEDUCING
THE WIDOW

by

Jane Walsh

2025

SEDUCING THE WIDOW
© 2025 BY JANE WALSH. ALL RIGHTS RESERVED.

ISBN 13: 978-1-63679-747-2

THIS TRADE PAPERBACK ORIGINAL IS PUBLISHED BY
BOLD STROKES BOOKS, INC.
P.O. BOX 249
VALLEY FALLS, NY 12185

FIRST EDITION: JANUARY 2025

CREDITS
EDITOR: CINDY CRESAP
PRODUCTION DESIGN: STACIA SEAMAN
COVER DESIGN BY TAMMY SEIDICK

Acknowledgments

Publishing a book takes the work of many talented individuals. Thank you to Radclyffe, Sandy, and Ruth for the behind-the-scenes magic, and to everyone at Bold Strokes for all that they do.

Many, many thanks to my editor, Cindy, whose kindness and patience are so appreciated. Thank you for encouraging me and for strengthening my writing. I have learned so much from you over the years.

Thank you to the Pickle friends for all the laughs, recipes, and heartfelt conversations. We don't see each other often enough, but when we do it's always amazing.

Thank you to my beloved cat, Macbeth, who sadly lacks the capacity to read this. You came into my life fifteen years ago when everything was topsy-turvy, and you have filled my days with purrs and warmth ever since. Thank you for being my faithful companion, and for keeping my writing chair cozy.

My gratitude knows no bounds for my lovely wife, Mag. I truly do not know how I could ever write these books without your support. You have given me confidence when I needed it most, and you have kept faith in me even when I lost it for myself. Thank you for Sunday mornings with coffee and conversations about books, for wonderful sunny afternoons on the Adirondack chairs, and dinners at our favorite pub. Lucky are we to share this journey.

For Mag, the delight of my days

CHAPTER ONE

London, 1813

"I don't need a blasted nursemaid, Cass."

Miss Cassandra Belvedere sighed. She brought her perfumed glove to her nose to escape the miasma of London air, redolent of coal fire, refuse, and manure, then clutched Victor's arm and dragged him out the door behind her.

Thank God their neighborhood seemed safe enough. She hadn't bothered to rouse a footman to walk ten minutes to the tavern, but she ought to have. Chelsea was a far cry from home, especially after midnight.

She walked fast, hardly caring that Victor wasn't sober enough to keep a steady pace. "Only two weeks in London and already you've pickled yourself beyond belief. I thought you were going to leave such behavior behind in the Cotswolds."

He laughed. "You know better than any that people such as ourselves cannot deny our nature."

She whirled around and glared at him. His cravat was loose and his waistcoat was as rumpled as his hair, and he was weaving on his feet. "I was speaking of your excess of drink. Nothing else."

It wasn't wise to speak aloud of other things.

"That's as much part of my nature as anything else, is it not?" he drawled, his eyes half closed. "Leave me. I'll be another hour at Queenie's, and home before you know it. You can even fix me a cup of hot milk and tuck me into bed like a good boy when I come up the stairs."

"I'll haul you home by the ear if you take one step back toward that tavern."

It wasn't an empty threat. Cass was strong enough to do it, and Victor knew it. Years of working with leather had rendered her arms most unfashionable to society, with hard biceps and sinewy forearms.

She had nothing against the Queen and Scepter. It had been established in 1742, according to the placard, which depicted a saucy-looking woman holding a suggestive-looking rod. It was a place where their own frequented, with as little fear as could be had. And though she was glad enough that they had somewhere so near to their rented townhouse, it did create an alarming proximity to temptation.

Temptation led to distraction.

"You need to focus, Victor. Not to forget everything at the first sight of a man's flagstaff. You are perfectly aware of what is at stake."

With eyes rolled heavenwards, Victor had promised her that very afternoon that he would spend the evening toiling away. But when Cass had entered the parlor after dinner, she had found piles of plain leather strewn across the table amid skeins of embroidery floss and packets of pins. The chair had been pushed away from the table, the room left vacant.

Those samples needed to be embroidered and sewn, and fast. How else could they show the *ton* what the Belvedere glovers were capable of?

He resumed walking with a sigh but stayed half a pace behind her. "I won't fail you."

He had better not.

Victor wasn't a bad sort. Truth be told, he was quite brilliant, and the dearest to her of all her cousins. They had been thick as thieves growing up and shared a devoted interest in the local glove-making industry that had made their family fortunes. But his thirst for spirits and fine gentlemen in buff breeches worried her.

Not the fact that he wanted a gentleman, of course. She couldn't condemn the very thing that she herself wished—a partner of her own persuasions. But she hadn't come to London to look for a lightskirt. She had come to work. She hoped that Victor would remember that should be his first priority, too.

They passed a pillory on the corner of the street, and Cass shuddered.

"I do wish to make it clear that I don't intend to spend all my time in London at labor," he warned her. "Not when there is plenty enough time for leisure."

"Even if we had such time—which, I will thank you to remember, we do *not*—have you forgotten that we do not have infinite funds?"

"A pint of beer is hardly a drain on our expenses."

"Pints lead to unsteady hands and thick heads in the morning."

Victor could sew and embroider a pair of gloves to perfection, but his fingers needed to be nimble enough to do it.

"This isn't just your venture," he shot at her. "I will thank *you* to remember that this is a family business, Cass."

"It was your idea for the artist renderings. They got us nowhere."

"Those drawings are beautiful and make our gloves look like the art that they are! How could we have predicted them to fail?"

They had arrived in London with a thick portfolio of illustrations and pamphlets, which Victor had been so sure would secure them the sales that they needed that Cass had brimmed with enthusiasm for an entire week after their arrival. But shop after shop on Bond Street hadn't been interested. It was apparent that the Belvedere name wasn't impressive anymore, now that over a decade had passed without their gloves being significant competition to the ones made in Worcester.

Cass had taken the mail coach back to the Cotswolds last week to gather what they needed to make samples to show what they could offer, and she and Victor had spent their days feverishly cutting and sewing ever since.

"These samples are integral to the success of our plan, and we are nowhere near ready to show them. I daresay I am not asking for anything excessive by requesting that we work more on them."

He laughed. "Like bloody hell you aren't! I can only embroider so much before my fingers cramp. Sewing up the seams of a single pair of gloves takes more than a whole day."

"And I can only cut so many pairs, but I'm keeping up with what we planned to do. Don't forget I'm helping with the sewing, too. The embroidery is all yours, but I'm a neat enough hand at stitching."

"Ah, how could I forget that I stand in the presence of the one and only patron saint of glovemakers? I presume that your halo, once it arrives, will be in the first stare of fashion. Why, such a thing would win you an audience with the queen." He put a hand on his heart. "All our problems shall be solved."

"I am far from a saint," she snapped. "But I am the one with connections, meagre as they may be. I made my debut fifteen years ago, while you balked at putting one toe past London Bridge."

He laughed. "Connections! You will be lucky to put *your* toe onto any fashionable ballroom floor now."

"Your pessimism is unwelcome tonight."

"As is your autocracy."

Her hands clenched into fists. The tan doeskin leather that rippled across her knuckles was as thin as a dream, thirty-two stitches to the inch creating the tightest seams she fancied England had ever seen, the gold embroidery floss on the back of each one as shiny and bright as a newly minted penny.

Of course, their gloves were worth far more than pennies.

Every member of the *ton* ought to be clamoring for a pair by the end of the Season. If only they could find an opportunity to show them off.

"We do have an invitation tomorrow night to dance at Mrs. Kingsley's." Cass glanced back at Victor, whose brows raised until they were almost hidden behind the mop of curls that flopped across his forehead.

They knew almost no one of significance in London, but when she had gone home to gather the materials they needed for the samples, she had pressed her mother into writing to her friend Mrs. Kingsley, who had somewhat reluctantly agreed to extend an invitation. It had been made clear that this was a favor, and an exceptional one at that.

They couldn't afford to squander it.

Cass caught herself wondering if Louise would be there, and her hands tightened into fists again. Did she still wear her hair in braids? Did her lip still curl when she spotted a social infraction?

"Tomorrow?" Victor frowned down at his cuffs. "I must ensure that I have a starched cravat for the occasion. Has our laundry come back yet?" He kept no valet and prided himself on the intricacy of his cravats.

"Please do not sacrifice all of your cravats in an attempt at something fantastical, for I plan to attend with or without you." But the thought of a ballroom didn't sit well with her. It had been a long time since she had donned dancing slippers and pretended to care about anyone's opinion. It was a damned good thing that her muscles were not the only part of her that had toughened over the years. Her heart might as well be made from the same iron as her awls at this point. "We shall attend. And we shall conquer."

Victor started singing a battle hymn dreadfully off key, as if he hadn't been the best singer in their town church choir when they had been young.

Cass looked around at the quiet brick townhouses and iron wrought fencing and smooth cobblestones. It was a far cry from the rolling hills of their homeland, and a reminder that they had only themselves to rely on now. They must be strong for themselves, for each other, and for the glovers.

A thousand snubs could not cow her, and the cut direct held no power in the face of her will.

❖

Louise, the Countess of Atwater, almost missed her trick when she heard the news.

There was never any deep play at Mrs. Kingsley's balls, though Louise always played her best no matter where she was. Any opportunity to sit down to cards was a good one, no matter how mean the stakes or how watered the wine or how dull the company.

As long as there were warm bodies with a modicum of skill across from her, any game was worth it.

And better yet if they were her best friends.

They were here tonight because Nell's cousin had wanted titles to grace the evening, given that their money was from trade. She would do anything to support her friends.

She placed the queen of hearts on top of the pile and was shocked when her hand trembled. After all these years, the name Cassandra Belvedere shouldn't have provoked any response at all.

"Distraction wins no points," Lady Darling murmured, tapping a finger on her cards.

"You of all people know there is no talking in whist, Darling!" Nell, Mrs. Fenhurst, stared at her. "God above, you've been playing it longer than I've been alive."

"These stakes are hardly interesting enough to call this a proper game."

Lady Isadore pushed up her spectacles. "Do let's concentrate. There are two rounds left and then it's time for supper."

Louise played through instinct alone, trusting her years of experience to know which card to play and which to keep. Darling was right—this crowd was uninterested in serious play. The steady drone of conversation sounded louder than usual in her ears, and one of the nearby tables whooped at faro, but such things never distracted her.

Nothing short of catastrophe could have shaken her focus.

The final trick was won and Nell and Isadore were declared the winning pair, which didn't surprise Louise but still rankled.

Even in a game of four on a team of two, she liked to be the single best.

Instead of clicking the polished ivory tabs down into their closed position on the wooden marker that they had used to keep count of each round, Nell shook the marker and collapsed the tabs with a clatter. "That was a good game," she said. "I think I've improved."

"You have indeed," Darling told her, patting her hand. "I thought your bluff on the spades was well done in the second hand."

Isadore took off her spectacles and tucked them into her embroidered reticule, then fixed her sight on Louise. "Had you not heard that Miss Cassandra had returned to London?"

Miss Cassandra. She had not married, then.

"No." Louise gathered the cards together and started to shuffle. Another game would be just the thing to settle her nerves. Not that they needed settling. Such a notion was absurd. "It is of no interest to me."

"It's time for supper," Nell said, craning her neck to watch laughing guests abandon their games and file out to the supper room. While Mrs. Kingsley never had the best of card tables, she served excellent beef and had a wine cellar to rival anyone. "We've had four rounds already. Come now, I promised my cousin that we would sit at her table, and you know she does not have half as many tables as she does guests. She will insist on hurrying the crowd along after the smallest bite of guinea fowl, so we do not have much time."

But Louise kept shuffling.

Darling made a low hum in the back of her throat. "You were quite the rivals in your debut Season, were you not?" She was fifty years of age with a mind sharper than most people Louise had met in the *ton*. Her dark hair was gray at the temples and framed her face in a dramatic contrast. Stoic, disciplined, and efficient, she forgot nothing about anyone, no matter how trifling a member of society they were. "Miss Cassandra did have an air about her."

She shuffled faster, cards slicing through the stack with neat precision. "People come and go in society. I do not notice each person's appearance or reappearance."

It wasn't strictly true. Darling might never forget a face, but Louise was the one with a reputation for being kind to everyone.

Nell pushed the tabs open and closed again on the marker. It was an expensive one, an elaborate checkerboard pattern engraved in the wood. "I've never met any such Miss Cassandra." She was the youngest of their group at two and twenty, whose doting husband gave her plenty of pin money to support her gaming habits. "Does she like cards?"

Isadore swatted the board away. "Impossible to determine. Miss Cassandra was in London for one Season only. I heard that she is the daughter of a formerly well-to-do squire, and her sole interest to us is that she tried to steal our Louise's husband before they even married."

This also wasn't strictly true, but Louise had never mentioned the details to anyone.

None of her friends could guess at the maelstrom of emotion whirling inside her at the thought of Cass's return.

For the first time in her life, the cards in her hands felt like meaningless paper. Queens, knaves, hearts. Which one was she? Which one was Cass? What did any of it *mean*?

"She was beneath my notice then and beneath it now." Yet another untruth, and Louise was a little ashamed at having said it. She steadied her breathing and dealt the cards. "We shall never be invited to the ducal whist tourney at the end of the Season if we do not put sufficient practice into the start of it. Let's play."

"I suppose there is nothing in life more important than winning a game." Darling's tone was dry as she gazed at Louise above the cards that she held.

Her friends indulged her for three more games, but Louise knew it tried their patience.

Nell pushed her chair out. "I am going for supper before there is naught but scraps left."

Nothing could compel Louise to walk into that room and choose cuts of meat and down glasses of champagne as if there was nothing on her mind except frivolity.

Not if Cass was there.

There was one strategy left to employ. *Escape*. "I am unwell," Louise announced. "I shall make my excuses to Mrs. Kingsley."

It was cowardly. She ought to have the courage to face Cass again, but after so many years had passed, she hadn't thought she would ever have to. Why was she at the ball tonight? How long would she be in London?

She ached to know, but at the same time could not bear thinking of it.

Darling knew her better than anyone and nodded at Louise with more sympathy than either Nell or Isadore, who looked perplexed. "I will call for the carriage and go with you."

Darling and Louise lived three houses away from one another and often shared carriage rides. Two widows sharing expenses, in a routine that they had established years ago, and yet Louise had forgotten it in an instant. "No, you should not cut your evening short because of me."

"My coachman can bring you to your home tonight if Louise wishes to leave," Isadore said to Darling. "It would be no trouble."

"If Louise is not well, then it's best if I make sure she gets home." Her chin was set firm. "You and Nell should enjoy the dancing." Darling had a motherly air about her, and it was a role she took to heart.

Louise took a deep breath. "Very well. But I wish to leave now."

She realized that they had dawdled too long when people began to trickle back into the card room, and she could already hear a growing din from the vicinity of the ballroom. Her spirits plummeted.

She fought to clear her mind of emotion and to think. This was not so disastrous. Now that she had advance warning, she could handle seeing Cass if it was from a distance. It was more to the point that she needed to avoid Cass catching sight of *her*. It would upset her, after all.

Or had she forgotten all about that long-ago summer?

Louise could recall every detail. Moonlight shining on Cass's hair. Stolen wine sipped amidst giggles at a garden party. The subtle scent of daisies and sun-warmed strawberries. The thrill of Cass's hand brushing Louise's thigh as they passed each other in ballrooms. Wrapped gifts and secret notes and whispered promises—*oh*. A lifetime's worth of memories, squeezed into a matter of months.

The years between then and now could have passed in the blink of an eye, for tonight Louise felt like that uncertain girl once more.

Oh, why did Cass have to come back?

Her chest ached. Maybe she *was* unwell. "Let's go," she urged.

Perhaps she would be lucky and they could make their escape unnoticed. Perhaps Cass had already left. Or perhaps she was dancing. She didn't remember her as a keen dancer, but this was a ball, after all. She would be on someone's arm, and Louise would duck out with little fuss.

But when they found Mrs. Kingsley to say good-bye, Louise had the great misfortune to meet a pair of smoldering brown eyes from across the room that beyond a shadow of a doubt belonged to her lover from a long-ago summer.

It was far from ladylike, but a fervent *hell and blast* fell from her lips.

CHAPTER TWO

The blond-haired woman at the entrance of the ballroom talking to Mrs. Kingsley was gone in a whirl of white skirts, but Cass didn't have a moment's doubt about who she saw. She recognized her by more than sight—she knew this woman in her very bones. A lifetime ago, when she had been a starry-eyed debutante with dreams instead of sense between her ears, Cass had thought that this woman resided within her heart.

Miss Louise Sheffield. Or the widowed Countess of Atwater, as she had become in the interim.

Her throat was tight. A silly reaction at the sight of a scrap of satin, given that Louise didn't mean anything to her.

God. She must have lied to herself all these years, because what were these sensations in her chest if not feelings? Fifteen years ago, Louise had been the wreck of all her well-laid plans. She had been dearer to her than the very heavens.

Louise *absolutely* still meant something to her.

It was simply that the feeling was no longer love.

"What are you staring at?"

Cass glanced at Victor. "Nothing. A memory."

Gone were the heavy eyelids and slurred words of last night's excess. Victor was resplendent tonight in a navy superfine tailcoat and cream kerseymere breeches. His white shirt points pressed against his jawline, and his cravat was folded in a neat de Bal fixed with an ivory pin, which Cass knew was because he had indeed discarded half a dozen cravats in failed attempts at a precise mathematical. He had never been to a proper society ball, but Cass knew that no one would guess it. Being a debutante so many years ago wouldn't have suited him, but he stood here now bright-eyed and sly, like butter wouldn't melt in his mouth but he would relish the effort.

She had never told him about Louise and had little desire to explain now, so she gestured at the ballroom. "Is it not extravagance itself, compared to the local assemblies in Rigby?"

Bright-faced debutantes sighed over the garlands of flowers that hung from every surface, their petals waxed and not daring to droop in the face of such fine folk. Matrons nodded their appreciation at the ice sculptures of exotic birds of prey. It was a lush and expensive display.

He gazed at the crowd. "It is impressive."

Cass had once been awed by such things. Yet since she had sunk herself deeper into trade, she thought more highly of the workers who had arranged everything than any lady who gave the order, or husband who footed the bill.

Hundreds of candles flickered from chandeliers set at dizzying heights, their light gleaming on jewels and satins and taffeta. People who wore their fortunes on their backs pushed past each other, without a care in the world. Young folk danced in the center of the room, skirts swirling and tailcoats flapping. Men laughed on the fringes of the floor, while their wives drank wine and gossiped behind their fans.

Vanity. Wealth. Prestige.

She was familiar enough with them. Could they not be used to her advantage?

"Does nobody have style anymore?" she asked Victor, feeling out of sorts as she scanned the room. Everyone looked the same to her tonight, like a sampling of dressmaker's dolls cut from the same cloth, each face stamped with a red-lipped smile and menacing eyes. "I seem to remember there being more arbiters of fashion when I was young. Perhaps our gloves will be wasted on people such as this."

Perhaps the *ton* had seemed more impressive to her because she had been so cowed by them, a country girl with no experience in a world that demanded perfection at every turn.

"You are looking at thousands of pounds' worth of sartorial splendor, and you think of *waste*? Now who is losing sight of the goal, my dear cousin?"

She bristled. "Impossible. I would never."

He patted her hand. "Of course not. And you will have plenty of opportunity to stake your claim here."

It was generous of him to say, given that no one had approached them other than a brief and chilly welcome by their hosts. Cass's mother's letter of introduction held limited appeal. They were looked at with a great deal of interest, but there were no smiles behind those eyes.

She was almost glad that she didn't recognize anyone tonight, for the debutantes that she had once bickered with over dances and favors would now be matrons moving high in society. Would they remember her? Would they treat her with more kindness now? Even if they did, she wouldn't care. All she wanted was to use whatever connection she could, not to become bosom friends with the girls she had once despised.

But something sparked inside her.

She had, after all, recognized Louise. And Louise had recognized her. She *knew* Louise had seen her. More to the point, Cass also knew that Louise wanted to avoid her. She was a woman of strict propriety and would never have left so fast otherwise—and was that not convenience itself?

The woman owed her, after all.

Cass wanted her gloves to adorn the hands of every single person in this room. But it wasn't for their benefit that she wanted it, nor even really for herself or for Victor. She wanted the work that it would generate for the people she loved at home. For the livelihood of the village she had grown up in, for the men who had taught her all they knew of their trade and who had become like family to her during her apprenticeship, and that long lonely decade after her debut. For the women who stitched the gloves together while sitting outside their cottages, gossiping with their neighbors on fine days with their sewing on their laps, and who always had a kind word for her as she passed. For the maintenance of the estate where her parents lived, aging more by the day as she larked about London.

For them, she reminded herself. Always for them.

But Louise's appearance tonight pulled at her. A shimmering vision in lace and spangles. Hair pulled up off her face instead of the braids she had once favored. Emeralds shining from her neck and wrists instead of a young woman's pearls.

This could be interesting indeed.

This could be an opportunity for gain. For *revenge*.

Maybe Cass wasn't in London only for her family and the glovers. Maybe she had come to London for herself, after all.

Was Louise still here somewhere? She squinted across the room, then lifted her quizzing glass from its chain around her neck.

"At least one of your accessories is garnering attention, though not the one we came to hawk." Victor nodded at a group of young people who were now gawking at them. "You will have a reputation for being eccentric by the end of the night if you do not put that away."

"You sound like my mother." She didn't mean it as a compliment.

"Perhaps it is the feathers that are a touch excessive and causing such a stir, and not the quizzing glass." Victor flicked at the four ostrich feathers waving from her pinned-up hair. "I thought we had not the funds to spend on such frivolity?"

She huffed and let the glass fall down on its chain. "Your waistcoat is worth twice my feathers."

"Too true, and worth each and every farthing."

"Then we are in agreement as to the necessity of fashion. Especially in our line of business." Insipid colors hadn't suited her as a debutante and would suit her no better now that she was three and thirty. Instead, her evening gown was *dashing*, and she loved it. It was a diaphanous dark green crepe dress that was open in the front to reveal white silk, and thin strands of jet beads and pearls were draped across the front from her bosom all the way to her hem. She had enough vanity to preen in her mirror when it had been delivered from the dressmaker, delighting in the clack of the beads as she moved. She strived for an expression of innocence. "If I cannot present myself as part of this crowd, then how will they ever trust me?"

"I thought you implied earlier that you were better than these people?"

"Well, they don't have to know that." She grinned.

"Pride goes before a fall, you know."

"Such harsh truths tonight."

But it wasn't pride to know one's worth. Besides, confidence was of utmost importance. The gloves were worth the investment, but first she needed to sell them. For a crowd of this caliber to be interested, *she* had to be interesting.

Cass flexed her hand in front of her. The light green lambskin stretched over her knuckles as slippery as if it had been oiled yesterday. Although her own skill at cutting leather had created the perfect fit to her hand, she had to admit that it was Victor's military precision and attention to the embroidery that made the gloves true works of art. Delicate vines and leaves of thread were embedded in the leather. "Who will admire my gloves if no one will approach me to notice them? I must look presentable enough to catch their attention."

Victor shrugged. "How should I know? I'm a mere tradesman." His voice was dry.

"You said it. Not I."

"Perhaps I am impeding your success here." His gaze kept wandering toward the door, and she guessed he was missing the company at Queenie's.

She swatted his arm. "I need you with me to keep me from doing anything too rash or foolish. Why, without you here, I may well stride straight up to that well-dressed gentleman by the ice sculpture and demand an audience with him posthaste."

"With no prior connections? Society shan't thank you for it. If we have not been introduced, we can do nothing but hope for someone to take pity on us."

Cass scowled. "I will never accept anyone's pity."

She wished now that she had spent more time in her debut year befriending the peers of the realm, instead of rolling her eyes at their affectations and manners. An investment in friendship would be paying fine dividends right now. But it was no use to fret over the past. She had spent enough time wallowed in regrets to waste another moment heeding them now.

She raised her quizzing glass again, and although she didn't find Louise, she was rewarded by the sight of someone she recognized in the shadowy corner of the ballroom. Cass took a step forward, then told herself not to rush. Summoning all her patience, she slapped her hand on Victor's arm and steered him toward the woman. She knew it looked best if she was on the arm of a man, even though Victor was a complete nobody in society. She wasn't much of anybody either, but her name should generate some vague familiarity. All she needed was one person to open the door to her, and then she could let the gloves speak for themselves.

"Lady Ingalls," she greeted the elderly woman as she approached her.

Startled, the woman looked up at her. Eighty if she were a day, with tight gray curls and fine lines creasing her brow. "Eh?"

"I am Miss Cassandra Belvedere," she said. "Do you not remember me? Sir John Belvedere's daughter?"

She hated to introduce herself this way. She was so much more than her father's daughter.

"Sir John Belvedere. That's a name I haven't heard in a long, long time." She pursed her lips. "You look like him."

She didn't like to hear it.

"May I introduce you to my cousin, Mr. Victor Belvedere?"

Victor bowed. "A pleasure, ma'am. I hope you have been enjoying this fine evening."

"Fine enough. Don't much care for interruptions, though, I'll have you know."

Had Cass still been a debutante, she might have blushed beneath Lady Ingalls's scowl. But she didn't care a pin for anyone's opinion anymore, so she merely nodded. "I don't much like them myself, ma'am. I will leave you to your musings, after I—"

"Come now, Elvie," the man standing next to her boomed out. "Who are these young friends of yours?"

"I would hardly call them friends," she said, eying them. "Nor are they quite young."

"I believe I lay enough claim to youth to protest that assessment, ma'am," Cass said, amused despite herself. "What is the age that you would consider one to be past one's prime?"

"It's in the eye of the beholder. But all I know is that I am well beyond its threshold." She tapped the arm of the gentleman beside her. "These old bones don't like to be out and about a moment beyond midnight anymore. Enjoy the evening, my not-quite-young friends."

The woman tottered off in a swirl of lavender perfume.

Disappointment crashed through Cass.

"It's more likely than not that she hadn't the eyesight to see the details of our gloves anyhow," Victor said.

"A woman of her age must know everyone. I had hopes she could introduce me." It must be grand to be a matriarch of her ilk and so free of constraints. No one could disagree with a woman of such consequence.

Why, one could say whatever one liked. "I seem to remember her having connections to an earl." In truth, her memory of the lady was dim, and she was not even certain that she had the correct title for her. But it didn't matter. A lady was a lady, whether she was a countess or a baroness. She had not refused to acknowledge the connection, and that was something Cass could use another night.

Cass frowned. She had spent too long tonight focused on finding new connections and ignoring the one that was ripe and ready to fall into her path.

As if on cue, Louise swirled back into sight, and Cass's focus shifted to her. She would not lose her again tonight. Not when it was clear that she would have to reenter society through sheer force of will.

Louise Sheffield was not her first choice, but she would have to do.

Louise moved in opposition to her, circling right when Cass moved left, dipping into the garden while Cass was distracted by a gentleman who had caught Victor's attention, skipping up the stairs on the arm of a friend to the retiring room when Cass passed within a foot of her at the refreshment table to get a glass of wine.

Louise moved differently than she had, her stride brisk where once she had been wont to linger. But she had the same radiance that she always had, that trick of making someone feel at the center of her orbit, ensnared by those crystal blue eyes. Cass could see it in the way she spoke to those who approached her.

It amused her to think that Louise was avoiding her when there was no real possibility of escaping her sphere. The *ton* was not so large that they could avoid each other forever.

Especially as Cass was now hell-bent on crossing her path.

Cass had no doubt that she would speak to Louise tonight. She sipped her wine and gazed at the staircase. Soon enough, Louise would have to come back downstairs.

And she would be waiting.

❖

"She's still here."

Louise crossed her arms and glared down the length of the ballroom. Cass was certainly in looks tonight. She wasn't at all like

Louise remembered her, but there was no mistaking those beautiful brown eyes that she had once lost hours gazing into. The dress she wore tonight fit her like a dream, the thin emerald green gown swirling around her hips and those strings of beads caressing her bosom.

"She's not going to leave until she talks to me."

She would be lucky if the shock of hearing Cass's voice again didn't send her straight into a faint.

"Are you certain Miss Cassandra noticed you? If she did, do you fancy yourself so important to her?" Darling frowned. "This isn't like you, Louise."

"You don't know her. Cass doesn't stop until she gets what she wants."

"What about what *you* want?"

Louise frowned. "What is that supposed to mean?" Her tone was sharper than she intended.

"Why are you waiting for her to catch you?"

"I am not waiting. I am biding my time until she leaves, or until I can leave without her notice."

"Would it not be easier to speak with her and find out what she wants?"

"I'm not in the least interested." But the truth was that she was afraid of what Cass might want. And how she might go about getting it.

A shiver went through her like an ice-cold breath.

Cass had once been very, very good about getting what they both wanted.

Darling sighed. "I suppose your other option is to pay her a visit. Or invite her to call upon you at your home. You have choices, Louise."

She swallowed. "Here. I should prefer to talk to her here." Lies, twisting inside her. In another lifetime, home would have been the natural choice. The terrain of privacy. Secrecy. *Lust.* "It's better to greet her in public."

She dreaded the encounter, but Darling was right. Why should she allow herself to be chased and hunted? The past had died, and so had the easily swayed girl that she had been. The woman she had become was stronger than this.

It took forever to force her way through the ballroom toward where she last caught sight of Cass. Everyone she knew seemed to want a word with her tonight, and she struggled to keep a polite smile on her face and to force pleasantries from her lips that she couldn't recall even a moment later.

In the end, Louise found Cass and her friend in the hallway beyond the ballroom. As they both still held wineglasses, Louise doubted that they were waiting for a servant to fetch their coats and call the carriage. Cass had indeed been laying in wait for her, then.

Well. She was not caught. Louise had been in pursuit too, hadn't she?

Now that she was close, Louise could see how well time had treated Cass. Her eyes were luminous as ever, pools of amber mixed with mahogany. Disdain filled them now instead of desire, but they were as lovely as she remembered. Her cheeks were less full, and the lines had deepened near her mouth. There was nothing soft about her. Not that there ever had been, but she had lost the coltishness of youth. Her body was lean and compact, almost feline. She looked strong.

She even smelled different. No longer like dandelions and vanilla. It was a sensual fragrance that she wore now, jasmine and almond and a hint of musk, evoking the thought of sultry evenings and poor decisions.

Somehow it hurt that Louise could no longer recognize her former lover by scent alone.

"Greetings, Countess," Cass drawled, a smirk on her face. "Do you still like what you see?"

Louise took a sharp breath. "You are as bold as ever. What is it that you want from me?"

Cass grinned. "Ever so much. Are you certain that you want all of my desires out in the open?"

She felt her face flush as a long dormant and most unwelcome feeling stirred in her abdomen. *Desire*. It pooled through her like a bottle of wine that had been dropped on the floor, broken and spilling out of control.

She had chosen unwisely after all. Home would have been the better option. She hadn't considered that Cass would refuse discretion in her speech. They had always been so careful when they were younger. Darling was near, and so was the man next to Cass. Anything between herself and Cass still required utmost secrecy.

She swallowed. "I care nothing about what you desire. I want to know what possessed you to chase me through Mrs. Kingsley's ballroom."

"I didn't realize that enjoying oneself at a ball amounted to chasing anyone." Cass's eyes were dark above the glass of wine as she sipped. How did she manage to make the ostrich feathers that bobbed from her hair look fascinating and cultured and intriguing? On anyone with less presence, it would have been ostentatious and ridiculous. "Or that you were paying such attentions to me. My word, I ought to be flattered."

She spoke differently too. Not her accent. Louise could still hear the faint burr of the country when she talked, but her voice was lower. Slower. Less impatient, unlike when her exuberance had hardly allowed her words to escape before she was on to the next thought that bubbled up out of her.

Everything about Cass was more deliberate now. The way she stood, her posture impeccable but her weight on one hip instead of standing straight. The way she held her glass, her finger caressing the stem as she gazed at Louise.

Louise swallowed hard again. Those fingers had caressed her once too. Oh dear Lord, she must be away before she erupted into smoke and flames right here and now. "Perhaps I was mistaken, Miss Cassandra. Pray do not allow me to interrupt your evening any further. I will take my leave."

"Miss Cassandra." She barked out a laugh. "It's *Cass*, dear heart. Or have you forgotten everything?"

Dear heart. That traitorous organ fluttered to hear it. "I forget nothing."

Cass's eyes turned serious and she leaned in so close that Louise inhaled the scent of claret on her breath and saw the flecks of amber in her dark brown eyes. "Then you must remember that you owe me. And I have come to collect."

CHAPTER THREE

C ass was gratified when Louise's eyes turned glassy. She had been cool and poised with her nose in the air and her pretty little lips in a tight moue of disdain during their conversation, but now her brow was creased and her breathing was shallow and her teeth caught at her bottom lip.

Triumph raced through her. The evening had started most inauspiciously, but everything had come together neatly enough at the end.

"I don't know what you mean," Louise said, her voice half a pitch higher than it had been a moment ago.

Cass caught the way her eyes darted toward her companion. Ah. So she had not disclosed the nature of their prior relationship to anyone, then. Wise of her. "I would be more than happy to review the details with you at a more convenient time."

One way or another, Cass would find her and talk to her, even if she had to ferret Louise's direction from a stranger at the ball. London was a sprawling city, but although the *ton*'s pull was strong, its orbit was small. The wealthiest and oldest titles inhabited a predictable few quarters of town. Louise didn't need to say that she lived in Mayfair for Cass to guess at it, but she was surprised when Louise provided her address.

"I will pay you a call. Soon, Lou."

Louise and her friend fled.

"Dare I ask what that was about?" Victor asked.

Cass had forgotten he was there. She had been so absorbed in

Louise that she had lost all awareness of where she was. It felt colder without her here. Less bright. She struggled against the feeling of disappointment.

"Someone I used to know."

"I gathered as much." When she didn't say anything further, he poked her arm. "Come now, there's more to this story."

She shrugged. "Does it matter? You saw how fine she was dressed and how many people came to greet her all night long. Lords and ladies and gentlemen who look like their pockets run deep. Someone like her could use a nice pair of gloves and could tell all her friends where she purchased them."

Cass would wring the connection as tight as she could until it ran dry, and she wouldn't care one whit after all was said and done.

The memory of how Louise looked the last time she had seen her was fresh in her mind. It had been thousands of tonights ago, but it felt almost as if it had been yesterday that the moon was full and bright and her heart was brimming with promise. Louise had stood in a place not unlike this very ballroom, like a princess flanked by guards of cackling debutantes and knights in shining Hessians with tongues sharper than swords, falling over themselves to bring her wine. Those blue eyes of hers had been cold and cruel.

That long-ago night when Cass had lost all her faith in innocence and goodness.

Victor went straight to Queenie's after they arrived home at half past three in the morning, and Cass was so distracted by thoughts of Louise that she did not take much notice. It wasn't until the faint light of dawn shimmered through her bedroom curtains that she fell asleep. Until then, she tossed and turned, her thoughts as unruly as her heart.

Nothing had prepared her for the reality of reuniting with the woman who haunted her dreams.

This time, things would be different between them. Cass was no longer that girl with stars in her eyes. She was no longer naïve and trusting. She would never allow herself to be taken advantage of. There was no chance of that.

Still, she hadn't expected the old emotions to be so strong. She was stronger, Cass reminded herself. She had made sure of it through the years. She didn't trust anybody anymore.

She had to stay in control and get what she wanted.

Revenge. Redemption.

And at the heart of everything—Louise.

❖

Louise's sitting room was as cheerful and tidy as the rest of her house, everything in perfect order to provide solace to her nerves. Almost everything was shades of cream and pale lemon, from the striped yellow Chesterfield strewn with decorative ecru cushions to the pastel floral Aubusson rug. Her midnight black cat, Socrates, was curled up like a coin in the center of the armchair beside her, on his worn flannel blanket that was not fit to be seen by anyone she did not consider to be family. He was dear to her, having been by her side through the long years of her marriage and subsequent widowhood. Flickering candles burned from their brace on the table, the light helping to banish the darkness of memory even if most of the room itself remained in shadows.

Cass's appearance at last night's ball had stirred everything up.

Oh, *damn* her for not calling today. Louise had not expected her to waste a minute's time in pursuit of her quarry. She had made sure everything was perfect in the parlor, rearranging the flowers at the window half a dozen times, and changing her frock twice.

Not that she was looking forward to Cass's reappearance in her life. What she wanted was to get it over with. She wanted to wrest the wound into the air where it could start to heal, long buried as it had been. She had wanted the visit to occur today so that it might be over all the faster, and then maybe tonight she could *rest*.

Instead, her nerves were worn as thin as the corners of her favorite deck of cards, tattered and torn from constant play.

Cards would soothe her. They always did. She drew out the worn deck that she always kept close at hand when she was at home—an Italian set, painted with so many intricate details that she saw something new every time she stared down at the cards. Wolves cavorted with harts, and pigeons flocked next to swans, and sly cats peered across the suite of clubs at mice who had been overfed with cheese. Unnatural bedfellows, all of them.

Nell had gifted the deck to her a year ago after she began her habit of sitting with Louise and her friends regularly at the whist table. She had given each of them a deck of cards that she said reminded her of them, and a pair of embroidered stockings. They were thin as mist and just as translucent, white netting scandalously revealing more leg than they covered, with hearts embroidered at the ankle. Shocked, she had taken one look and then shoved them in a drawer, not letting them see the light of day since.

The cards tumbled as fast as her thoughts as she shuffled. Whenever Cass did choose to call, Louise would have to humble herself before her. Cass deserved an apology. And if Louise's dratted temper could stay banked during the visit, she thought she could manage to do it. Then all would be well. The past would be healed. She could move on and put it behind her.

Louise took a deep breath. She rubbed her thumb against the edge of the cards she held in her hand. There was no reason to lose her temper. She had outgrown such outbursts. Besides, they were two adult women who would be in the same room for perhaps a quarter hour. Hardly long enough for anything to happen, let alone to have any sort of deep feelings erupt. After all, it wasn't as if Cass would want to stay for a cup of tea.

She wondered how Cass took her tea these days. Was she still partial to honey?

Louise was still shuffling a quarter hour later when her maid brought Darling to her room.

Although it was past eleven o' clock, neither Louise nor Darling stood upon ceremony with each other at any time of day or night. Louise had always found it difficult to sleep. It had worsened after Atwater had died, which had led Darling into the habit of stopping by for a hand of cards (which often turned into half a dozen) after she came home from whatever social engagements she had scheduled. Living so near one's dearest friend was handy indeed.

"Where did you find yourself tonight?" Louise asked, dealing a hand of whist without even asking.

It was a relief to stop the churning of her thoughts and to turn her mind to the game. Two people at whist wasn't as engaging as four, but she and Darling had sharpened their skills together over the years by such regular practice. Louise never turned down the opportunity to play, though they didn't always heed the rules when it was the two of them, particularly when it came to being quiet during play.

"The Robertsons' soiree. You were invited too. We spoke of it last night." Darling picked up her cards and gazed at them, inscrutable.

"Ah. Of course."

Though Louise was indeed always invited, she suspected that Lady Alice Robertson little expected her to ever appear at her soirees. She had been part of that dreadful debutante circle that Louise had been friends with when she had been young and foolish. Louise had grown up since then, and found little enough to recommend the connections of her youth.

Darling took the trick with a neat flourish and pushed up the first tab on Louise's old, scarred whist marker to keep score. There were five tabs for points and three to count the games in a rubber. "It was a pleasant enough evening. Venison for supper. A fine champagne was served. Lord and Lady Robertson bickered enough while dancing to catch everyone's attention, so do not be surprised to see coy mentions of it in the gossip rags."

"I pay no heed to gossip," Louise protested.

Darling glanced up at her. "And yet you are the same woman who delights in knowing everything about everyone?"

"Curiosity is natural. One may even say it is healthy." It wasn't as if she was nosy. She was simply *social*.

Socrates roused himself from sleep to wind his way around Darling's ankles until she picked him up and settled him against her.

Quiet descended, save for the cat's purrs and the hush of cards moving against each other.

"How many nights have we spent like this?" Louise asked, looking up from her hand after two more rounds had passed in comfortable silence.

Darling shuffled and dealt a new hand. "Scores. Hundreds. Who could say? At my age, I find it easier to track the seasons of the year than the nights in a week. So many come and go."

"The nights are easier with company." Louise tapped her finger against her cards. "I am grateful for yours."

Darling had been there for her forever. Ever since Louise was a girl who married in her first Season and who thought she knew everything—and subsequently learned that she knew nothing at all.

There was very little of that girl left.

Louise frowned and sipped the green tea that Darling preferred, and which the maid had brought to them in a habit as old as their friendship. "I have been thinking about age," she confessed. She looked up and met Darling's eyes. "As time continues to pass us all—does it ever get easier to reflect back on your regrets?"

"It's easier to forget one's regrets when they are no more than a little thing. A thoughtless turn of phrase, an unintended slight where one didn't mean any harm." She sighed, and her face was troubled. "But there have been times in my life when I wished I had done things differently, and it gets no easier to think of them. I wasted opportunities when I thought I would be granted more. I suppose our poor husbands are proof that none of us are guaranteed the time we think we will have."

"That's true enough. I thought my life with Atwater would be longer than the span of seven years. I thought we would grow old together. At least long enough for him to tease me about the silver I might someday get in my hair." She touched her curls. He had loved her hair.

"What has brought this introspection on? Is it seeing Miss Cassandra again?"

Louise might have preferred a less perceptive whist partner tonight, but that was Darling's great strength at cards as in life, and she could not be expected to behave against her nature.

"That doesn't trouble me." But Louise tossed a ten of clubs down where she should have dropped a knave, and she flinched at the careless mistake.

"Hmmmm." With the deck dwindling before them and with her impeccable memory, Darling would have surmised that she held the knave and had caught her error. "I didn't hear what you said to her last night, but I saw how you looked at each other."

Her mouth was dry. "Whatever do you mean?"

No one knew that Louise had succumbed to a reckless passion that had consumed her every waking thought that summer. No one could guess that her thoughts had been fixed upon a fellow debutante instead of her dream earl.

"There is unfinished business between you."

She forced herself to laugh, though she could tell from Darling's face that she wasn't convinced by her insouciance. "We are old friends who have some catching up to do."

"Hmmmm."

But Louise would say no more and took the last trick.

CHAPTER FOUR

Cass followed the maid through the hallways of Louise's townhouse to a parlor tucked away at the back. She assumed that Louise meant this as some subtle slight, given that the maid had guided her past larger and more ornate receiving rooms for more prestigious and respectable guests.

After the maid left, Cass stilled upon entry to the empty parlor. It was strange to step foot in the house where Louise had been living during all these years. There were flowers in the window, a tasteful arrangement of roses and lilies, but nothing of the room beyond the delicate blooms reminded her of Louise. The chairs were black leather and the curtains were sober navy twill, where she might have expected white or pink or perhaps pastels.

Louise, for all her personal faults, had flawless taste, and had been elegant and refined at the ball earlier in the week. Cass had expected her house to be resplendent with the latest furnishings and fabrics.

She was not a gambler, but she would bet that none of this was Louise's taste. Not the mahogany desk or the brass lamp or the books on the shelf or the elegant candlesticks on the mantel.

Which meant that this had all been chosen by Atwater, or perhaps by his mother or sisters when he had first inhabited the townhouse as the earl instead of the heir. Cass hadn't thought of Atwater in years, so why should it send shivers down her spine to sit on a chair that he had once sat on, perhaps with one of his cigarillos in hand, laughing in that hearty way of his that had been so infectious?

Oh God, she hadn't been prepared to rouse ghosts today. She had only planned to settle things with Louise. The air was too still here, the hair raising on her neck when she caught sight of a miniature of Atwater himself on the desk. She wanted to pick it up, to gaze upon his dear face again, but she didn't dare reach out her hand. How was it that he was so much easier to forgive now that he was gone? Why had she wasted the last of his years in anger at him?

Cass was caught off guard when Louise appeared at the door, solid and warm and *breathing*, banishing all thoughts of spirits from Cass's mind. It was almost curious that her anger still burned bright for Louise even though it had turned to ash at the thought of her late husband.

But then, if not for Louise, Atwater would have been hers.

Cass embraced the anger that flooded her at the sight of her former lover, relying on it to remind her of her purpose.

She had no reason to forgive, or to forget. She was here to *take*.

"It is kind of you to call," Louise said, her hands clasped in front of her. "Were you unwell yesterday?"

It had been petty of her, but unsettling Louise was indeed why Cass had not bothered to call yesterday. It was gratifying to know it had the intended effect. "Did you miss my presence during your visiting hours? Alas, I have many more important things to occupy my time than to pay court to you." She sat in the black leather chair without invitation, Atwater and his very much alive wife be damned.

"There is nothing of courtship in your manner," Louise said, eying her with suspicion as she took a seat across from her. "To be clear, I would neither expect nor welcome it."

Cass had said it to ruffle her feathers. Louise was as beautiful as she had always been, but there was a remoteness to her now that soured the attraction. She had been approachable and eager once upon a time, her eyes sparkling with interest and full of high spirits and enthusiasm. Now she was cool and rigid, shielded by prickly hedgerows where once the field of her heart had lain open and yielding.

Cass didn't want to waste any more time needling Louise. It would be better to settle this business between them, and then to leave as fast as she could. Memories were best left in the past.

"May I interest you in tea?" Louise asked, surprising her.

"So that you may lace it with hemlock? I think not."

"Do not be absurd." She rolled her eyes just as she had done a hundred times that summer, and Cass saw a glimpse of the girl she had been. "There are poisons far more sophisticated than found in those Gothic romances you used to read."

Cass hadn't expected humor.

Louise glanced down at the sage green rug. "I need to say something to you." Her face was pale, her lips as tight as her fists were. "I need to apologize."

She hadn't expected this either. Instead of the words landing like a balm to soothe a long-ago hurt, Cass felt the sting of them like a slap. "I don't need a damned apology," she snapped. She didn't want to hear the justifications that Louise had invented over the years.

Louise's chin lifted. "I would appreciate it you would listen—"

"Now you are telling me what to do? How to feel?" She gave a mocking curtsy. "I beg your pardon, but I shall do nothing of the sort."

"I wish to apologize for—"

"What *I* wish is for you to wear my gloves."

Louise's eyes raised to meet hers, and Cass could see the hurt and bewilderment in them. "Your…gloves?"

"I should have known that our conversations that summer meant so little to you. My family has always promoted and sold the gloves that our county is known for, and I have now made it my mission to revive the business."

Cass fished out a box from her reticule and tossed it onto the ebony table between them instead of handing it to Louise. It was rude, but she found she did not care.

"I want you to wear a pair of gloves and tell people where you got them," she said, enunciating every word. "I expect this isn't too much to ask."

Louise stared down at the box, then prodded it with one finger to move it toward Cass by an inch. "Gloves are a common gift between lovers. Are you paying court after all?" Gone was any trace of softness from her face, as imperious as an empress.

A most tempting empress, with fire in her eyes and a rosy glow on her flawless cheeks.

But those thoughts were better off pushed down as far as she could manage.

"You flatter yourself. I'm not offering more than gloves," Cass said through gritted teeth.

"Did you think you would find me pining for you?" Louise folded her arms across her chest, her eyes narrowed. "Did you hope I had a miserable marriage and that I would appear before you as a wreck of a woman?"

"I would never wish for someone's misfortune." Cass leaned back and considered her. "In your case, I might make an exception, but I would never have wished misery upon Atwater."

"Good, because he wasn't unhappy," Louise said, and Cass wished she could believe it.

"For God's sake, I'm offering you a gift." Cass grabbed the box and withdrew the gloves, then slapped them on the table. If Louise wanted to look at them, she could pick them up herself.

They were *gorgeous*. Light blue sheepskin, with snow white embroidery pricked into the leather at the wrist, and ornamental engraved silver buttons at the outer edge. They would be a most arresting sight during a promenade.

"I must confess that I have enough gloves." Louise waved her fingers at Cass, which annoyed her because as Louise was dressed to receive visitors in her own home, she was not even wearing gloves. "From the very best of manufacturers. Dozens of pairs of French kidskin. Gloves trimmed with Irish lace. York tan riding gloves, Limericks for most any occasion, and fingerless mittens of finest netting. What need do I have of Belvedere sheepskin?"

"No one ever has enough gloves. Not like these. Look at the quality! Thirty-two stitches to every inch!" She wadded them back up and shoved them into the box. "Why, I ought to walk the streets of Mayfair and find another woman who would appreciate such a gift."

"I suggest you do just that. In fact, I wish you well on your endeavors."

Louise *then* had been uptight and prim, but she had also been confident and fearless. A shining pillar of goodness and light, a person who had never done wrong and who had every sensitivity and vulnerability in the right amounts. A girl who cried over robins who fell too soon from the nest and who believed in fair and proper treatment for all.

Louise *now* was jaded and hardened.

Cass's eyes bored into Louise's. "There is one thing you are forgetting. You owe me," she growled.

"I owe you nothing."

"You took the husband I should have had. The *life* I should have had."

"Atwater offered me marriage and I accepted. I took nothing from you."

"You knew he would have made me an offer that night at Vauxhall if you hadn't interrupted us."

"His partiality was weak indeed if it took one evening with another woman to sway him."

❖

Louise took a deep breath, but it did little to calm her down. "I told you I wished to apologize."

Cass looked bored. "And I told you I don't wish to hear it."

Before joining Cass in the parlor, Louise had struggled to come up with words that could explain what had happened that long-ago night. She yearned to tell Cass how much she had changed since they had known each other, how much she regretted the past. And yet, were they words to ease Cass's pain? Or her own?

Oh, the weight of this guilt was suffocating her.

"You broke your word, and you broke my heart." Cass laughed, but there was no humor in it. "I don't need to know more than that. But worry not. It isn't grounds to call a magistrate, Lou."

"Don't call me that," she whispered. It was too intimate by half.

"I am asking you to wear a pair of fucking gloves. Is it so much to ask? I don't enjoy this any more than you do. But my connections are sparse—so I need you."

Louise had once needed this woman with every fiber of her being. Gone was any softness of lace and silk that Cass had worn when she was younger, replaced with sturdy twill and frogging and epaulettes, her hair in tight ringlets close to her ears. Gone was the uncertainty in her eyes.

And gone was any trace of the girl she had been enamored with.

"Why should I help you?" Louise asked.

She willed herself to pretend that Cass was not as attractive to her as she had been fifteen years ago. She couldn't understand it, but this arrogant woman was as compelling to her as the earnest girl had been so long ago.

What cruel fate was this? Were they bound to be attracted to one another forever, no matter how much time had passed? She could never have expected this terrible irony.

"Do you not wish to atone, Lou? Is that not why you wanted to apologize? Perhaps I need your actions more than I need your faithless words."

Louise swallowed her retort. She picked up the gloves and studied them. They were as soft and delicate as the first tulips in springtime, as intricately embroidered as a painting in the British Museum, and dyed a beautiful robin's egg blue.

Cass was right. She deserved atonement. It was a small thing that she was asking, wasn't it? Louise wore gloves every day of her life. It would not inconvenience her to wear this pair instead of another.

She opened her mouth to agree, when Cass spoke again.

"If you do not take said action, I may be inclined to tell people how you prevented Atwater from coming up to scratch. Stealing another woman's intended bridegroom wouldn't do you credit."

That was the catalyst to unleash years' worth of anger. Louise could not remember when she had last felt the surge of rage in her veins, the pounding in her heart that reminded her that she was alive.

No, no, no.

But the blood racing through her whispered *yes*.

Her temper was a beast to rein in once it had been loosed, and Cass had pushed and prodded her until the frayed leash snapped. Every ounce of goodwill fled. How *dare* Cass threaten her?

"You were never betrothed," Louise snapped, rising to her feet. "He could have chosen as he wished."

"And you never did anything to persuade him? I doubt anyone would believe it if they had known how close I was to marrying him. I certainly don't." Cass shrugged. "But even if it were true, if the truth doesn't serve me, then a falsehood will do as well."

"So you admit to dishonesty." Louise clicked her tongue. "My, how you have changed."

Cass raised a brow. "Is it dishonest to take what I am owed?"

"I owe you an *apology* and nothing further!"

Cass's eyes lingered on Louise. "I admit to being rather partial to taking what people say I ought not have, or what they proclaim to be forbidden."

Oh, if only this exchange were not so thrilling. Louise moved, putting the chair between them and gripping the back of it tight. This could not be happening. Not to her. Not by *Cassandra Belvedere*.

"Play your games elsewhere. I am not interested."

But Cass stepped closer, and she swallowed. The heat from her body was overwhelming, her jasmine scent overpowering, her height intimidating. She was taller than Louise. Stronger. Why, Cass could sweep her up right now and carry her to her bedchamber and—

"Not interested?" A glint appeared in Cass's eyes.

"No," Louise said with as much dignity as she could muster. "Certainly not."

"Hmmm. Time will tell on that front." Her eyes flicked down her bodice. "And what a lovely front it is."

She gasped and took a step back.

"You will regret this, for I will haunt your every event," Cass told her, her eyes cold. "Every ballroom. Every soiree. Every play, at every theater. You will never be free of me." She leaned closer. "You will watch as I triumph and bring my gloves to the *ton*."

Louise half-closed her eyes with a show of indifference that she did not feel. "And?"

"And you will wish every damned day that you had said yes today."

"Yes to what?" Louise dared to ask.

She smiled. "You know *exactly* what."

Cass took her leave in a swirl of dark laughter, leaving Louise disconcerted.

She hadn't been so flush with desire…well. Since that one summer. But she would have preferred to lose a thousand hands of whist than admit it to Cass.

What on earth had she gotten herself into?

She had made little progress on the apology that she knew Cass deserved, even if she did not want to hear it. Oh, if only Cass had not been so infuriating!

Louise had entertained no romantic thoughts during the past few years. She had no desire for a second husband, and even less interest in a paramour. Not when the greatest pleasures of her life were forbidden to her—for they had come in the arms of another woman, and how could she take such a risk again? That kind of behavior was for reckless youth, not for mature women who knew what they were about!

Cass looked like she would relish the opportunity to risk it all again, though. Not with *her*—Louise was sure that Cass had been trying to aggravate her, not seduce her—but from the easy sensuality of her gaze and her manner, she realized that Cass had taken other lovers after their own tryst. She had seemed comfortable with flirtation.

It was eye-opening.

She had never thought to wonder if Cass had ever found another lover, and had in fact assumed what they had experienced together was rare. She hadn't thought much about Cass's life after she had left London.

She supposed that was selfish of her.

Louise almost wished that Cass had left the gloves behind. The Cass of yesteryear did deserve the favor.

And yet, if she was planning to resort to blackmail to get it…that meant the Cass of today was a cad and deserved nothing.

In an effort of self-preservation that she thought was positively valiant, Louise resolved to steel her heart against Cass's machinations.

As intriguing as they might be.

Chapter Five

True to her word, Cass appeared at every engagement Louise attended. Louise wasn't sure how she had managed it, but whenever she greeted her hostess, there Cass was, glowering from a corner with her cousin.

Not that it was having the impact that Cass desired. Though she had been invited, she wasn't quite *welcomed*. Louise was gratified by the chilly reception that Cass was granted.

"Whyever are you not fueling the flames of Miss Cassandra's dislike with well-placed gossip?" Nell asked, swirling her glass of wine.

Louise hadn't told Nell or Isadore about her history with Cass, but they had noticed the disdain that emanated from them both when they so much as glanced at each other. It was difficult to miss Cass, after all. She may not be popular, but she had a presence that announced itself with little need of the butler calling out her name when she arrived.

Cass was either glaring at her or waving down the barest of acquaintances, bursting with pride and the conviction that her gloves were the best that anyone could imagine. Even though every lord and lady had their own glovemakers that they patronized, some of them for generations, Cass was brash enough to try to sway anyone who would listen.

It wasn't necessary for Louise to be within earshot of Cass's endeavors to know what she was doing, because plenty of her friends recounted their conversations with her. The Belvederes were proclaimed to be most peculiar and were met with reactions that varied from mild amusement to sharp censure. More than once, Louise heard Cass described as vulgar and opportunistic, someone who was a gentlewoman by name only.

Louise met the accusations with the barest murmur of disinterest. She did not wish to engage in any conversation surrounding the Belvederes, lest she draw any attention to the fact that they had once known each other.

Despite everything, Cass's magnetism held a certain appeal. Louise could acknowledge it to herself if to no one else, though it made her uneasy. This business between them remained unfinished, and yet Cass had not approached her all week. Not that Louise wished for her attentions, but the tension was becoming unbearable. Even if Louise was not looking at Cass, she felt her eyes on her all night. She felt marked. Or rather, *claimed*. A shiver went up her spine, and she would have been embarrassed to admit that it held more than a trace of excitement.

She could not afford for her tempers to be unleashed again, or for other feelings to be unlocked.

She had to remember that this woman represented a dire threat. Would she spread rumors about her? Louise couldn't be sure.

But she did know one thing. She would never provide grist for the mill regarding Cass. "I would never gossip about Miss Cassandra," she announced. "There is no need for it."

"You should consider it," Nell said, gazing across the room at Cass. "She looks like a woman who would do such a thing in a heartbeat. If you won't, I could."

"You could do what, exactly?" Louise asked.

"Ruin her," Nell replied. "I would do the same for any friend."

"Rather bloodthirsty," Isadore said to her with a frown. "Can you not let things be?"

"Never," Nell said cheerfully. "To fight unto death is my family's motto. I follow it in all things in life."

"Your husband is your family now. Surely he is not amenable to such an approach?"

"I believe he is aware of who he married."

"There is no need for such theatrics," Louise said. "No one is talking about death, Nell. Miss Cassandra isn't worth my time, nor yours. Let us be off to the card room, I beg of you."

Cass had always been an indifferent card player. Louise was

grateful that although she could little escape her glares at supper or in the ballroom, she would be spared her attendance at cards. She could not bear the notion of sitting across from her former lover at whist, attempting to divine the cards she held or her preferred method of play, and spending altogether too long trying to understand her mind.

Many of her acquaintances considered a late-night stroll around a garden to be the easiest path to romantic temptation, but for Louise it was the card table. What better place to deepen one's connection and foster a sense of compatibility? The subtlety of play, the brilliance of strategy, the tension and emotion of a hard-won game. *That* was seduction indeed.

Even knowing that Cass wouldn't find her in here, Louise couldn't rest easy knowing that she was somewhere at the same event. Sharing the same space. Breathing the same air.

Oh, why could Cass not have stayed in the Cotswolds?

Darling was already at the card table when Louise, Nell, and Isadore arrived. After a half hour of whist with other friends—for Louise liked to play with as wide an array of people as she could—she joined her friends at a table for four.

Louise was surprised by the fatigue on Darling's face, and then by her inattention to the hand that she was dealt. She knew her friend so well after so many years that she could tell in an instant that her mind was not on the cards in front of her. Darling's gaze wandered about the room, landing on nothing in particular. There was a crease between her brows that Louise recognized from when she used to recount the most frustrating exploits of her sons when they had been busy sowing their wild oats.

After Louise and Isadore won the round, they joined the throng for supper and made up their plates with a choice selection of savory jelly and quail and a refreshing bounty of cherries and peaches. "What would you wish for, if you had the opportunity?" Nell asked idly, after they had seated themselves at the table with their gloves folded in their laps. "My husband has a hunting box in Scotland, and yet I've never been beyond the Midlands. Why should I not have a hunting box of my own?"

"Because you dislike hunting," Darling pointed out. "You mention it each time your husband travels north."

Nell waved a finger. "A trifling detail."

Isadore propped her chin on her hand. "I would quite like to be a princess," she announced, and then frowned as they laughed. "I could become accustomed to being served and always having my way."

Darling smiled. "That is no laughing matter. I do not wish to be served, but I would wish for a life above consequences. To have the freedom to do as I wished, with no one to pay the slightest attention to what I do."

"No attention? That sounds like hell rather than heaven," Nell said. "I would prefer to be adored."

"I want to be invited to the duke's house party at the end of the Season, and to win his whist tournament," Louise announced. She frowned into her empty wineglass. Seeing Cass again didn't just rouse unwanted emotion and memory. It forced her to reflect on who she was. What she wanted.

And what she really wanted—what she had *always* wanted—was to win.

She had won Atwater on her own merits, little as Cass wanted to believe it. Her competitive spirit had been roused by the accusation that she had stolen him away from Cass, and she felt restless.

"It seems unlikely." Isadore raised a brow at her. "None of us have ever been invited, though you are considered to be an excellent player."

"This shall be my year." She stared at her plate and willed it to be so. "This is my opportunity."

The duke hosted the tournament every year, but the invitation was extended to a very few select individuals. Although she had longed to be invited, Louise had never thought it a likely proposition.

But something made her believe in dreams again.

If she could prove her worth, maybe she would finally be included.

She knew it would be difficult to achieve, but it would make victory all the sweeter.

What had Darling said the other night about regrets? Opportunity, once squandered, rarely came around again. If Louise wanted something, she must make it happen for herself.

A long time ago, she had needed to make a choice. The pocketbook of the Earl of Atwater, or the love of Miss Cassandra Belvedere.

She had once been so certain that she had chosen well.

But what use was it to look to the past? If Cass didn't wish for her to make amends, then Louise could leave it all buried where it lay. She didn't need to reexperience the hot flush of shame that overtook her when she thought of that long ago Season. She didn't need to remember the mistakes and the follies of youth, the bitter words and betrayals. She needed to look to the future.

She needed to choose *herself.*

The social whirl that Louise maintained was exhausting. When Cass had left Louise's townhouse last week, she had spied the silver salver near the entryway that held all of the calling cards that visitors had left for Louise when they had found her not at home. She had been angry enough to do something that a gently bred country squire's daughter such as herself should have considered unthinkable—she had stooped so low as to have searched through the pile of crisp ivory cards covered in elegant black script, and then had employed a servant to find out if any of those grand houses were hosting balls in the next week or two. She managed to bully her way into each and every event that she could. It had meant exploiting any connection she could conjure up from that first ball hosted by Mrs. Kingsley, but it had been well worth the effort.

At first, Cass had wanted nothing more than to ruin Louise's peace by appearing where she would be least wanted. But she also knew that Louise's connections were impeccable. Anywhere she was invited was sure to be filled with the cream of the *ton*, and they were the sort of people who deserved to patronize the Belvedere business.

Mrs. Kingsley's ball had been a misstep that Cass vowed not to repeat. Her ballroom had been resplendent but crowded largely with new-money connections, the fringes of high society. Louise must have been granting someone a favor to have deigned to grace them with her presence.

The events that she had forced her way into were a very satisfying cut above.

And yet it had been a bittersweet week. Disappointing in that she had endured more snubs and snide looks than she had expected. Aggravating because she bore witness each night to how much everyone loved Louise, where they ignored herself and Victor. Angry that no one had any desire to listen to her conversation about gloves.

But the letter that was waiting for her on Thursday afternoon when she came home from a stroll in Hyde Park was by far the worst experience of the week.

She and Victor had transformed the little parlor on the first floor of their rented townhouse into a workshop of sorts. It held the odor of the almond perfume that she favored for the leather, and the coppery scent of metallic threads that Victor worked through the gloves with such patience. Samples were scattered across the desk and side tables, and more often than not there was the risk of sitting upon a pair of cutting shears or pointed awls on the cushions of the Chesterfield where they both liked to work, albeit at different parts of the day.

Victor preferred the dreamy evenings before his jaunts to Queenie's, citing that his creative powers were at their most potent between glasses of dinner-time wine and evening-hour rum punch. Cass liked the sharp morning light, which aided her to do her best precision work.

The parlor held the fragile imagination of their dreams as much as it did the physical reality of the samples that they manufactured, and so it was the natural refuge that Cass sought upon reading the letter.

Victor was already ensconced in the chair by the empty fireplace, sipping at the expensive whiskey that Cass regretted spending money on, given that they had few visitors and even fewer prospective clients to pay them a call.

Cass tossed the unsealed envelope onto his lap. "We have a letter from home." She heard the flatness in her voice, but there was no use disguising it.

She threw herself into the chair opposite her cousin but was unable to sit still long enough for him to read the missive. She sprang up and poured herself her own whiskey.

"This isn't bad news."

"Indeed it is. The leather will be ready soon enough," Cass said. "And yet *we* are not."

The hides were currently being conditioned in lime pits before they could be dressed and tanned. They would stay there for some weeks before being scraped and cleaned, and then soaked in water and manure to render them soft and supple before being washed and scraped again. Then the leather would be soaked in alum, salt, and egg yolk, or in extracts of oak bark to dress and dye them.

It was daunting that there were only another four or so weeks before the fellmongers would be ready to dispatch the leather to the glovers. There was more to their business endeavors than regaining the prestige of their lost name. There were livelihoods at stake and bellies to feed. A whole village that depended on gloving to survive was waiting on tenterhooks for her word to proceed, for her assurance that she had received orders in hand from the *ton*.

Otherwise, they might need to sell the prepared hides to others who were ready to use them and recoup their investment that way. The herd had been expensive.

"We need one more week and then we shall see results," Victor promised her. "It will be easy." He tossed the letter to the table and sipped his whiskey.

"How?" she cried, rising from the chair. "How do you think it will be easy, when nothing yet has gone in our favor?"

"I finished another pair this afternoon."

How could one more pair be enough to save them from ruin, when they had no *clients*? Victor's dear face was beaming at her, confident and assured. How was it that Cass felt so unmoored in the face of his certainty?

Seeing Louise again had shattered her confidence.

Anger simmered beneath the surface. She could not allow it. The glovers were worth more to her than these ridiculous feelings about things that had happened fifteen years ago. And what was worse, those feelings were tied up with guilt.

She should have been resourceful enough to find a way to wrest Atwater from Louise.

She should have been his bride.

The sheep farms that he had owned should have been *hers*.

But because they were not, and because her father had been dazzled by the false promise of largesse that the gaming hells of London offered to guileless country squires, Cass had ended the Season with empty pockets and no ring on her finger. Her father had lost both farm and fortune at the hells, so there would be no more sheep to provide leather to work with. Cass had failed to marry into the promised land that she had expected. The glovers had been stripped of their livelihood almost overnight.

If Louise had not been such a threat to Atwater's affections, maybe

Cass's father would never have wagered everything on cards in a bid to sweeten Cass's dowry. Her own father had not had the confidence that she could succeed without incentives being offered.

Cass should have been ruthless.

She should have been like *Louise*.

Anger simmered in her belly, mixing with the whiskey.

Victor took one of the gloves into his lap and stroked the soft leather. "I have outdone myself." His arrogance was unmatched. Impatient by her lack of response, he shoved the glove at her, and she picked it up. It was, as always, expertly embroidered, but she hadn't expected the motif.

A snake eating its own tail.

CHAPTER SIX

A n ouroboros might not be of broad appeal to the *ton*." Cass frowned down at the glove.

"A niche market, perhaps." He shrugged, his eyes dark.

She blew out a breath. "Is there something you wish to say, Victor? Because this snake is telling me more than you have since we arrived in London."

He rose to his feet. "When will you remember that this is our business, Cass, not yours alone? It's a family affair. I am *family*." His eyes were bright with anger, his chest heaving beneath his elaborate waistcoat. His face was flushed, and he pulled at his cravat to loosen it.

"I never said you weren't."

"Then why don't I have more of a say in how we're going about things? I didn't even know you had told the skinners to start their work, and now I see from the letter that the hides are already in the lime? Should we not be deciding together?"

"No one knows the business like I do! It was always me, working side by side with the glovers. I was the one who apprenticed and learned all I could at every opportunity. I would give my life's blood for those men."

Old Mr. Ferguson, who had taught her how best to make sure that the fourchettes aligned properly in the middle of the fingertip to prevent the fingers from twisting on the hand. Young Hamish, who was seventy if he was a day, who had shown her how to pull the leather with consistent strength and tension so that the glove would fit as snug as could be. Mr. Branagh, who was renowned for squeezing five pairs of gloves from a single sheepskin.

They had listened to her and encouraged her as they taught her, and she had felt more at home at their hearth than she had among her own family.

"And you think I would not?" Victor peeled his gloves off and slapped them on the table. "Look at my forearms. My fingers. Are those not the pricks from oversharp needles and scrapes from gemstones worth more than my own blood? Do I not bear enough scars from the gloving trade to prove myself to you?"

Infuriated, Cass tossed her own gloves down and thrust her forearms up. "I have my share of scars from scraping leather and cuts from the shears I could hardly pick up when I started as a girl of thirteen. Do not speak to me of proving yourself."

Victor glowered at her. "When I was thirteen, things were rather different for me."

She sobered. That was the God's honest truth if she had ever heard it.

Victor had grown up as Clarabel, striving for years to be the perfect young lady that his parents expected. He had refused a debut season five years before Cass went to London for hers, which had put additional pressure on her to marry well. She had been one of the very few that he had confided in when she had begun her unusual apprenticeship with the glovers, as he had wondered if she had the same feelings about herself as he did about himself. It was altogether odd for a girl to be drawn as she was to the masculine world of gloving. Although gloves were almost always stitched together by women, it was almost unheard of for a woman to be a master glover who cut the leather.

It wasn't simply that it was unladylike—which it was. Or that it could be dangerous—which was also true. It was a man's trade, and women were not expected to participate except as sewers and embroiderers.

As it turned out, Cass didn't feel the same way as Victor did. But she had other inclinations that he understood. Thoughts about other girls, which she dared not speak of to anyone except to him. It had secured them in steadfast friendship ever since.

It wasn't until he turned twenty that Victor had run away to London and sowed his wild oats at Queenie's for the first time. Cass had missed him dreadfully. She had plenty of family, but with him gone, there was no one who understood her. When he had returned almost two decades later, he had done so by declaring that he was a distant cousin of the Belvederes. It had been the only way he could think of to live as *himself*.

Neither branch of the Belvederes would acknowledge him in the year since his return to the Cotswolds, and so he had agreed to come to London this summer with Cass. She had worked through the years to scrape enough money together to purchase a herd of sheep, and this would be the first year that the leather would be ready. All they needed now were sales.

"Your genius is in the designs," she told him, her anger evaporated. "I thought our arrangement was working well between us. I don't understand why we need to change this."

Victor bowed to her, his face cold. "Then I beg of you to continue your contemplation of the matter while I step out for a drink."

"We still have so much to do. And we have an invitation to dinner for tomorrow. Please do not be too late coming home lest you be bleary-eyed when it is time to leave again."

"To go as I please is a gentleman's prerogative," he called out to her over his shoulder.

Cass picked up the glove again. The brushed suede was soft, the satin trim around the hem smooth. The glossy green threads of the snake undulated over the thin leather, and a sly yellow eye peeked at her. They were marvelous and clever, but would anyone be interested in such a thing?

Cass had seen Louise at every damned engagement she could wrangle through grit and determination, but it had turned out to be a distraction that she could little afford. What was this obsession that coursed through her like poison?

Louise represented the loss of everything. Innocence. Happiness. Faith. She was a reminder of everything that had gone wrong in her life.

Cass had been too soft, not approaching Louise again after their first meeting at her townhouse. As if Louise were some untouchable princess, some ethereal being too good for this world, instead of a cold-hearted snake.

The glovers were depending on her to succeed.

At the very next event, she vowed to have the Countess of Atwater agree to wear the Belvedere gloves. As if her life depended on it.

Cass could not afford for Louise to be the ruin of all her plans. *Again.*

❖

Louise was finishing her toilette and choosing her jewelry when Darling was announced. Emeralds seemed to be the very thing she needed tonight. She told herself it was to match her spring green muslin gown, and not because she wished to impress anyone. Especially no one by the name of Cassandra Belvedere.

The very notion was absurd.

Darling was waiting for her in the sitting room by the time Louise was ready.

"Fancy a hand of cards?" Louise suggested. She glanced at the clock on the mantle. "We have enough time for a rubber of whist before we leave."

"I don't wish to play tonight."

"This is the fourth night in a row that you have not wished to play." It was most unusual of her, and she felt a pulse of alarm. "You have been distracted of late," she said, as gently as she could. "We have both wanted a chance to be invited to the whist tourney at the end of the season. Have you changed your mind?"

If she had, it was best that Louise find out now. It was time to dedicate herself to practicing more than ever, if she was to have any chance to be invited. Darling had been her most consistent whist partner for years.

"I have given enough of myself to others," Darling announced.

Louise blinked at her. "I have not meant to take advantage of your kind nature," she said, but felt a twist of guilt beneath her breastbone. Had she expected too much? Had she taken their nocturnal visits for granted? She was ashamed to think that she might have.

Darling waved a hand. "I am not speaking of our friendship! In many ways, you are like the daughter I never had. But at fifty, one takes stock of one's life." She paused. "I have given much thought to our recent conversation about regrets."

"As have I," Louise admitted.

"I have discovered that I am ready to stop waiting for a re-invitation to the grand ball of life. It is past time I put on my dancing slippers again."

Louise stared at her. "You were married for twenty years. You have four fine sons, and soon to be six grandchildren. You have plenty in your life."

Darling's eyes glittered. "That is precisely what I mean. Am I to be valued only through my relation to others? Where is Sarah Finch, the woman? I assure you that I am more than Lady Darling—wife, mother, and grandmother."

Louise took stock of her appearance. Darling wore a white Venetian crepe gown with a daringly low neckline, and sheer silk sleeves that billowed down her arms over her long kidskin gloves. There was a fire in her eyes, and her lips were pressed together in determination.

She was not young. There were a few creases across her forehead and gray in her curls. She was indeed still a beautiful woman, regal and sophisticated.

Louise took her hand. "I am so sorry. I never meant to reduce you to your title. I cherish you as my closest friend. Your patience and kindness have helped me through the worst times of my life. You have inspired me to be better than I am, and I am grateful for it every day."

She meant every word. Darling was dear to her.

Darling took a deep breath. "I trust you," she said, and her eyes bore into Louise's. "You may be shocked by what I am about to say, but I trust in your discretion, and I trust in your support of me."

"Whatever you wish to say, I will always be here to listen."

"I am going to take a lover this Season."

Louise's shoulders relaxed. A *lover*. This was not so very shocking. She had been worried that some dire confession was forthcoming. "That's a wonderful idea. I know how deeply you loved Henry, but it has been ten years now. There is nothing wrong in seeking companionship."

"I am not talking about a husband."

"I have never spoken of it, but I myself took a lover once." Louise had trouble getting the words past her lips. She had never uttered them before to anyone. But for Darling, she would bare her soul—with the exception, of course, of revealing who that lover had been. No one needed to know that detail. "Before my marriage, I engaged in certain relations. I would never judge you."

"I am also not talking about a man."

CHAPTER SEVEN

The silence in Louise's sitting room was louder than a room of the most raucous people cheering a game of faro. Louise could hear the blood rushing in her ears and Darling's unsteady breathing. The sound of Darling's kidskin slipper tapping against the hardwood floor. The crinkle of her own taffeta dress as she shifted on the chair.

Louise cleared her throat. "Not—um, not a *man?*" Her voice squeaked and she winced.

Darling looked dignified. "I warned you that it would be quite the shock." There was almost a hint of pride in her voice. "I may be a mature woman, but I am a woman still. And I have had these feelings for as long as I can remember. There have been moments of my life when I thought I might grasp at the chance to embrace them, to have some fleeting moment of joy or passion, but I lacked the courage to reach out and try." Her chin lifted. "No more. I have plenty of life in me yet, and I shan't waste another moment in regret."

Louise struggled to compose herself. Darling was like *her?* She had not thought *anyone* she knew was like her.

Darling stood and shook out her skirts. "Now, shall we go to the Twyfords'?"

"I beg your pardon?"

"We have a party to attend, do we not?"

"Oh—yes. Of course." She felt dazed. She fumbled for her reticule, then set it down again as she realized that she was still ungloved.

"Tonight is the perfect opportunity to see what is available to me."

"Whatever do you mean?" She paused, one glove dangling from her hand before it dropped to the floor.

"If I am to take a lover, I cannot do worse than to approach a woman I already know."

Louise was alarmed. "If you are rebuffed, the scandal would be enormous."

Panic clutched at her throat. This could *not* be happening! She and Darling were stalwart members of society. Such gossip would be unthinkable.

"Well, what is your suggestion? Visit a lady of the night?" A thoughtful look came across Darling's face. "The idea does have merit. I don't know much of the petticoat trade, but I would assume there must be someone who would accept a client such as I."

Louise gaped at her. "I don't know if I would recommend either action. Can you not simply *think* about it for now?"

"I am done with thinking," she announced. "I wish for action. Scandal shall not touch me. Who would believe such a thing of me? What better opportunity than tonight? Lady Twyford always collects a witty coterie around her dinner table. They love to invite artists and intellectuals." She smiled. "I might well find a kindred spirit."

They argued in the carriage all the way to the doorstep. Louise felt helpless as Darling swished her way past their hostess and started greeting her friends with more warmth than Louise was accustomed to seeing from her.

If only Nell or Isadore were here tonight to help. Not that Louise would ever breathe a word of Darling's desires to them, but she needed strength and support of her own. Their friendship would prop her up when she already felt like sinking through the floor with exhaustion, the evening barely started.

Oh, dear Lord. What mess could Darling get into? Louise would be honor bound to prevent the worst from happening. Darling had not thought this through. She had asked for Louise's support, but surely preventing her from proceeding until she had more time to consider her options would be the best support she could give her?

❖

Lady Twyford's soiree was a smaller gathering than Cass had become accustomed to. There was no card room, she was relieved to note. Louise could not hide from her tonight. If she even showed up.

Cass had been here for an hour and spent much of her time trying to interest the gentlemen in talk of business, to little avail.

After yet another man broke away, Cass spied elderly Lady Ingalls across the room and strode over to greet her.

"Lady Ingalls, it is good to see you again."

Cass was irritated to see that she was alone again. Lady Ingalls was often alone, standing about watching the crowd with a smile on her face, but her family seemed content to bring her places and then escort her home, with little enough attention paid to her during the evening itself. Cass had taken it upon herself to fetch her wine every now and again. Lady Ingalls had her friends that she spent time with, but a woman of her stature and age ought to be catered to.

"Elvie," she corrected her vaguely.

"Of course. Elvie." Cass repeated it obediently, as she did every time she saw Lady Ingalls. She felt it almost disrespectful to call her by her Christian name upon such little acquaintanceship but acquiesced each time upon the lady's insistence.

"Where is Mr. Belvedere tonight?" Lady Ingalls asked. "I always like to see a strapping young man about."

Victor would adore hearing that from her later. If they mended their ways, anyway.

"Oh, my cousin is here somewhere." Cass wasn't sure where. They had arrived together in chilly silence, and he had stalked off to smoke a cigar in the garden almost immediately. He might still be there, or perhaps he had found acquaintances of his own.

"May I bring you anything, ma'am?"

"Do you feel a dreadful chill in here? I had a shawl with me when I arrived. If you could fetch it for me, dear."

Cass found a servant to bring out the shawl. She also asked him to shut the windows in the room, conscious that Lady Ingalls would have a fit of the vapors if she saw that fresh air was invading the sitting room. She didn't seem to be a believer in London air, citing it as responsible for many an ailment. She brought the shawl back to her and helped settle it around her shoulders, then guided her to a chair where she could watch the dancing. Lady Alice, one of her friends, came over and Cass arranged a chair for her. She then brought them both sherry when Lady Alice's son wasn't looking, as she had discovered during a previous engagement that she was not supposed to have it. But Cass did as she was bade, and soon the ladies were cackling together.

Cass returned to the other room. Louise had arrived when she had been fussing over Lady Ingalls. She accepted a glass of wine from a passing servant and sipped as she watched Louise flit from person to person. Her movements were frenetic, her color high. She laughed and touched someone's arm, then moved to another and bent her head low to speak to them. Her head kept jerking up and down, as if she were looking for someone.

A flutter started deep in Cass's belly. It must be her own presence having such an effect on Louise. She was the one who had come to disrupt her life, and it looked like it was working. Deeply pleased at the notion of having bothered her, Cass drained her glass. She wasn't finished distracting Louise.

Perhaps she would never be finished.

At dinner, Cass praised the workmanship of her neighbor's gloves as he tucked them onto his lap and was disappointed that he was not interested in furthering the conversation. She tried to engage the men on either side of her, who dismissed her almost to the point of outright rudeness at every turn.

Cass knew she made them uncomfortable with her direct manners, but she refused to be cowed. Not even for the glovers would she allow herself to feel lesser than she was. She could see Victor across the table talking to a young woman who looked up at him with stars in her eyes. She felt proud of them for a moment, dining with a select crowd of elegant people in London society. They were not seated near anyone of social importance, but they were here nonetheless.

They *belonged*.

Cass struggled to hold on to the feeling as she looked over at Louise. She was ensconced in a chair very near to the head of the table, and her neighbors to each side of her were paying her every attention. She was beloved by them in a way that Cass and Victor never would be.

And yet Louise was gripping her soup spoon as if it were a bayonet. There was a smile on her face, but it was tense.

Was it only Cass who noticed? Had Louise made such an imprint in her mind that Cass could still tell her mood, the small signs that she was upset when no one else knew?

Did no one else at this table know Louise the way Cass once had?

Cass stared down at the venison on her plate. She didn't need to worry about the Countess of Atwater, who had enough people in her life to fawn over her. It would do Cass no good to be *concerned* for her. The very idea.

After dinner, they gathered in the parlor where a young lady began to play the pianoforte, and Cass saw Louise slip out of the room. Finally, this would be her opportunity to speak with her. She followed Louise to the garden. It had rained while they were at dinner, and the air was fresh and cool against her cheeks and bosom, and sweet with the scent of lilies. The shadows that played on Louise's fair skin and hair were captivating.

Cass had been proud of their garden exploits back in their youth. She had never squandered an opportunity for a kiss when they had the flimsiest excuse for privacy. She would have taken every advantage of a moment like this one.

"I was looking for you," Cass said.

Louise kept looking over her shoulder. "You were?"

"Yes." She waited a beat. "As you were looking for me."

"Was I?"

Now Cass was thoroughly irritated. "I saw you looking everywhere for me."

Louise touched her throat. "Oh. I suppose."

She was flushed, a pulse beating in the base of her throat, and Cass was in flames. By the end of this night, Louise would be wearing her gloves. It was a simple matter of persuasion.

And she knew she could be persuasive indeed.

Louise was certain that her neck would be strained in the morning after all of the exercise it endured as she kept an eye out for Darling tonight. She had managed to keep close to her for most of the evening, but there were moments of panic when she lost sight of her.

Darling had done everything for Louise when she was first married to Atwater. She had never failed to provide wise counsel and had given Louise the courage she needed to become the woman she wanted to be.

She would not allow Darling to fall into social ruin. She would protect her no matter what. She owed her no less.

"We need to talk." Cass stepped closer.

Louise was too agitated to be upset about Cass choosing to be a ceaseless thorn in her side. Not when Darling could be throwing away her good name at this very moment with some ill-chosen paramour.

"I am busy," Louise said.

"Ah. Of course. It takes a great deal of occupation to talk to everyone in London as if they are your very dearest friend."

Louise blinked at the sarcasm in Cass's voice and finally looked at her instead of searching for Darling. It proved to be a mistake, as Cass's eyes were as captivating as they had ever been, and Louise had to pause for a moment to regain her train of thought. "Is not the purpose of a party to talk to people? I do beg your forgiveness if the notion offends you. Now, if you will excuse me, I should return inside where people who actually like me wish to spend time with me." She tried to push her way past Cass, but she didn't move and they bumped shoulders.

The connection stopped her in her tracks. Cass was so close that Louise could smell that heady new scent of hers again.

Oh, blasted Cass, why was she blocking her way out of the garden? Louise had come outside to find Darling, but she didn't see her on the terrace or in the garden. Then again, she supposed anyone could be beyond the shrubbery. It wasn't difficult to hide in a garden.

She and Cass had done it enough times.

Cass glowered at her, her eyes hard and flinty. She didn't like Louise, and Louise certainly didn't like her. But liking was not the same as trusting, and if there was any other person in all of London that she could talk to about Darling...surely it would be the only other sapphic woman she had ever known.

It was time to take a risk and bet stakes as high as she dared.

"I'm having trouble," Louise blurted out.

Cass snapped to attention, and her strong arms tensed beneath the satin cap sleeves of her dress. "Who is bothering you? Where are they?"

"Not that kind of trouble. I'm having difficulty with a friend of mine."

Cass's expression eased into boredom. "What business is it of mine?"

Louise swallowed. "Cass, she is like *us*."

"And you are looking to me to solve your lady troubles?" She laughed. "Good luck, dear heart."

"Don't call me that!" Louise snapped. "It's not what you think. My friend is determined to take a lover, and to find one here among the *ton* tonight. It's the very height of folly."

"Again, it's not my business." Cass held up her hands. "My business is gloves, as well you know. And you still owe me."

A hundred thoughts warred for precedence in Louise's mind. She was accustomed to quick thinking and strategy, which had served her well through thousands of games of whist. "Maybe I'll wear your gloves," she said slowly and tried to ignore the way Cass's eyes lit up as if she were a child who had been promised their favorite sweet. She held up a finger. "One time. One pair. If you can introduce my friend to someone who might be suitable for her."

By the way Cass's eyes flickered and her lips tightened, it seemed that as many thoughts were flying through her head as through Louise's own. She didn't want to say yes. Louise would have wagered a hundred pounds on it. Cass loved to be in control as much as Louise did. She would far prefer to demand favors from Louise instead of bargaining with her.

But Cass surprised her by grasping her hand and pumping it with vigor. The warmth of her touch through her gloves went all the way up Louise's arm and straight into her chest.

Not her heart. That was ridiculous. But her chest was as hot as if she had been served whiskey at dinner instead of wine.

"I can find a friend for your friend. There will be nothing easier." Cass grinned. "But you owe me more than one pair of gloves."

"We can discuss it another time." Louise shook her hand free. "Now I must find my friend before she gets into trouble."

Cass stepped aside, and Louise fled back into the house.

A rush of exhilaration coursed through her. No matter what game was in play, there was nothing that compared to the satisfaction of winning a round when the odds were well-calculated. It would have been easier to endure Cass's glares for the rest of the Season instead of forcing herself to see her again, but she hadn't been thinking of herself.

She had done it for Darling. Darling could now have a reasonably safe conversation with someone of like-minded interests, and maybe share a kiss or two—Louise wasn't certain if Darling wanted more than that.

All Louise needed to do in return for her friend's happiness was wear a pair of gloves. They would not be unlike the dozens of pairs in her wardrobe, or the hundreds she had worn in her life.

Simply because Cass had designed them, and touched them, and cut them, would mean nothing.

But Louise's heart was in her throat for the rest of the night. After she went home, it took over an hour of shuffling cards before her mind was calm enough to sleep, Socrates purring on the pillow beside her.

CHAPTER EIGHT

Cass prowled around the library of the townhouse for half an hour after Lady Twyford's soiree. She was too tired to join Victor at Queenie's, but too restless to call for her maid and put herself to sleep.

She didn't like leather work at night, preferring to focus early in the morning when she felt fresh. But there was no time like the present to make a new pair of gloves for the haughty Countess of Atwater.

None of the gloves that they had already made were suitable for the purpose. They were meant to showcase different techniques and to display their fine craftsmanship. Each glove had been cut and sewn and embroidered to be functional and practical, as well as beautiful.

In fact, she and Victor had been concentrating on men's gloves first, hoping to secure orders for riding gloves and hunting gloves, which she hoped would yield larger quantities as they wore out quickly. Even the pair she had tried to offer Louise earlier had been suitable for a promenade, not for a fashionable evening. The leather from their herd of sheep was sturdy. But there were plenty of hides that she had brought to London that were delicate.

Proper.

Perfect for a lady's needs.

Gloves suitable for the ballroom were almost exclusively cut from white French kidskin. Many glovers imported the leather and cut and sewed it in England, but Cass had never dabbled in imports. If they must concentrate their efforts, they had a better chance of success by targeting a different client. But perhaps she had been too hasty to make such an assumption.

Lambskin, after all, was an appropriate leather for fine ladies' gloves.

If Louise would only agree to one pair, Cass wanted them to be worth the wear.

Not that she had any intention of relenting. There would be a way for Louise's will to be shaped to her own. She simply had to find it.

Cass forgot the lateness of the hour as she rummaged through the sample materials that she had brought back with her from home. She took her time looking through the variety of hides, not so much thinking as feeling her way through each one. Each piece of leather was brushed into suede on the inside, and all of them were beautifully dyed. Cass was a master at her craft and knew that she would recognize what she wanted when she encountered it.

Accessories like gloves and hats and handkerchiefs needed to complement the fashion of the wearer. The most beautiful glove on the most elegant woman could still be a sartorial disaster if it suited neither the woman nor her outfit.

Louise had once worn typical debutante dresses of white muslin. It would have been easy as anything to make a white glove for such a girl, perhaps with pearl buttons and a delicate lace edge. Now the countess favored elegant dresses of fine gauze, in an array of colors. Some of the fabrics were pale, but some were dark and dramatic. None of them reminded Cass of yesteryear. She sighed. She needed to be sure that what she was doing would complement Louise's style because it was imperative that she already own something to match the gloves. If that meant opening up long-locked memories, then so be it.

Cass was willing to bare herself to the bone for the sake of the glovers.

She thought about Louise's hands. Once she thought she had memorized every crease in those palms, the length of each finger. She could remember how those hands felt beneath her lips, but what had been their shape? Smaller than her own, she remembered.

It would be best if she had the measure of Louise's hands, and she could afford to wait another day to ask Louise to send her one of her own pairs of gloves so that she could work from them.

But Cass didn't want to.

Perhaps it was stubborn pride, but she wanted her own mark on the gloves, with no hint of another's mastery. If that meant that she was forced to work by memory, then dammit, she would.

After handling half a dozen hides, Cass gazed at the deep blue lambskin that she held in her hands, noting the imperfections that she would need to cut around. She could get two good pairs from it, if she was careful. It would be prudent to cut panels for all four gloves tonight and give the very best ones to Victor tomorrow for embroidery.

She began to stretch the leather, pulling it with firm strokes against the edge of the table to make it pliable, then turning it and pulling it against the grain. It needed to be well stretched in all four directions before cutting, or the fit would be terrible.

They would be as long as she could make them, almost fully encasing Louise's arms. The effect would be dramatic and eye-catching.

And entirely inappropriate for full dress at a ball.

It was uncommon enough to see pale colors instead of plain white kidskin in a fashionable ballroom. Midnight blue would cause everyone to stare at the infraction. Midnight blue with embroidery all the way up the sleeve would be a bold statement indeed.

Which would result in as many eyes as she could wish on the gloves. It would do Louise no favors, given that she would be the subject of scrutiny and gossip, but she spared no thought for how she would feel. Either she would be hailed as a rare arbiter of fashion, or she would be ridiculed, but either way—everyone would remember the Belvedere name.

Cass scored the leather with a blunt-edged tool before picking up a pair of sharp shears and sliding them along the indented lines with ease. Working quickly, allowing intuition to guide her hands as she kept the thought of Louise and her body in her mind, she cut out fourchette panels and gussets for the fingers, and then the thumb panel and the quirk, which would be attached at the juncture of the thumb and palm. She left the hand panel uncut with only the score lines to indicate the shape that she would need, for Victor would need a large enough piece of leather to fit in his embroidery hoop. It was a delicate business, as it was easy for the wooden hoop to scuff the surface of the leather.

After sorting through the pieces, Cass took an awl and began to punch holes where the seam would be. After two decades of experience, she didn't need to measure to know that each hole was perfectly spaced as she pierced the awl through the leather.

She would ask Victor tomorrow to embroider flowers. Cass had given Louise daisies once, the day after their first furtive kiss—but no. Daisies were too innocent. She needed a more sophisticated motif. Perhaps something with leaves or vines. Green, like their long-ago love.

Rosemary, for remembrance. Yes, that felt right. Every time Louise looked down, she would remember Cass and what she had done and what she owed her.

This would be the penance Louise deserved.

It was late when Cass finished, and her thoughts turned to her side of the bargain.

It had been a bit of a bluff to tell Louise that she could find a lover for her friend. Cass had enjoyed enough passionate nights through the years to know that it was not so very uncommon to find willing women. Usually, they were spinsters with whom she had a casual understanding. They were in no rush to wed, comfortable with their lot in life and wholly disinterested in the idea of marriage.

But in London, she knew more men of such persuasions than ladies. The ladies she *did* know were not of the class that Louise would likely prefer for her friend.

Cass thought for a moment, then scribbled a note with plans to send it with a footman to Louise straightaway upon waking. She had always found that quick action was the best prevention for regret, as it allotted less time to dwell on any potential outcome.

Not that she had many regrets in life, much as she wished she had never set eyes upon Louise Sheffield's cherubic face at the cusp of eighteen. Now that Cass was older, she considered it a dangerous age. She had more bravado than sense at the time, and yet had been expected to make a flawless match and to dazzle her contemporaries with beauty, grace, and wit.

It wasn't such an impossible task for some women. Louise was proof enough that it could be done. She had been scintillating. Captivating. She had charmed barons and dowagers and intellectuals.

Cass had only been one of her conquests.

She thought she had been the only one who had been intimate with Louise, but then again, how well had she really known her?

Had she been a pretty face with an ice-cold heart?

Or had she simply acted with the selfishness of youth?

After all, Louise was showing her friend a surprising amount of kindness by asking for help from Cass, whom she despised.

It would be interesting to see what sort of game Louise planned to play.

❖

"I asked you for one introduction for Darling," Louise grumbled. "One woman." She grabbed Cass's arm to steady herself after she stumbled out of the carriage.

"Did you expect that I keep a list of women available for such occasions? I do apologize, but this is the best I can offer you."

Cass's arm was afire where Louise touched it, but all she said as she looked down at her hand was, "I really will be doing you a favor by gifting you with a pair of gloves. Belvedere leather is excellent, you know. Much superior to what you are wearing now."

Louise glared at her. "I swear, your pride will be the death of you. Could we please focus on Darling tonight and not on business?"

"As the lady commands," Cass murmured, and pink washed across Louise's cheeks as she removed her hand from her arm.

Lady Darling tripped out of the hack behind them and made a trilling sound when she saw the placard. "Oh, the Queen and Scepter! This sounds *delightful*."

When Louise had told her that she had a friend with sapphic desires, Cass had assumed it might be scholarly Lady Isadore, who perhaps was feeling inspired by such goings-on from scandalous histories that she might have read. Or the limpid Mrs. Fenhurst, who was young enough to throw caution to the wind for the joy of seeing where it may land.

She hadn't expected the distinguished and elegant Lady Darling.

It had felt like a lark to issue an invitation to Queenie's, but now Cass wondered if she should bundle them straight into the hack with strict instructions to the driver to return them from whence they came.

It was too late, for Lady Darling had already wrenched open the door and bustled inside.

"Is this a wild establishment?" Louise tilted her head back and studied the placard that hung above the door. The woman painted on it was winking broadly as she stroked the scepter, but Cass refused to be embarrassed.

If Louise had expected introductions to be arranged over luke-warm tea and an insipid tray of biscuits, she had asked the wrong woman for help.

"Neither you nor your friend will be in any danger," Cass assured her. "Admittedly, there may be some crass language. But Lady Darling is an experienced matron with four grown sons. I would expect that she has heard worse in her time."

Even so, perhaps this had been a bad idea. Louise would be uncomfortable in a tavern filled to the brim with drunken mollies.

But then, what did she care for her comfort?

Cass warmed to the idea of Louise being in a place where she was every inch as intimidated as Cass used to be in the high society ballrooms. At Queenie's, Louise would be far away from the gentlemen who catered to her every whim and the ladies who wished to befriend her. Cass held the power in such circles.

"You didn't waste any time, so do not think me ungrateful," Louise said to Cass before opening the door. "You have already made Darling very happy."

"Unlike you, I pay my debts promptly."

Cass studied Louise as she entered the inn and saw curiosity, interest, and more than a hint of unease play across her face. Queenie's must be unlike anything she was used to. The best-dressed fops and fawning ladies of the *ton* were nothing like the denizens who frequented here.

It was late evening and the tavern was filled with the usual crowd of students and lawyers and booksellers and bricklayers, some with starched collars high enough to rival the most fashionable dandies, others in plain suits. But there were also plenty who dressed in a manner that Cass knew Louise would find most peculiar, for they donned particles or whole outfits of women's clothing.

Regardless of how they dressed, Queenie's catered primarily to men who often enjoyed the company of other men. Enough of them were like Victor, who lived as the men they were, despite having been brought up to be debutantes or wives. He had embraced the tavern as his second home when he had fled the Cotswolds, and it was the reason why they had chosen a townhouse so near to it.

Cass touched Lady Darling's back and led her to a table near the bar. Louise didn't need to know it, but Cass took her responsibility seriously toward others of their persuasion. She would never do anything to jeopardize Lady Darling's chances to find someone that suited her here, or to do anything that would tarnish her enjoyment in their community. If that meant also welcoming Louise into a space that she considered almost sacred for her, then it was worth it.

I can't see people like us being happy together. Louise's girlish voice from fifteen years ago rang through her ears as clear as a bell, and Cass flinched. One evening might turn Darling into a regular visitor here, but Louise would never again step past the threshold.

"I would be happy to fetch you a drink," Cass told Lady Darling. "Anything you like."

Her face was dreamy. "Rum punch, please."

Cass strode up to the man behind the counter. Her Majesty owned the tavern, made the drinks, and ran the place like it was the best establishment in London. It was Vauxhall within these walls sometimes. It was the Theater Royal. It was the best of places where one could be exactly as one wished.

Her Majesty was a Black man with a towering powder-white wig and a black beauty patch on his face above his bushy brown beard. A plain leather apron protected his dove-gray wool tailcoat and snowy white linen shirt.

"I'll have a round of rum punch for the table."

"Right you are. How many are you tonight?" Her Majesty grabbed a crown punch bowl and a bottle of rum and then almost dropped it when Cass pointed to the table where she had left Louise and Lady Darling. "Why the fuck have you brought us *society ladies*? That sort doesn't sit well with these kind of folks outside the tavern at the best of times." He poured the rum and slammed the bottle on the bar. "Our folk have *professions*, Cass. They have their *dignity*. I won't hold with anyone tittering behind their fans at them. Your ladies there are about as useful as potted plants."

"Don't speak of them like that, please." Cass was surprised that she was defending them. Lady Darling did not seem the type to gossip, but she could not be certain that Louise would not do such a thing. A sense of unease spread through her. Had she made a terrible mistake tonight? She vowed to keep watch on Louise.

"I like you and your cousin well enough, but you have to vouch for your guests. It's how things work here. You're responsible. Fuck, Cass, they had best not bring the night watch here tomorrow."

Cass hadn't even thought of that. She reached for the rum that Her Majesty had set down and poured herself two fingers, then downed it. "Of course, Your Majesty."

"We don't even have that many women here of an evening, as you well know! What are your friends to *do* with themselves? They look like they are ready for a fancy dress ball. Those gloves are almost all the way up to their armpits, and their muslins will not hold up well to a tankard of ale if anything should happen to spill on them." Her Majesty frowned down at the punch that he was mixing. "I might not wish them to be here, but if they are here, I want them bloody well entertained. This tavern has a reputation to uphold. The best of times are had here. Hell and dammit, Cass, you've thrown everything into a pickle."

He was fretting like a mother hen now, scowling over at their table. Cass was touched and grabbed the glasses from him. "Don't worry. They're looking for a taste of life, that's all it is. I will be surprised if they do more than blush the whole time they're here."

Louise wasn't quite blushing when Cass returned, but she wasn't far off from it. She was studying the table as if fascinated by the nicks and dents in its pitted surface. Even when Cass handed them their punch, she hardly looked up.

Cass felt gratified. She had been right after all. They would cause no trouble. Meek as mice, they were.

"Is this the type of establishment where one might make love to another woman?" Lady Darling asked, beaming at her.

Perhaps they were not so meek after all.

CHAPTER NINE

"There are rooms upstairs if one takes a fancy to someone," Cass admitted. "It is not so uncommon."

Louise gasped and stood. "If that is the case, we are leaving the premises immediately."

Lady Darling tugged her back down. "This was your idea, was it not?"

"But I certainly did not choose this location!"

"No one will recognize you here," Cass said, locking eyes with Lady Darling. "You are among friends and perfectly safe. There will be no gossip. No consequences. We do not need to use your titles here, if you do not wish it."

"No consequences." Lady Darling mulled this over as if she were savoring Her Majesty's best whiskey. "I like this."

Louise frowned. "It is still dangerous."

Cass excused herself and returned with one of the few women present tonight. "May I present Miss Adelaide? She is an artist with very fine sensibilities." Cass had met her half a dozen times here in the past few weeks. She was a charming woman, but although they had engaged in a mild flirtation, Cass had not been inclined for more.

"I am Miss Lovelorn," said Lady Darling. "I am ever so delighted to meet you."

Louise was silent, so Cass shrugged and said, "This is Lou." It earned her a glare as sharp as a brand-new awl, but it was worth it.

"The pleasure is mine," said Miss Adelaide.

She slid onto the bench beside Lady Darling, and they soon bent their heads together and were speaking in low tones and laughing as if they had known each other for years. There was no place for Cass to sit except beside Louise, so she went to fetch more drinks to fortify herself before the endeavor.

They sat in silence for a moment.

"Are you enjoying yourself, Lou?"

"You know I am not. And do not call me that."

"Would you rather I used your title?"

"I would have liked the option to choose my moniker."

"And what shroud of mystery would you have cloaked yourself in tonight, if I had given you such a chance?"

Louise sipped her third glass of Her Majesty's rum punch as calmly as if it didn't put grown men under the table each night. "Diana."

"Goddess of the hunt, and of the moon?" Cass allowed herself the luxury of looking her fill at her. Her Majesty was right in that Louise was overdressed. She would have fit in at a rout or a soiree better than she did on a bench sticky with beer. Her cream muslin dress was sheer enough that Cass could see her skin through it where it lay against her body, tantalizing her with glimpses of her arms and her bosom where her shift did not cover everything. Louise was flushed now, perhaps from the heat of the room, or from the liquor. Or from where Cass's thigh pressed against her own. She nudged herself closer and saw Louise's color deepen, with a jolt of satisfaction. "It is an apt name indeed."

"I always admired Diana. A hunter gets what they want. Besides, I am very partial to the moonlight. I show to great advantage in it."

Cass remembered all too many encounters with Louise on shadowy terraces to deny that the moonlight indeed suited her. "Diana was also the virgin goddess."

Louise laughed. "That is not so apt." Her own drink finished, she took Cass's glass and drank from it.

Cass smothered her smile behind her hand, a laugh half-strangled in her chest. The punch had done its job, and then some. Louise's hair was unkempt from where she had run her hands through it earlier, and one of her diamond combs was snarled in a mess of curls. Bright spots bloomed on her cheeks, and her chest was heaving with laughter.

She was magnificent.

But then, Queenie's always brought out the best in people.

She simply hadn't expected to be so charmed by Louise.

❖

Louise's head was swimming in a very pleasant manner, but her sight was not as focused as she would have wished. Especially when Miss Adelaide brushed a lock of hair from Darling's face and murmured something in her ear that had Darling throwing back her head and laughing in a manner that Louise had never heard before.

"Are you all right?"

She blinked, and Cass's face was closer than she expected it to be.

"Of course I am."

"You sighed."

"Oh. Did I?" She didn't think she had, but then realized with some alarm that she was not certain. She frowned and pushed Cass away, but Cass was strong enough that she didn't move an inch. Louise tried to ignore how attractive she found her tonight in her white kerseymere dress with its white braiding looped around the bodice and the silk epaulettes on her shoulders. Cass was far more relaxed here than she was at any of the society events. "You needn't stay so close to me, you know. I can take care of myself."

"I do not relish calling a lady a liar, but I would be loath to leave you alone in the state that you are in. The rum has taken a sudden liking to you, I fear, or you to it."

"I am not alone. Darling is right here."

"She left a few minutes ago."

Startled, Louise looked around and saw Darling in a shadowy corner of the tavern—and was she *kissing* Miss Adelaide? There was no mistaking such a tender embrace.

Unexpected envy sparked in her heart.

"I am not dancing attendance upon you by choice. I am keeping an eye on you as a favor to Her Majesty. He seems to think that ladies, left to their own devices, will turn his tavern upside down."

"He is quite a character," Louise said, studying him. Imagine having such confidence to wear such an outrageous wig! It was elaborate in the fashion popular with ladies some decades ago, with a ship stuck in the midst of its white curls.

Darling returned with a smile so radiant that Louise forgot every trepidation she had felt about coming to the Queen and Scepter tonight.

This was worth every discomfort in being surrounded by men behaving in manners toward each other that were at once very shocking—and yet so familiar that she recognized them in the beat of her own heart.

She herself was *one of these people.*

Louise had denied it for so many years that the idea of belonging in such a place was strange and uncomfortable, as if she was wearing a dress that was too tight and she could not breathe. Or was it the other way around? Had the rest of her life been so restrictive that only now was she feeling the uneasy freedom of having her stays loosened and her dress unlaced?

These thoughts were as dangerous as Her Majesty's rum punch.

Mr. Belvedere came over to them, arm in arm with another man dressed in a modest cambric day dress.

"Settle a bet for me, Cass," he demanded, his eyes half-lidded. "Who is better dressed? My friend here, or that lout by the door?" The lout was a handsome young man in a double-breasted navy tailcoat and tan trousers who grinned at them and raised a tankard of beer to his lips, downing it in one long swallow. "The winner may well deserve my affections."

"You know I don't wager," she said. "Victor, I'm here with gentle-women."

Mr. Belvedere looked down and blinked when he saw Darling. "Indeed you are. To what do we owe the honor, ladies?"

"I am here for a lover," Darling announced. "And I think your friend here looks very becoming in cambric, so my vote is for him."

Louise felt a headache coming on. Perhaps Her Majesty had been right and the tavern had turned topsy-turvy since their arrival, for Darling was never so forward.

"Lovers abound in places such as these. But be warned that the gentlemen may not be to your tastes."

"Who are you to guess at my tastes when you do not even know my name, sir?"

He grinned. "Ah, so you wish me to examine the evidence before me. Well, Lady Mysterious, I can observe with my own two eyes that you have a taste for rum punch. Shall I fetch you another?"

"Be careful," Cass said. "These are society ladies. They are unused to such spirits."

"Darling is right. Who are you to assume anything?" Louise asked

Cass, indignant. "For all you know of us, we could be downing a bottle of brandy apiece every night."

"I do not think so," Cass said, eying her.

"Even more to my liking," Mr. Belvedere said, and winked at Darling. "I will be right back."

"Not you pandering to them, too, Belvedere!" Her Majesty bellowed as Mr. Belvedere approached him.

"They're friends," he said simply, and Louise was touched.

"They're *ladies*."

"We have ladies here, now and again."

"No, what we have are women," Her Majesty corrected him. "Not ladies like these. These fancy folk will soon be expecting minced beef and lemonade, and do you think we look like a lemonade type of establishment? I don't bloody think so!"

"We wouldn't take it if you offered it," Darling called out. "We have more spirit in us than that! And I am very pleased to drink such spirits instead of lemonade."

Louise glared at Her Majesty. "I think we *should* be offered lemonade if we decided to order it. I am a countess, I will have you know."

"Leave off, Lou." Cass's eyes held a warning.

"In fact, I would love a glass of lemonade! Whyever not?" It sounded like the loveliest thing in the world all of a sudden, cool and tart and refreshing.

"What outranks a countess round here, lads?" Her Majesty shouted.

"A queen!" they roared, and he held his apron out and curtsied to applause.

"You may choose between spirits or beer, lady."

Louise clambered to her feet, then realized she needed more height. She braced a hand against Cass's shoulder and hopped up onto the bench. "Are we not all equals here?" she cried out, and felt the truth of it with a burst of pure joy.

"That's enough." Cass helped her down, sliding her against her hip as she set her to rights, and a shiver ran through her. Oh, how she had missed these feelings, roused by a touch so sweet it could not be believed.

Louise didn't move away, but instead leaned closer and gazed into Cass's eyes. "Maybe I'll take a lover of my own."

"You'll do *what?*"

"I believe you heard me."

"You'll do no such thing."

Her eyes narrowed. "You would recommend Darling to find a lover here, and not me? Whyever not?"

"If you need a lover, you have one right here."

It seemed the rum had loosened Cass's tongue as much as her own.

Louise stilled for a minute, then bent over with laughter. "What a lark," she said, gasping for air and wiping at her eyes. "Lovers."

"Is it so funny?" Cass growled.

"To be intimates again would imply that we liked one another, and I am quite sure we do not."

"That's true enough," she acknowledged. "But you won't find anyone else here."

"Again, I must ask why?"

"You're off-limits here, dear heart. To everyone." She leaned in. "Except for me."

Chapter Ten

Spending an afternoon on Bond Street with Nell was just the thing to take Louise's mind off her whirling thoughts from the previous night. She was unsettled and uneasy, coiled like a cat about to pounce.

What she wanted to pounce on, however, was somewhat of a mystery.

The very air at the Queen and Scepter had a sort of magic to it. It was different from any tavern or inn where she had spent the occasional night while traveling to one of Atwater's estates in the country. The people she had seen last night were somehow *themselves* in every way that counted. Their mode of dress was rather surprising, and their behavior was even more so—but there was something almost painfully honest about the entire night.

Louise wasn't accustomed to such naked emotion. She had learned to keep hers to herself, as close to her chest as the cards she played nightly.

She hadn't over-imbibed like that since she had been young. She knew how much to drink without losing her head—how could she have allowed herself to be so careless last night? And in front of Cass, of all people?

She was mortified.

But the real mystery she had encountered had been Cass herself. How dare she suggest that they become *lovers*? It must have been a jest, for there was no other logical conclusion for it. Cass delighted in her discomfort, after all.

"What do you think of this scent?" Nell thrust a vial of perfume at her. She sniffed her wrist where she had peeled back her lace glove and applied a drop of fragrant oil. "It's sumptuous."

Louise inhaled warm vanilla and honey, with a faint floral note. "Lovely. But when purchasing perfume, the most important question is—do you like the scent, or does it truly suit you? They are different things."

She thought of Cass's perfume. Why had she changed it? Did it mean that she was so different from her past self? Last night had proved her to be kinder than Louise had expected.

Nell shrugged. "I feel as if I change from one moment to the next. Perhaps this shall be the perfect scent for me one day. Why not accumulate as many options as I can, so that I may have anything I may want at my fingertips?"

Nell had a dizzying amount of pin money each quarter from her husband. She had been more than happy to answer Louise's invitation to shop.

"I never knew you felt that way." Louise stoppered up the perfume and they wandered to another section of the store, their maids trailing behind them. "You always seem so sure of yourself."

"I am who I choose to be in each moment," Nell said. "But I must admit that it helps to be properly adorned so that I may play the role more aptly. Do you not love fashion?"

"I like it well enough. One must be clothed, after all, and I have a preference for what I place next to my skin. But it's not what makes me happiest in life."

"I am happy enough. My husband gives me everything I ever wanted. Fashion is but part of what I spend my fortune on." But there was a hint of sadness in her voice.

Louise frowned. This was not what she had expected when she had invited Nell to spend the afternoon at the shops with her. She had wanted light conversation and idle gossip, but now she felt guilty that she had thought of Nell as soon as she had wished for ease and simplicity. Nell had depths like anyone else.

"Are you certain that you are happy? You know I am here to listen if you wish to talk about how you feel."

"You know I don't prefer to talk of anything serious," Nell said with a sniff. "I am a creature of indulgence, nothing more. Why do I need anything else?"

"You have a sharp enough mind to know why," Louise said.

"What use does a woman have for a mind when she has already won a rich husband and secured her position?" Nell asked, flicking open a fan and fluttering it in front of her face. "Oh, I like this one. I should have to buy a new frock to match it. Do you wish to go the draper's next?"

Her eyes were overly bright, and her smile was hard.

Louise was determined to push past her reluctance to speak more of serious things. "Perhaps you would like to join a lady's committee?"

"Card play gives my mind enough stimulation. I do not wish for more," she said with a shrug. "I hate to consider what mischief I could encounter if I used my time for thought instead of leisure. Besides, do I not already have what every girl in London dreams of?"

That had indeed been her own dream when she had been Nell's age, and then she had learned the pain and suffering of skating along the surface of life instead of being disciplined enough to live it how one ought.

She had broken Cass's heart.

And it had taken painstaking years to rebuild her life and her very self in the aftermath of her self-destruction.

If she shared it with Nell, perhaps she could prevent her from experiencing the same heartache.

But she couldn't bring herself to talk of her long-ago love affair, and with another woman no less. It wasn't wise in the least. It must be Cass's influence that she felt so close to speaking of things that she had kept secret for so long.

"Maybe you do have the life you dreamed," Louise said. "But it is good to remember that there is more to life than pleasure."

"Not everyone wishes for a virtuous life. Especially when there is money enough to cushion the consequence."

"I am not so virtuous as all that."

Nell burst out laughing. "You! Not virtuous! You are a stickler, my dear Louise. You have the most thunderous frown on your face when someone slips into their seat one moment after the violinist begins to play at a concert hall. You are entirely correct in your dress and behavior, and almost stoic in your approach to life. You have your one glass of sherry of an evening, and you talk to absolutely everyone about exactly what they want to hear."

She supposed that was a credit to her dedication to change, in that it seemed to all the world that she was this way by nature instead of by force of will. After her marriage to Atwater, she had vowed to transform everything about herself. Her habits. Her friendships. Her life.

Nell sobered and touched her arm. "It's a charming quality," she said, and her eyes were soft. "You have been a good friend to me, and I have needed your stability and sterling character in my life. Who knows what would happen to me if I were not so often at cards with you and Isadore and Darling?"

Had Louise become Lady Darling without realizing it? The staid, older friend? The one who prevented others from getting into trouble? For all that Darling was her very best friend, she didn't want to end up with the same fate, with all her recent talk of regrets and missed opportunities.

Louise had been shown an unexpected amount of opportunity at the Queen and Scepter. Why should she not help herself to what was being freely offered? What harm was a little trouble, if one was careful?

Maybe she *should* take a lover.

Maybe she could indulge in one area of her life without the entire thing unraveling.

One thing was for sure.

It certainly wouldn't be with Cass.

"I am looking forward to seeing Samson and Katherine," Louise told Darling after she joined her in the carriage.

Returning to the bosom of her family would help to settle Darling. Louise well understood her yearning to be more than a matriarch, but it was too dangerous to visit the molly house again. It was the very height of scandal to have done it once. It was unimaginable to do it again.

Why couldn't Cass have brought a woman to meet Darling at a reputable establishment like Gunter's for an ice or a candied orange?

"My Samson does love to entertain. I shall have to go upstairs to see darling Nancy and little Paul when we arrive. I promised them a hug before dinner starts."

They always arrived unfashionably early when visiting with her family for this very reason. Louise loved each of Darling's four sons like brothers and had been enveloped into their family life for well over a decade. Samson in particular had become great friends with Atwater after their marriage.

There was a lump in her throat that wouldn't go down.

Atwater.

How could she consider taking a lover? And yet, he had been gone for seven years now.

They had made each other laugh. She had known all of his little preferences, such as being partial to the opera instead of Shakespeare and liking venison more than steak. He had indulged her with jewelry and had accompanied her anywhere that she wished to go, without complaint. Had that not been happiness?

What if there was more of life to be enjoyed instead of holding onto the memory of what she once had?

Samson and his wife Katherine greeted them warmly. Darling retreated upstairs to visit with the children, and Katherine ushered Louise into the parlor for a glass of ratafia before dinner.

"I do enjoy having a nice coze with you before everyone arrives," Katherine said. "It is a small gathering tonight—only eight to the table. I find I am unable to host anything larger given that I am ever so tired these days."

Katherine was in an interesting condition but not yet at the time of confinement.

"I am so delighted for you and Samson. I know how much you had wanted another baby."

The lump in Louise's throat felt thrice the size. She had never been able to give Atwater children. Although she knew that Atwater had never blamed her, she wished the title could have gone to his own progeny instead of to his brother and his family.

She gave Katherine's hand a quick squeeze before they were joined by more guests, but then her hand flew to her throat when she saw who those guests were.

Cass and Mr. Belvedere.

Chapter Eleven

As skilled as Louise was at hiding her emotions at cards, she knew she hadn't kept the shock from her face when she realized that her mouth had opened.

They were a handsome pair with their chestnut brown curls, Cass's piled up and secured with pearls and a single bird-of-paradise feather, and Mr. Belvedere's carefully rumpled across his forehead. Cass's dress was a startling ruby red silk with a deep neckline edged in a crisp white starched ruffle, and her white gloves, embroidered with poppies on the back of her hands, drooped fashionably on her upper arms as she had not bothered to tie them. Mr. Belvedere was dressed more finely than Louise remembered from the tavern. His light blue tailcoat was open to reveal a striped double-breasted waistcoat, his elaborate cravat spilled over the ruffles of his shirt, and his shirt points pressed against his cheeks.

"Are you looking forward to joining us at the opera next week? I have not been to the theater in an age, and I confess I am looking forward to a nice evening of looking over all the latest fashions with my quizzing glass, from the comfort of my seat."

Katherine's bright chatter broke her focus. Louise closed her mouth and managed to wrench her eyes from the newcomers and to look at her hostess again. "Of course. I will be delighted to attend."

But her attention was divided, as she was unable to stop herself from stealing glances at the Belvederes as they spoke with Samson.

When Darling came downstairs, Louise pulled her aside at the first opportunity. "What is the meaning of this?"

"Is it not clear? I fancied spending an evening getting better acquainted with Mr. Belvedere."

"By introducing him to your family?"

"There are other guests here." As Darling spoke, more people entered the parlor and proved her point. "Have they not been to every event that we ourselves have been at? The Belvederes may not be popular, but they certainly are respectable."

"We have both heard from a great many people recently that they consider Miss Cassandra and Mr. Belvedere to be rather vulgar, steeped as they are in trade despite their birth. Are you confident that you wish for them to be dining with your son?"

"Shame on you, Louise. We spent a perfectly pleasant evening with them, and I thought they were charming. You have never been a snob."

Her throat felt tight. Had she been too preoccupied with fears of losing the good opinion of others? She was uncomfortable around Cass given their previous history, but she did not consider her to be vulgar. It was not well done of her to gossip. "I am not one now," she said quietly, staring down at her hands.

"Then why are you behaving this way? I have not seen this side of you since the early days of your marriage."

Louise flinched.

Darling huffed out a breath. "If you cannot bear to be in the same room as Miss Cassandra, though you were happy enough to enjoy her hospitality at the tavern, then I beg of you to please feel free to cry off with a stomachache."

She gritted her teeth. "I dislike her."

"Be that as it may, they are my son's guests at my specific request. It is the least I can do to thank them for inviting us to the Queen and Scepter. It's common courtesy."

"I do not know if it is common enough to return a night at a molly house with a seat at the family table."

Darling lifted her chin. "Then I am happy to declare myself uncommon."

She sighed. "I did enjoy myself, but I wish to make sure you are not making a mistake by furthering the acquaintanceship. Cass does not care for me, and I do not know her cousin. I would have appreciated you warning me that they would be in attendance tonight."

"Would I have then experienced the pleasure of your lecture in the carriage instead of here in my son's parlor?"

Louise was chagrined as Darling stalked off to greet the Belvederes. She hadn't meant to sound ungrateful. She wanted to protect Darling from making a mistake—for it was entirely possible that Mr. Belvedere was cut from the same cloth as Cass. With the way Darling was looking at him, she didn't want for her to suffer a broken heart as a consequence.

She watched as Cass had the nerve to brush a kiss to the back of Darling's hand, and Darling laughed at her pretense of gallantry.

What if it had been *her* hand that Cass kissed?

Her skin tingled at the very thought.

When they had been debutantes, the merest brush of Cass's hand against hers had almost brought her to her knees as they jostled in place for the supper dance with Atwater.

Cass's behavior would win her no favors here among the fine families of the *ton*. A private dinner was one thing, but such boldness would have no place in the ballrooms that Cass insisted on attending.

"You still are wearing inferior gloves." Cass didn't bother to say hello when she approached her, merely shook her hand in a way that left Louise feeling like jelly. She lifted her hand up to peer closer at it. "The satin could be cut closer at the fingers to give a tighter fit."

"I thought you specialized in leather, not cloth."

"You cannot begin to know one product so intimately without being familiar with its competition."

Louise withdrew her hand. "You are being overly familiar with me."

Cass's eyes bore into hers. "Would you prefer instead that I be intimate?"

Louise didn't deign to answer and instead turned to curtsy to her cousin. "Mr. Belvedere. It is a pleasure."

Mr. Belvedere bowed. "The pleasure is mine."

He was a very handsome man, but when he said such things, Louise didn't feel anything in particular. It was only when Cass said them that she trembled.

Louise could not escape Cass's presence at such a small gathering. The dinner table was not so large that she couldn't hear Cass's laugh from the opposite side of where she sat. After dinner, Cass maneuvered herself to sit beside Louise as tea was poured.

"You have three minutes for whatever insult you have prepared for me," Louise told her. "The Darlings always play vingt-et-un after dinner, and I am keen to join them."

A maid was already drawing out decks of cards and lighting candles by the tables near the windows.

"I wanted to give you this." Cass drew out a slender box from her reticule and passed it to her.

The box was light and small, and plain. "What is it?"

"You know what it is. I expect you to honor your side of the bargain. Wear them to Lady Aislington's ball on Wednesday next."

Louise willed herself to feel disinterest, but she wished to rip open the box. Had Cass thought of her and chosen gloves she thought she might like? Or had she shoved whatever pair she had close at hand into the box? It shouldn't matter.

But she wished to know so badly that she ached with it.

She didn't want Cass to guess at it, so she slipped the box into her own reticule with barely a glance. "Are you angling for an invitation there as well? I feel as if I have seen you everywhere as of late."

"I don't care about society or balls," Cass said. "I only care that people see the gloves."

"If you aren't in attendance, you'll have to trust that I'll wear them."

Cass cocked her head. "Trust is in scarce supply between us. I suppose it's good that I already secured an invitation."

"You trust me so little?"

"I trust you not at all. I don't recall your honor."

"I truly am sorry," she said quietly.

Cass looked away. "I'm sure you are. Fifteen years ago, such words might have mattered. Go attend to your card game. That's all that matters to you now."

Katherine called out to her to make up a table with them, and Louise rose to join them. When she looked back, Cass was already gone.

It took every ounce of patience that Louise possessed, but she waited to open the box until after her maid had undressed her and she was tucked into bed. A single candle flickered on the table, and the breeze that flowed in through the window and ruffled her curtains also served to fill her lungs with much-needed air, because it turned out that it was hard to breathe when she looked at Cass's gift.

Louise had expected them to be beautiful. After all, she had seen the gloves that Cass and Mr. Belvedere wore. They were impeccable. But these…Louise touched the leather, as soft as a dream, and then lifted them free of the box. These were gorgeous.

But had not Cass asked her to wear them to a ball? These dark blue gloves would give the sticklers of society pause if they saw her wear them to such a formal engagement. She had never worn anything but white kidskin if she was in full dress. It wouldn't only raise a brow. She could expect to hear nothing else but comments about it for the whole night.

Would she be considered eccentric? Or would she be made a laughingstock?

Neither option was very desirable. Louise's mouth was dry as she thought of a ballroom filled with ladies hiding their mockery behind their fans.

She could not wear these gloves to a ballroom, no matter what she had promised Cass. She could not bear to be ridiculed.

And yet, they were so very lovely.

She brought one glove closer to the candle so she could better see the motif. Was that rosemary embroidered in intricate glossy stitches? Spiky and delicate, with small bluebells tucked into the greenery. Her breath caught in her throat. It must be a message. Cass always used to code the gifts they passed between them when they had been young.

Well, if Cass wanted her to remember, then maybe she *had* been serious about asking her to be her lover?

There was much to think about.

But it would take more than memories to seduce her.

Unless she was trying to interpret too much from the gloves. After all, they were not a gift, but an exchange. The embroidered rosemary was a reminder of her obligation. Of course it called to mind their past, because this was payment for it. The gloves were beautiful, but not because they were meant for her as a person. Their beauty was meant to exalt the workmanship and nothing more.

She wished that fact didn't prickle at her.

❖

Cass didn't much enjoy the social whirl of London, but there was something to be said about it when Louise was in attendance. She was beautiful every night that she ventured out into the serpent's nest of lords and ladies, gleaming and shimmering in jewels and lace.

Cass didn't have to like someone to like the look of them. She had a taste for beautiful women. There was nothing wrong with having discerning tastes. Of course, there might have been something rash about expressing such a thing to Louise the night that they were at Queenie's. But perhaps she had so much to drink that she didn't remember. That would be for the best, for admitting that she was available as a lover had been a colossal mistake.

It didn't mean that it wasn't true, but tonight, Cass's heart burned with desire for another reason—the satisfaction of finally seeing her gloves on Louise.

She would have liked to have seen Louise's face when she opened the box. Had she admired the fine stitching? Had she been impressed by the quality of the dye, and the softness of the leather where it had been brushed inside?

Had she been horrified at the idea of donning blue gloves to such an elegant evening?

Louise must have given some thought to the gloves, for she had chosen a fine navy muslin with cap sleeves so short that they might as well not have been there at all. They accentuated the dramatic length of the gloves that covered most of her arm, for instead of leaving the glove ties loose and allowing the gloves to slip below her elbows as was the fashion, she had tied them tight around her bicep. Her sapphire earbobs and necklace were a perfect match to the dyed leather.

"Your pride towers so high that it can hardly be contained in the length and breadth of this ballroom," Victor remarked.

Louise had been a woman of her word after all, donning the gloves. Cass respected that she honored their bargain. She was most gratified that they indeed seemed to be garnering attention. Cass had lost count of how many times men had bowed over Louise's hand tonight and simply stared down at her gloves.

"It feels good that our hard work is paying off."

Victor flexed his fingers. "Not a moment too soon. I spent hours working with silver floss this afternoon, and my hands are still cramped."

He paused. "I haven't seen Lady Darling return to Queenie's." His voice was a touch too casual.

"I wouldn't have expected her to return. I hadn't invited her or Louise except for that one night." There was an unwelcome knot in her stomach. She didn't much like the idea of them going to Queenie's without her there.

"They are widows and free to roam wherever they please. Neither of them needs your escort."

"They are not so worldly as all that. Besides, Her Majesty was not pleased that I had brought them. If they are there, I need to look out for them."

He narrowed his eyes. "I'm capable of doing that, thank you. You want to keep an eye on *me*."

Cass couldn't protest that it wasn't true. "If you drank less, I would worry less."

"Your worries are better served elsewhere."

"Yes—such as on Louise and Lady Darling. If you like, I'll talk to Lou tonight and ask if they wish to come later this week."

Regardless of what she felt about Louise, she liked Lady Darling. She owed it to anyone they met to foster their inclinations and show them what was possible within the tight constraints of society and prejudice.

Besides, she was feeling charitably inclined. Louise was wearing her gloves, and all was right with the world.

Louise was dancing with some fop who was of no threat to anyone but who did look like he spent a good deal of money on clothes. Hopefully, he would admire the workmanship, the detail, the luxury of the lambskin—

And then the set ended, and Louise flounced off.

Cass's eyes narrowed. That wasn't part of the plan.

"Excuse me," she said to Victor, and pushed her way past him to follow her.

Louise had left the attentions of the dance floor for the relative seclusion of the card room. Cass didn't like cards or gambling and liked the idea of fewer eyes on her gloves even less.

What she liked least of all was that no one wore fucking gloves at cards.

CHAPTER TWELVE

The card room was full, but Cass found Louise without trouble. She was already seated at a whist table with another lady and two gentlemen, in studied contemplation of the hand being delt in front of her.

Cass didn't see the point of whist. There was no talking permitted and thus no conviviality, which made the evening pass slowly. The rules were simple enough, and though Cass was aware there was more skill than what the rankest amateur such as herself could achieve, it wasn't very interesting to spend hours staring at a pack of painted cards. Her time was better spent doing anything else than playing games.

It was a fruitless pastime unless one was in it for the money, but gambling was its own hell. If Louise had any skill at it, then she might make herself a tidy enough income at the table. Maybe she needed to. Maybe Atwater had left her without as large a jointure as Cass would have expected. He was a cad if that was the case. A woman like Louise deserved to be kept in finery.

If Cass had kept her, she would have found a way to give her the moon and more.

She couldn't imagine that Atwater had managed the estate so poorly, however. It abutted her father's land, and she had spent countless afternoons as a child shrieking after Atwater and his sisters in the fields of both of their estates. He had always been clever, and responsible. The least sensible thing he had ever done was to marry Louise instead of herself.

The masterpieces of Louise's gloves were folded on her lap, out of sight to everyone.

Cass's blood heated. This could not be borne. It was a direct insult to her, she knew it.

She managed to wait out the game, with nothing more to do than watch Louise play. There was no denying her skill. She was thoughtful and composed, efficient and graceful in her movements. She was quick when it was her turn, as if she had thought out her move long before it was her time to put down a card and was rewarded when she and her partner won the rubber.

As soon as Louise rose from the table, Cass was there to put a hand under her elbow and steer her into a darkened alcove.

"I see you have not changed at all since 1798. Selfish to the core. Was this your plan all along? To humiliate me in front of your peers?"

"Of course not." Louise's eyes narrowed. "And I assure you, I have changed a great deal."

"You aren't wearing the gloves."

"No one wears gloves when playing cards!"

"I know. And as our sole arrangement is based upon you wearing the gloves I provided, it is an affront to me that you chose to do something that necessitates removing them."

Louise took a step back. "Am I not to be separated from the gloves for even one minute? What nonsense. If I sit to dinner, I shall remove them there as well."

"It causes affront. Supping is de rigueur, but sitting to cards is a choice."

Louise's mouth was tight, and her nose flared. "My usual whist partner has been too busy to play much these days. I *must* sit down to cards and practice somewhere. It is no more a choice for me than supper."

"Then I agree that you have changed, and not one ounce for the better. Gambling is now so important to you that you cannot even go one evening without it?" Cass shook her head. If she had needed a reason to ruin her attraction to Louise, she had found it.

"That isn't true. Besides, how would anyone think that this could be an affront to you? I don't mean to be rude, but people don't really know who you are."

Her cheeks burned hot. That was true enough.

"In fact, these gloves are an affront to me. *Blue*, Cass? You must have had a laugh while stitching them. I have had little other conversation tonight than the provenance of such unusual gloves, so I suppose you have won your point. I will further admit, as I have to all and sundry, that they are the most sumptuous pair of gloves that I have ever worn. But is it something to be wondered at that I sought some small relief from the attention by joining the card room?"

"Indeed I do wonder at it. There is nothing that ought to compel you so strongly to card play."

Louise drew the gloves on, finger by finger, the soft supple lambskin enveloping her hands in as close a fit as Cass had wished for. Her eyes were soft as she looked up at Cass. "Are you upset because of your father?"

Cass jerked back. "I don't know what you mean."

"I remember that he lost a lot of money at the card table that summer."

"I never think of it," she snapped, which was the biggest lie she had told herself since arriving in London. There had been entire years of her life where she had thought of little else. Her father's actions had influenced her own since that day, and even now she was struggling under the weight of them.

She didn't have time to dwell on the sins of her father.

Louise waved her hand. "Look, I have the gloves on again. Are you not pleased?"

But her pride in the evening had soured like milk in her belly.

"You should come back to Queenie's," she said sharply.

Louise raised a brow. "You have such a charming way of issuing invitations that make them so very easy to turn down."

"I think Lady Darling enjoyed herself, so it is more for her benefit than yours," she said. "But you could come, too."

"Why? So you could try your hand at seducing me?"

Cass gritted her teeth and leaned in. "If I truly wanted that, then you would not be immune, dear heart."

A pulse throbbed in Louise's neck. "Don't call me that."

"Fine—Lou."

"Don't call me that either."

Now that Louise was unnerved and off balance again, Cass's mood improved, but she felt like an utter heel once she realized it.

Her behavior thus far in London simply wasn't like her. Louise had been kind. She shouldn't answer back with cruelty.

She vowed to do better.

"I suppose you wish to invite us so I would be obliged to wear another pair of gloves." Louise looked down at her hands, then shrugged. "I would consider it, you know. These are the nicest gloves I've ever worn."

"Yes—that's what I want," she said. Oh, lies upon lies. Truth be told, she didn't want Louise wearing her gloves.

She wanted Louise wearing nothing at all.

❖

"I don't know why I'm looking forward to this," Louise said to Darling as she took her seat across from her in the carriage. "I maintain that it is scandalous in the extreme, and I am not one to court scandal."

They were on their way to the Queen and Scepter again tonight. It had felt daring the first time they had gone. Louise had held her breath on the carriage ride to the point that she had thought she would faint when they arrived. Now she was breathless again, but not out of fear.

"I admit to being filled with anticipation myself." Darling smiled.

Louise felt almost eighteen again. She had spent almost as long dressing tonight as she had for her very first ball. "I feel like everything is new again."

"When you grow older, it can feel like there is nothing new to discover in life. The opportunities never really go away, but you may reach the point where you simply forget to look."

"I suppose one becomes comfortable once one has discovered enough about themselves," Louise said. "I remember when Atwater poured me a brandy for the very first time in our first week of marriage, and I was astounded that I liked it. Now I think nothing of it, so accustomed I am to the drinks that I prefer or the dances that I most enjoy or the books that beckon to me of an evening. I don't seek out things outside of my preferences."

She was surprised to realize it, but it was the truth. Although she had changed her life upon her marriage, the majority of those changes had occurred within the first few years. The past five had been very much like the five before that, and she had given no thought to the next five being any different at all.

Now it was like a new landscape was before her.

"I am having a grand time doing exactly that," Darling declared. "I thought I knew everything about myself, but these evenings are proving to me how little I do know."

It was a public tavern, so Louise supposed she and Darling could have returned at any time, but she wouldn't have wanted to go alone. Cass had been gruff when issuing the invitation, seeming almost embarrassed at their exchange at the ball last night.

Maybe she should not have mentioned Cass's father. She had meant to express sympathy, for she remembered the gossip surrounding Sir John being fleeced within an inch of his life at cards, and how badly Cass had taken the news. She had told Louise about it the very next morning, her face white and her eyes haunted.

Cass had arrived to call on her an hour after Atwater had left her father's study to ask for Louise's hand in marriage, but Louise had not known it yet.

It was clear that Louise speaking of Cass's father had distressed her. She would be sure not to do it again. For despite what Cass seemed to think, she had no intention of hurting her.

The carriage pulled up to the tavern, and it was like another world opened up when they entered it. Outside was dark and quiet, but inside was a riot of light and noise and laughter.

It was joy, Louise realized. There was joy here, among these people, inside these walls.

She had forgotten what that felt like. Like ice cold spring water sliding down her throat and shaking her whole body awake with its freshness.

There could be opportunity here for her, too. It didn't have to all be for Darling, who took to it as easily as a foal learning to walk. Darling was already beaming at Her Majesty and embracing Miss Adelaide in a most familiar way, while Louise hesitated by the door. Unsure of herself. Wanting something, feeling restless, but nervous to reach out her hands.

"You came."

Cass's voice was low and velvety in her ear. Louise hadn't even noticed her approach, but here she was, her hand low on Louise's back. It felt possessive and intimate.

She wanted more.

SEDUCING THE WIDOW

Louise swallowed. But just because Cass was here and felt so good did not mean that this was what she needed. There could be more opportunity for her here than returning to an old habit. Besides, Cass didn't truly want her. She might want a physical release—they had always been more than compatible that way—but she didn't trust her. Louise deserved a lover who liked her, at the very least.

But then why did her legs tremble as Cass guided her to a table, where a pitcher of lemonade was waiting beside a tray of biscuits and sweetmeats?

Cass poured a glass and shoved it at her. "I may have been overhasty last night in my accusations," she said stiffly. "I apologize for leaping to conclusions about your gambling habits."

Louise almost spat out the lemonade in shock. "Thank you. I do prefer to play for the love of cards, and not for money. The stakes are never of much interest to me." She took a deep breath. "But I too must apologize. It had been selfish of me to disappear into the card room. The truth is that I had indeed planned to stay there for some time. It was difficult for me when some of the most important women of the *ton* took me to task for daring to flaunt my supposed disrespect for society's rules."

"It was not disrespectful in the least!" Cass's eyes were hard. "Those gloves were gorgeous, and every stitch of them ought to have been admired."

"And they were. But not by everyone. I found it hard to endure such intense scrutiny." It was hard for her to admit, and she took another sip of lemonade, then peered into the glass. "This is stronger than I expected."

"Her Majesty allowed the presence of such an insipid drink and even let me keep a block of ice here to cool it, but he was outraged at the idea that it could be served without rum. He rectified the problem most assiduously." She pushed the tray at her. "I thought you might like these."

"I have loved gingerbread biscuits since I was a girl." Louise bit into the crisp biscuit, savoring the flavor of warm spices and orange on her tongue.

"I know. I remembered."

Cass was looking at her with hunger in her eyes, and Louise was delighted that the hunger was not for food.

• 99 •

"Are you still partial to marzipan?"

"Are you perchance remembering when I ate so much of it that I almost cast up my accounts in an earl's garden?" Cass shook her head. "I do still enjoy marzipan, but with more temperance now."

"And then I stole a bottle of Madeira and brought it out to you and was distressed that it added to your misery."

"I was impressed that you didn't mind drinking from the bottle. I can't imagine you doing such a thing now."

"When one is young, one has fewer standards. And sometimes a lot more fun." Louise sighed. "I miss those days sometimes."

She took another bite of gingerbread and licked her lips. Cass was staring at her, and warmth spread through her as potent as the spice and as heady as the lemonade.

Darling slipped into the seat next to her. "I do hope I am not interrupting anything."

"Not at all." Cass poured her a glass. "Please join us. I do warn that the lemonade is not the same as you are accustomed to at Almack's, but I think you may enjoy it."

"Is Mr. Belvedere in attendance tonight?"

"Somewhere." Cass shrugged. "I shall leave you ladies to chat."

"Does she not like me?" Darling asked, fishing out a buttery Prince of Wales biscuit from the tray after Cass left. "Or was I indeed interrupting something interesting?"

"I don't know how interesting it was," Louise said. "But we are not here to talk about me. I have no stake in this place."

"Do you not?" Darling murmured. "I wonder how true that is."

Louise forgot to breathe for a moment. "It is truth indeed."

"You forget that I can tell when you are bluffing. You lean forward but a fraction of an inch, but it is still noticeable to those who know you best." Darling rapped her knuckles on the table.

Louise struggled to keep her emotions off her face.

Darling leaned in. "That lover you said you had before your marriage. It was Miss Cassandra, wasn't it?"

She gulped from her glass and found enough strength in the rum-laced drink to confess. "It was indeed. I've never told anyone."

"With the way you look at her, you don't need to say anything."

Louise froze. "Is it so obvious? Not here—but I mean—at the balls?"

"Oh, I doubt anyone would take any notice at the balls." She dropped her voice. "Mr. Belvedere told me all about the gloves she gave you. A lover's gift, is it not?"

"Absolutely not. We may have been lovers once, but not since our youth."

"She's a fine-looking woman."

"No one would deny it. But the gloves are a favor for an old friend."

Darling pursed her lips. "Interesting."

Louise wished to change the subject. "You were asking about Mr. Belvedere." She hesitated. "But, Darling, I thought you wanted a woman? Was that not the reason for all of this?"

"I did kiss a lady last time, and again tonight. I wanted to explore these desires of mine, and I have done so—I have enjoyed myself. But I think what I want is the society of like-minded people, and that's what surrounds us here." Her eyes were soft and dreamy. "I had not dreamed such a place existed, and yet it feels as natural as coming home."

Home. That was the right word for it.

If that was the case, what was the harm in indulging their desires in the safety of the tavern, among people who would not blink an eye? Encouraged, Louise decided to fetch her own drink from the bar. If Darling could feel so comfortable here, she could too.

"Back for more, Countess? I suppose I'll grant the royal pardon." Her Majesty winked at her. "If you have come groveling on bended knee, that is."

"I shall never do such a thing," she vowed. "But if flattery would appease, Your Majesty, might I compliment you on the fine spread that was set before me?"

"Bah, that was all Cass," he said, rolling his eyes. "Came in here at half four with a tray and strict instructions to keep it for your arrival. Said she didn't think I would take kindly to having biscuits and fancy bonbons on the premises, but I did try one of those lemony ones. Wasn't bad."

Cass came up to them. "Is Lou causing you trouble, Your Majesty?" she asked, leaning an arm against the bar. She was close enough that Louise could feel the heat from her body, and it took everything she had not to lean against her warmth.

"Not one whit, and you know it. She's a nice enough lady. Can't say I have many complaints, not when her coin is good and there seems to be plenty of it."

Louise laughed. "Such a high recommendation. I am gratified." She turned to Cass. "If I may have a word with you?"

"You are always free to speak to me. What may I do for you, Lou?"

"In private, please."

Her Majesty whistled, and Louise swatted at him. "I take back my compliments. You are uncouth, sir," she told him.

Louise led Cass to a quieter corner of the tavern.

"Did you want to go up the stairs?" Cass smiled at her.

"No." She put her hands on Cass's hips and heard her sharp intake of breath. "What I want can be done right here."

Cass raised a brow. "I am ready for anything."

"You were right about yesterday. I'm sorry I went to the card room. It was selfish and thoughtless."

Cass sighed. "I may have been selfish as well, in choosing that color for the gloves. I did expect you to encounter some degree of censure, and it was not well done of me. You are free to do whatever you wish. I should not have expected you to eschew every pleasure in pursuit of my business."

Louise paused. This part would be much more difficult. "But it is not just for last night that I want to apologize. I need to apologize for the past."

Cass's face darkened. "I don't want to speak of it. Here I thought you were angling for a kiss."

The heat between them was an inferno, but it could not have been further from hell. The pleasure that burst from her heart held all the sweetness of heaven.

"Oh." Louise smiled. "Yes, I want that too."

Cass pulled her closer and pressed her lips against hers for the first time in forever. Louise remembered the silky soft feel of her lips, the slide of her tongue against the corner of her mouth, the way her breathing slowed. She remembered the dip she felt in her belly, the restless ache that built between her thighs.

The rest of the sensations were new.

Neither she nor Cass were inexperienced women any longer, fumbling their way through the first forays of pleasure together. Instead,

Cass was holding her tight, her fingers digging into her hips in a way that she had never done before. Her body was more powerful now, hard and muscled instead of thin and sinewy, and Louise delighted in running her hands up her arms and feeling her biceps bunch.

Cass's lips were hot and fervent, and Louise clung to her, inhaling the scent of her jasmine perfume. These kisses were revelatory, exposing her desires to their very core. If she had any doubts about the strength of what they had felt for each other once upon a time, they were erased by the sweetness of Cass's lips against her cheek and neck.

She hadn't ever felt passion like this for anyone else, man or woman. It was Cass alone who could do this for her, and it filled her with a need that longed to be satisfied.

Louise had never felt more powerful or more sensual than when she pulled back and saw the dazed look in Cass's honey-flecked eyes. She smiled. "We are not as rusty as I thought we might be."

Cass gaped at her, and Louise walked on unsteady legs to where Darling and Mr. Belvedere were sitting.

"Quite the exhibition with someone you insist on describing as a friend," Darling said dryly.

Mr. Belvedere smiled. "My cousin doesn't have many such intimate friends, you know. It is a mark of great favor."

Cass sauntered up to Louise as she and Darling were preparing to leave.

"Oh—I almost forgot." Cass shoved a paper-wrapped parcel into Louise's reticule. "Think of me when you wear them."

She winked and left in a swirl of satin, her perfume lingering in the air along with her laughter.

CHAPTER THIRTEEN

Cass had received another letter. The leather was close to being ready, and the glovers would be looking to pick up their tools again. She had made promises to them before she left, and now she worried that she had been too ambitious, bolstered high by her own arrogance.

What if her promises had been as lofty now as they had been when she had been so determined to marry Atwater? She had let everyone down then. Maybe she would again.

She thought of Mr. Branagh, who had been so patient as he taught her to calculate the gloves she could get out of each hide. How to look for imperfections, how to cut economically and precisely. How to pierce the leather with the awl to make the holes for the seamstresses to stitch the gloves together.

He was seventy now, retired with arthritic fingers, and had seven strapping grandsons who all wanted to do him proud. Cass had grown up with those boys and had learned to tan leather by their side, and had competitions to see who could scrape leather the fastest.

She couldn't let them down any more than she could disappoint their sisters who sewed the gloves, or their aunts who carried the packs of glove panels from the cutting workshops down to the cottages where they were sewn, and then brought the packs of finished gloves from the cottages to the manor house where the Belvederes would arrange the wholesale to the London shops.

Cass and Victor had made progress, but with no interest from the shops for wholesale orders and no sales to the gentry for commissioned work, the time and expense spent in London was useless.

Although something inside her was twisting and changing, and it had everything to do with seeing Louise again.

She had thought she had been comfortable in the Cotswolds. For years, she had directed all of her attention toward gloving, learning the craft and finding solutions to keep enough work in the village to sustain those that she considered friends and even family.

But that didn't mean that her life was cut out and neatly punched like a perfect sample for a needle to follow, with straight lines and even edges. Her life was not yet fully embellished and decorated, either.

She had spent so much time dedicated to her family and restoring their livelihood that she hadn't taken much time for herself.

Cass had buried memories and emotions for too long, and kissing Louise had brought them boiling to the surface and itching to erupt. It had been a mistake that she could ill afford. Such feelings were a distraction from her mission. But Louise had been so vibrant and full of mischief. At Queenie's, she was a different creature than she was in the ballrooms. She was warm and inquisitive, her eyes wide and shining and her lips parted in wonder.

What person possessed such social graces that she could fit in *anywhere*? Cass had wanted Louise to be uncomfortable at Queenie's. She had wanted to be sure that she would be on even footing and Louise would be kept off balance, reminded that this was Cass's environs.

Instead, Her Majesty doted on her, and the crowd had accepted her without a murmur.

Louise had certainly taken to kissing by the shadowed stairwell as naturally as if she had been there half a dozen times before.

What had that been about? The allure in her eyes had been irresistible, and Cass had been ensnared in no more than a heartbeat.

It was one thing to want to seduce Louise. But to be kissed like that…This wasn't seduction. This was altogether more tender. Delicate. This reminded her of love.

Or rather, it was a distant memory of the most vibrant emotion she had ever felt in her life. What she felt now could never compare to how enthralled and enraptured she had once been, for the girl who had experienced such things was long gone.

Cass hadn't allowed herself to remember any of the good things from that summer. If she let herself think of it, it tore at her heart.

Because Cass had everything she had ever wanted that summer.

Louise had *been* everything that summer to her. She had been pretty, and popular, but also kind and surprisingly funny. What had started with enmity had become something of a jest between them. Louise had wanted Atwater because he was handsome and her overbearing father wanted the match. Cass had wanted him for his sheep farm, which meant her own father had a shrewd interest in the match.

She and Louise had been rivals from the start.

Cass hadn't liked anything about her. She didn't like that Louise had set her eyes on the one man that Cass had decided she could stomach being married to. She didn't like Louise's soprano warbling or her insipid choice of Italian arias as she jostled to be the first to sit at the pianoforte after any dinner, eager for any attention she could attract.

Cass had particularly disliked that she couldn't take her eyes away from Louise's intricate blond braids or the warm flush on her cheeks or the way her gowns dipped most invitingly over her bosom as she danced.

Cass had been a wallflower, gawky and awkward in plain white muslin dresses that she hated, standing next to other debutantes that she hadn't liked any more than she liked Louise. Some of them had been snide, and others had been snobbish, and all of them had laughed at Cass for her forthright manners and blunt way of speaking.

But although Cass cried into her pillow each night, she had vowed never to appear anything but confident in public. She had been so sure that Atwater would choose her. After all, she had something that none of the other girls could have predicted. She was his *neighbor*. They had grown up together, while their fathers hunted deer and grouse and their mothers paid incessant house calls upon each other.

They had spoken of a match between them, before the Season started. Admittedly it had been mentioned in passing, and though Cass now wondered if he had ever remembered having said such a thing to her, Cass then had clung to it as if it had been writ into law. It would be a sensible choice, a union of like-minded people who were also friends.

But Louise was beautiful. She had been charming, and ever so sweet. She crooned over a bird that fell from its nest one evening, and Atwater had tenderly put the robin in his handkerchief and tried to nurse it to health for her. Cass was too practical for such things.

For years after Atwater had married Louise, Cass had lived in dread of her visiting the estate. She had expected Louise to lord it over her. To insist on taking precedence at the local assemblies and at church. To preen in front of the other gentlewomen of the village, while Cass looked from afar—because after that summer, their family had sunk in consequence with the loss of so much of their fortune and the collapse of the gloving business.

But as far as she knew, Louise had spent the vast majority of her time in London.

Cass had shoved it all from her mind. But now she could not help but wonder if Louise had been happy in her marriage. Had she grieved her husband?

Cass didn't want to think of her in pain.

Truly, she should be kinder to Louise. She had apologized, after all, at that very first visit at her house.

She hadn't explained things, though. Cass hadn't thought that she wanted an explanation about how love had turned sour, knowing it would wound her to think of it again. But perhaps the pain would be in lancing the wound, and after the initial cut, it could start to heal.

❖

Darling had invited Louise and their friends to Hyde Park, as Mr. Belvedere had told her that he enjoyed a stroll of an afternoon. She thought she might have the opportunity to meet him on their walk.

Louise spent more time than usual choosing a promenade dress. It had to be the right color to complement the gloves that Cass had tucked into her reticule. To her delight when she opened the package, she had discovered a smart pair of tan riding gloves and two pairs of pretty wrist-length gloves for day wear. They were tasteful and beautiful, but more importantly, they had been given without any hint of expectation of where to wear them, or when.

These were a *gift*.

If Darling was hoping to see Mr. Belvedere today, there was every chance that Cass would be there too. Louise tried to stop the flutter in her heart at the thought, feeling for all the world as if she had drunk one dish too many of the strongest brewed tea.

More than anything, she looked forward to fresh air and daylight and sunshine. Most of her new memories of Cass were in candlelit rooms, or shadowy alcoves, or moonlight gardens. It created opportunities most tempting. The afternoon air would keep her head clear enough to prevent her from doing anything foolish.

After all, she had been able to think of little else than the kiss they had shared. Foolish in the extreme, and yet the most thrilling thing that had happened to her in years.

"I have yet to meet Mr. Belvedere by chance anywhere," Darling confessed after Louise sat down in the carriage. "I know we have seen him at the balls and the tavern, but I wish for an opportunity to converse with him." Her eyes were soft, but her brow was creased. "I hope he would like the same for me."

"This will be a good opportunity, then." Louise patted her hand. "Who does not enjoy a healthful stroll? The Belvederes look like the sort to enjoy a vigorous walk, and I feel sure that they are taking as many opportunities as they can to show their gloves to their best advantage. I would bet anything that Mr. Belvedere will draw attention to his by using a cane as an affectation, and Cass will have a parasol."

Louise had not yet had much of a chance to speak with Mr. Belvedere. She had every reason to have a good opinion of him, but she was conscious that they knew very little of him. She hoped he had as good a character as Darling thought he did.

"I hadn't expected to like him so much," Darling said. "I know I had hoped to take a lover, but instead he has been so gentlemanly with me. He has not tried in the slightest to impugn my honor." She fluttered a hand over her heart, her face shining. "That's how he phrased it. He's concerned for my *honor*."

"That is to his credit." Louise hesitated. "But given the circumstances in which we met him…Are you sure that he would be interested in anything else? I mean to say, with a woman instead of a man? Have you indicated to him that you might have warmer feelings?"

Her cheeks pinked. "I have. By the way he grinned, I think he might share such feelings. Oh, I had wanted something wild and furious and impetuous, but Louise—I think I like this slow dance best of all."

"Then I wish you happy, and I am certain that Nell and Isadore will as well."

"It would be nice if they liked him. Samson seemed to when I invited him to dinner. Perhaps I ought to invite him to Alexander's dinner table next."

Alexander was her second son. Darling's feelings were serious indeed if she wished him to meet all of her children.

"I am here for a purpose," she told Nell and Isadore as soon as they saw each other at the park. "I have met a man, and I will be looking for him. I would be happy for you to meet him."

"A man!" Nell looked interested. "I had no idea you were hanging about for another husband."

Darling smiled. "Marriage bells are not ringing in my ears yet. He is a friend. A companion with a like mind."

"Oh, does he enjoy cards?" Isadore asked.

Darling considered. "You know, I don't think I have asked him." Her voice held faint surprise.

"Well, does he at least dance?" Isadore's face was doubtful.

Darling laughed. "I suppose he must, but I have yet to dance with him to determine whether or not he has feet of lead."

"I don't care what he likes to do at a ball," Nell declared with a sly smile. "I think it's more to the point what he is capable of doing *afterward*."

Louise frowned at her. "We don't need to investigate every detail of Mr. Belvedere's nocturnal habits."

"There is every need," Nell protested. "It's very important."

"Oh, I am not in the least worried. I have every expectation of satisfaction."

That sent them all into peals of laughter, and Louise marveled at the change in Darling. She had never looked so carefree as she had these last few weeks.

It was always nice to stroll with one's friends in the park in such clement weather. There were gentlemen on horseback, and an absolute crush of carriages moving inch by inch down the fashionable lane. Children laughed on the bank of the Serpentine, and a few people had well-trained dogs trotting at their heels.

After a half-hour stroll without their quarry in sight, Darling clutched Louise's arm. "He's here," she breathed.

Cass and Mr. Belvedere were making quick work of the gravel path, setting a pace more ambitious than a stroll. But why should they be expected to adhere to society's standards of pace, when they eschewed so very much else?

It was almost strange, seeing them in the daylight. It ought to have changed nothing. After all, they looked the same, whether lit by candles or by sunlight, but it felt different seeing Cass's face, shadowed by a smart straw bonnet as the sun shone on the silver epaulets fixed to her navy spencer.

Everything all at once felt less fraught.

On a beautifully sunny day like today, Louise could almost believe that *this* was their first meeting after fifteen years. It stripped away the nighttime encounters and left her with joy seeping into her limbs like sap after a long winter.

Nell and Isadore greeted the Belvederes with avid interest as they joined their party. When they kept peering at her and Cass, Louise realized with a start that they expected enmity between them as much as they expected affection between Mr. Belvedere and Darling. Nell went so far as to wedge herself between Louise and Cass, as if they might do each other some damage if they were not kept apart.

She caught Cass's eye behind Nell's back and smiled an apology. She could tell Cass understood when she winked at her before she turned to her other side to talk with Isadore.

She and Cass had *always* understood each other without the need for speech. More than anything, this reminded her of those heady days of falling in love.

Isadore strolled beside Cass when they resumed walking, while Nell interrogated Mr. Belvedere.

"Do you belong to any clubs, Mr. Belvedere?"

"Alas, a second son is perpetually embarrassed of funds," he said, touching the brim of his hat. "I hate to raise the topic of commerce among such ladies as yourselves, but I think perhaps you are already aware that my cousin and I are in London because we are the makers of very fine gloves, and we are seeking to replenish our funds. Perhaps someday I might boast of fortune enough to join one of the more respectable clubs."

A very satisfactory answer. If Cass could talk half as well as her cousin, she would have had more success by now.

"If I were a man, I should like to join Crockford's," Louise said. "I should never be in want of a whist partner again."

Cass's lips tightened. "Deep play at Crockford's," she said, her voice short. "You may never be alone at the table, but you may well leave without your shirt."

Isadore beamed up at her. "May I say that your frock is positively dashing, Miss Cassandra? You may be known for your gloves, but your style of dress is impeccable."

Louise was shocked to feel a prickle of jealousy, when she knew Isadore was trying to change the subject to ease the tension between them. But *she* was the one who wanted to compliment and be complimented in return.

When they drew near to the keeper's lodge where refreshments could be had, Mr. Belvedere insisted on fetching them all a syllabub, and Cass strode off with him to help.

"They are both so gallant," Isadore said.

"Mr. Belvedere is handsome." Nell grinned at Darling. "You have chosen wisely."

"Is he not a trifle young?" Isadore ventured.

"Not so very young! He is a man of experience, and within ten years of my own age," Darling said. "Do not allow the sight of my greying hair to age me one minute more than my fifty years, my dear. Although I do assure you that this is a time of life best enjoyed without a care for the thoughts of others, so I counsel you to keep your opinions to yourselves."

"If I were to marry again, I would have considered a title," Nell said. "Mr. Fenhurst is a fine husband, but a title would be dashing. Mr. Belvedere is certainly from a good family, but I daresay that he does not have the fortune that one might hope for. Of course, you already are a lady, Darling."

"Were I interested in such a thing as marriage, I would not consider such a match imprudent." Isadore pursed her lips. "A respectable mister has plenty to offer."

"I am most interested to hear *exactly* what he has offered, in all manners of courtship." Nell lowered her voice. "Has Mr. Belvedere written any letters to you? Stolen any kisses?"

Louise's attention wandered as Nell and Isadore continued to tease Darling, who tried to admonish them, but the smile that played on her lips betrayed how pleased she was at their encouragement of the match.

The sunshine and fresh air had not distracted Louise from her attraction after all. If anything, her desires were enhanced by the sight of Cass in the daylight. Her proud posture as she walked with determination beside her cousin, deep in conversation as they joined the line for refreshments. The way her brown hair had hints of tawny gold in it where the sunshine landed on her curls. The military-inspired frogging and cording on the spencer that clung to every inch of her magnificent bosom, and the soft flowing muslin skirts that twisted between her legs as she walked unfashionably fast.

"I wish to speak with you." Cass thrust a cup of frothy syllabub at Louise upon her return. "Let us stroll to the Serpentine."

Her eyes were dark with emotion, and Louise felt powerless to refuse.

More to the point, she didn't want to refuse. She wanted to hear her out.

Oh God. How she *wanted*.

Where Cass led, she worried she would follow—and that they might end up in her bed.

CHAPTER FOURTEEN

Cass watched as Louise sipped the sweet cream and wine from the metal cup. She hadn't purchased anything for herself, as she and Victor had only enough hands between them to fetch beverages for Louise and her three friends, but she wished she had figured out a way to have done it so that she might have something to do now with her hands.

She clasped them in front of her instead and stared across the Serpentine instead of looking at Louise's full lips. The water wound lazily by, and a few meters away, a few children were entertaining themselves by throwing stones into its depths.

Cass cleared her throat. "We shouldn't have kissed."

She had meant to broach the topic with more grace, but Louise ought to know who she was by now. She had not changed so much after all from the blunt youth that she had been.

"Oh?"

Cass wasn't sure what that meant and wasn't helped by the fact that Louise's bonnet was wide-brimmed enough to cover half her face.

"It was foolish of me. And rash. I know you dislike impulse."

"Did you hear me complain?"

"I suppose I did not."

"I believe you staked your claim when you told me that if I were to take a lover, it ought to be you."

Cass felt like a cad. "You oughtn't feel that way," she muttered. "You are free to choose whatever you want."

Louise cocked her head. "If I were to kiss another woman, you would take no umbrage?"

The very thought rankled.

She peered up at her from beneath her bonnet. "You needn't answer. I can see it plain as day on your face." Her voice was rich with satisfaction.

"You should not be constrained by my feelings. Not that I have *feelings*," Cass rushed to add.

"Nor I," Louise murmured.

"You have been very obliging about the gloves. I appreciate it." She felt awkward admitting it, but it was the truth.

"It is the least I can do. Darling is very happy."

They looked over at their friends. Victor had said something that made them all laugh.

"Is that all it is between us, then? Gloves? And other people's happiness?"

"There has always been more." Louise hesitated. "And I must admit that I am as changed as Darling these days."

Cass snapped to attention. "What is that supposed to mean?"

"I am enjoying myself." Louise looked faintly surprised. "I thought I had been having a grand time in London, but I am struggling to remember anything of any particular note in recent years. Except for Queenie's."

"It has that effect on people. Have you considered it might be the rum?"

"I thought perhaps it was the company." Her voice was scarcely above a whisper.

"Yes, the clientele is memorable."

"I meant *your* company." Louise scowled at her, and Cass couldn't help but laugh.

"I suppose I can admit that I don't dislike your company either."

"Such high praise."

"Do you not deserve the highest?"

"This conversation is a good deal more foolish than the kissing."

"Then perhaps we ought to try the kissing again."

Louise grinned up at her. "I could be persuaded to share a friendly kiss now and again." She pursed her lips. "Do you think perhaps we could be considered friends?"

Cass's breath caught. "Maybe. Yes. I suppose we could."

There had been good moments between them when they were

younger, although those memories had always been overshadowed by the bad.

The ending that they had never talked about.

The hurt feelings that still gnawed at her.

For all of her plans, she hadn't had the courage to address it. It still hurt too much. And what good would it do her, anyway? They could move on from the past without speaking of it.

Cass was worried that she wasn't feeling in the least bit friendly, after all. For underneath the layer of heavy memory that pressed hard against her heart, something a good deal warmer and altogether more alarming was scrabbling inside to be free.

❖

Louise had come to appreciate Cass's presence in the ballrooms.

She never danced, but she and her cousin now had a small coterie of acquaintances who passed the time with them in passionate discourse. Cass was nothing if not opinionated, and Mr. Belvedere was cut from the same cloth. If she were honest with herself, Louise could admit that what she appreciated most was that every so often, Cass would swing her head up, set her quizzing glass against her cheekbone, and search the room.

Looking for her.

Louise knew it because each time Cass found her, she would tilt her head the slightest degree upward in recognition, and then drop the glass and return to her conversation.

It didn't matter if Louise was talking with Nell and Isadore, or if she was in the midst of a country dance with a duke. Whenever she met Cass's eyes, a thrill raced through her and she wished for nothing more than to stop what she was doing and go to her side.

She never did, of course. That would be making too much of their fragile friendship.

Cass's crowd consisted of minor gentry and eccentric offshoots of family trees, due to her own insistence on following whichever conventions she preferred instead of society's standards for female behavior. Mr. Belvedere attracted a bevy of younger sons with style who wished to buck the trends of their titled fathers. Louise knew them all by reputation if not by direct association, and none of them had enough of their own funds to purchase gloves for a week let alone a season.

Louise had promised herself that she wouldn't venture into the card room tonight, though her toes itched to walk over to where she could find any number of companions willing for a rubber of whist.

She would keep away from cards as a matter of principle, for she owed Cass a great deal for Darling's newfound happiness. Darling had always been an excellent companion and a woman of gentle wisdom, who always knew the right thing to do. Louise knew Darling had not been unhappy before, but there was a sparkle in her eyes now that was delightful to witness. She laughed more easily and seemed to be more carefree.

Darling no longer haunted the card room with her. She also wasn't coming round in the evenings to Louise's townhouse as often as she used to, either, and when she did, she played an indifferent hand and then wanted to speak of her blossoming feelings for Mr. Belvedere.

In fact, right now she was standing with Mr. Belvedere and Cass, deep in conversation with an earl's daughter who was known to be rather fast and something of an artist. It was not someone who Darling would have ever even noticed previously.

Was this how Darling had been in her youth? How intriguing.

And it was all courtesy of Cass.

Nell appeared at Louise's side, a vision in pale pink taffeta, fluttering a white lacy fan in front of her face. "It is dreadfully warm in here," she said, and closed the fan with a snap so that she could tap Louise on the shoulder with it. "Do play cards with me. I peeked in the card room earlier and was dismayed not to find you, but I did notice that the room boasts two French doors that are wide open to the gardens. It's much cooler."

"Thank you, but I am more inclined to dance tonight," Louise said. "Isadore is here with her mother, and I am sure they would be happy to join you."

Nell pulled a face. "I am uninterested in mothers tonight. My mother-in-law is in London and staying with us, and as she never hesitates to tell me her much-varied opinions of me, I have escaped here while my husband escorts her to the theater."

"Isadore's mother will surely not share the same opinions."

"Mothers rarely have good opinions of me. Cheer me up and spend the rest of the night with me at cards, please. I have been practicing."

"I regret that I cannot." It pained her to say it, because there was nothing more that she would rather do. "I have agreed to dance with Lord Williams."

"You cannot be serious! Dancing in this heat isn't enjoyable in the least. Besides, do you not wish to practice for the tourney? How will you ever win if you do not focus?"

"I have not yet even been invited. Besides, there are other things that are important."

Nell started fanning herself again, watching Louise's face over the lace. "If you consider dancing so important, then perhaps you have followed Darling to the husband hunt?"

"I assure you that I am uninterested in a man." That was true enough.

The worst part of having card players as friends was that they could often guess when she was bluffing.

Nell gazed around the room. "Lord Williams is not the type of man I would have chosen for you. He is too young and too serious."

Louise was interested, despite herself. "What kind of person do you think I should be looking for instead?"

"I think you would do well with someone that you could have fun with." She grinned. "Someone with real passion."

"Atwater was nothing like that."

"You cannot marry the same man twice." Nell poked her with her fan. "It would do you good to be with someone altogether different. But if you are disinclined toward marriage, then I do not see why you are hanging about the dance floor tonight. After your dance, come find me in the card room."

Maybe Cass wouldn't notice her absence. Whist was a quick game, after all. Louise could even play a rubber now and return before the musicians began to play the next set.

But that wasn't the point. If Louise wanted to help encourage sales, it necessitated her talking, which could not be done at the whist table. The Belvedere gloves were magnificent and deserved the highest praise she could give them.

She would dance with Lord Williams and she would tell him all about the Belvederes.

And she would *not* follow Nell into the card room.

"Please, Louise?"

The problem was that she did still want the invitation to the tourney, and had not found much time for practice. Nell looked so forlorn, and Louise hated to disappoint her.

Before Lord Williams approached her for their dance, she saw Cass in a heated argument with Mr. Pierce. He came from a very old fortune and loved nothing more than to remind others of his wealth by entering bets at White's for exorbitant sums. He was a fashionable man who took great care with the cut of his trousers and was a rather wretched person. Louise had never liked him.

Ignoring anyone who tried to stop and greet her, Louise darted through the crowd to Cass's side in time to hear Mr. Pierce insult her.

"I daresay I have no idea how you were even invited here tonight if this is how you behave. If your sole conversation consists of nattering on about trade, there are places more appropriate to do so, Miss Cassandra. Such as the shops. Or one might think of the gutters, perhaps?"

Cass's hands were clenched into fists, and Louise had a horror of her throwing a punch.

"Mr. Pierce, what is this fuss about?" Louise smiled up at him. The sneer on his face took her aback, but she knew it was more important to cool his temper with as little fuss as she could manage. He was an influential man and petty enough to do a good deal of harm. Her own temper was rising, but she breathed deep and straightened her back and thought of cards. This was no more than a game and could be won with the right stratagem. "Are you implying that my dear friend is bothering you with shop talk, of all things?"

"Lady Atwater, she speaks of nothing else!" he cried. "I have never been more relieved to see your face so that this tedium may end."

Louise held out her hand, and he took it automatically and brushed a kiss at her knuckle. "You may see for yourself what fine work Miss Cassandra speaks of," she said, refusing to lower her hand even after he had released it.

Her gloves were pale pink and embroidered with tiny roses in various stages of bloom. They had not shocked onlookers as the navy gloves had, though they were an equally odd choice for a ballroom. Louise still felt like she had to make amends to Cass and could not deny that colored gloves caused much more interest than if she wore plain white kidskin.

"These gloves are made from her own hand. And in my mind, she speaks not of trade—oh no, Mr. Pierce." She looked at the people around her and laughed, encouraging them to laugh with her with some success. "Miss Cassandra speaks to you of *fashion*! Are these gloves not the most fashionable thing you have ever seen? Such delicacy. Such fine leather." She beamed at Cass. "Is not fashion the very best and most interesting thing to speak of at a ball? I think there is no topic more suitable for discussion."

His mouth snapped shut. Louise curtsied, then bumped Cass's elbow with her own to get her to follow her to the bay windows where they could find some solitude. People murmured to each other with interest as she passed them, but that mattered less to her right now than Cass.

"Was he being a boor for very long?" Louise asked as soon as they were out of earshot. She kept an eye on the crowd but couldn't see where Mr. Pierce had gone after they had left him. Uneasiness snaked through her. He was a powerful man.

"It is of no import." But Cass's color was high, and her brows were knitted low over her eyes. "I do not care for the opinions of oafish men."

"Be that as it may, perhaps you might wish to take a moment alone to calm down."

Louise took a deep breath as she settled her back against the wall for a moment. The plaster was cold against her shoulder blades, the thin muslin of her dress doing little to protect her. She disliked confrontation.

"I don't need to calm down." Cass took a step away. "I need to *sell*."

Louise tugged on her hand. "I know, but—"

"You don't understand at all!" Cass cried. "People are depending on me."

No one was paying them the slightest mind, so Louise didn't release her hand. She stroked her palm with her thumb. This was a matter of some delicacy. "I do wonder if perhaps it is possible that you are using the wrong approach to speak to people." She gentled her tone. "The reality is that these people are here to gossip, and to dance. They do not wish to speak of sales in the ballroom."

"Not all of us were born with the gift of speech like you were." Louise stared at her. "I don't have any particular gift."

"Of course you do! You have always been beloved. From when we were debutantes, you had all the other girls eating from your hand. None of us stood a chance with any gentleman when you were around. And in the end, I fell under your spell the same as the rest of them." Her smile was bitter.

"There was no spell," Louise said softly. "But if there were, I succumbed to its charms too. I was bound to you the same as you felt bound to me."

Cass's breathing was shallow, and her eyes were dark.

"Come home with me." Louise squeezed her hand. "Let us talk."

"I do not have time."

"Please, Cass."

As Cass settled into an armchair in Atwater's library, all she could think of was how very odd it all felt. The brandy that Louise was pouring into a crystal snifter for her had likely been chosen by Atwater himself for his cellar. The kisses that she and Louise had shared had been before his marriage and after his death, but sitting here with his widow and drinking his brandy felt like a trespass against her old friend.

She swirled the brandy and sipped, needing the fire to run through her veins to soothe her heartache. So many of the memories from her debutante Season were tangled between Atwater and Louise and the confusion of emotion that she had felt for them both.

"Are you upset about tonight?" Louise was looking at her with sympathy in her eyes, but it deepened the pain in her heart.

"I told you that I don't care what people think of me."

"It wouldn't be so surprising if you cared tonight. Mr. Pierce can be awful."

"You came to my rescue." Cass drank deeply and shifted in her chair, resettling her skirts around her. She didn't like relying on someone else for help. "Thank you."

"You don't sound very pleased about it."

Louise and her insights could go to hell. "I could have handled it on my own."

She lowered her eyes and Cass felt a prick of guilt.

The truth was that she wasn't thinking of tonight's ballroom. When she closed her eyes, all she could see were the shadows of ballrooms past. Dancing with Atwater and grinning at Louise from over his shoulder as she tapped her foot with impatience from the sidelines waiting for her turn in the next set. There had been dozens of strolls in Hyde Park, each of them hanging on one of his arms and trying to pretend as if she were the only girl he was with. Once he had rowed them both into a lake at a house party, where they had entered the kind of high-spirited and completely silly debate that young people enjoyed, about the merits of each summer fruit and which tasted best when enjoyed at a picnic.

Now Atwater was gone, and Cass and Louise sat drinking brandy that had aged more than he ever had.

"Next time I shall leave you on your own." Louise's tone was cool. "I apologize for overstepping where I was not wanted."

Cass swallowed her pride along with the next sip of brandy. "I am sorry. It is difficult for me to ask for help, when I have expected so little of it in my life. I am accustomed to doing many things on my own. But I appreciate what you did for me tonight. You were always better with people than I was."

"Perhaps not better. Different," Louise said with a small smile.

"Better," Cass corrected her. "You are a kind woman."

She was quiet for a moment. "But I wasn't always, was I? I wasn't kind to you fifteen years ago."

"You already apologized for it." And it still hurt, but talking about it was sure to hurt worse.

"But I never explained. I was still angry when I apologized. You deserved better, Cass."

"Why did you choose Atwater? You could have had anyone that summer." Cass swallowed. "You could have had *me*."

CHAPTER FIFTEEN

L ouise didn't say anything.

"I loved you. And you did nothing but betray me."

"I loved you too, Cass. Did you think it was so easy for me to choose Atwater? Did you never realize how much I cried? But my family was relying on me to say yes to him."

"So was mine," Cass shot back. "But at one word from you, I would have chosen to forsake everything. We had the chance to have done something daring. Something *real*. Something that we could have been proud of when we looked back on our lives. But you chose marriage. You chose the safe option."

"What is it that you could have offered me? What kind of life would we have had? No security, no money. No home of our own." Louise rose from her chair and paced the room, her skirts swirling around her ankles. "A life between us could never have been real. It was a dream. A *beautiful* dream, and one that I didn't wish to wake from. But that's all it was." Her eyes were bright with unshed tears, and her hands had clenched into fists.

Cass felt as if she had been slapped. "Our summer together meant nothing to you, then? The nights we had together were not real?"

"I didn't say that. But you have to understand that you were asking me to make an impossible choice."

"You made plenty enough of them. You wed the one man I could have married. If you had borne any love for me at all, you would have chosen someone else and left me with Atwater. Instead, you broke my heart and stole my one chance at a husband." She raised her glass in a mocking salute. "Not all of us were peerless beauties."

Louise sighed as she fell back into the armchair and pressed a hand to her forehead. "Do be reasonable. You could have had someone else."

"Atwater's land has the best sheep in the county, which would have been a priceless advantage for the Belvedere glovers. My family had planned for us to wed for years, though nothing official had ever been drawn up between our fathers. He was meant for me." She lifted her chin. "Besides, no one else wanted me. I received no other offers."

"I am not to blame for that." Louise gazed at her steadily. "I am not responsible for your father losing a fortune at a gaming hell."

Cass jerked back. "His loss is why an old family friend was the only person who could have overlooked my father's shortcomings, but you had already ensnared him by the time I found him and begged for his help."

The expression on Atwater's face had been so very kind when he had told her that he had already proposed to Louise. The shock of it had sent her reeling, and the crowd of debutantes that Louise had gathered around her to celebrate the engagement had laughed and laughed at her. Gauche, awkward Cass, who had little enough to recommend her and who had lost the support of the two people she had trusted that summer.

Louise had not said a word. She had stood as tall as a queen, as certain as a judge. She had won her game, and Atwater was the trophy.

It was the last time they had seen each other.

"I know you feel like you were entitled to marry him." Her face was soft. "But what kind of life were you offering him, Cass? Would you have given him love and affection? Would you have borne his children?"

Louise's face was white and pinched as she gripped her glass and brought it to her lips. Her hand trembled. Cass remembered that Louise had never had children, and for the first time she wondered how she felt about that. Did she feel it was a loss in her life? Or a relief, that there was no reminder of her late husband? Had she wanted children? She could not recall having ever discussed it in the hours that they had spent talking in the corners of ballrooms and in shadowy gardens when they should have been dancing.

Maybe their conversations had not been so deep after all.

Maybe she really hadn't been able to offer the world to Louise.

"I would have done my duty." But Cass knew that although it was true, it would have never been more than duty, and an efficient and cold one at that.

Louise had been willing to offer her heart to him, as bruised as it had been from Cass's rough treatment of it.

It was all so long ago now. They were no longer in the first blush of youth, but neither of them were yet in the grave like Atwater. He had been a good man, and gone too soon.

Cass stared into the brandy. "He only had eight years left after your wedding day. Knowing that...I am glad that he spent them happy."

"Thank you," Louise said, her voice just above a whisper. "It means a lot to think that I made him happy. I did love him, you know. Not at first—not like I felt for you—but I grew to love him."

❖

Louise sat with Cass in silence. She could hear the rustling of the leaves through the open window, and the ticking of the grandfather clock in the hallway, and she almost thought she could hear Cass's heartbeat from where she sat across from her.

But there were no more words.

What else was there in life but to have loved and to have been loved in return? Hadn't she lived through riches to have earned the love of two people, however temporary it had been? Cass's love had lasted but a summer and Atwater's less than a decade. But both had enriched her life beyond measure, and she could not be anything but grateful when she thought back on those halcyon days when they had all been so young and so alive, flush with the success of the Season and in experiencing a taste of adulthood for the very first time.

She and Cass would always have those memories. For the first time when Louise thought of them, she didn't ache with the weight of guilt and shame.

"That summer was not all bad," Louise said finally. "I remember a lot of laughter."

Louise had been so entranced by the balls and the men and the dancing, and the friendships that she had discovered had been waiting for her. It had taken her too long to recognize that she had been too easily influenced. As the youngest of five daughters, she had never felt as if her family listened to her, but London had been a different world from where she had grown up in Cumbria.

In London, she was no longer the youngest and least significant Sheffield. It was a golden world of opportunity, where every grace and favor was granted when one was young and beautiful.

It had gone to her head. She could admit it now, but she had been too willing to believe in dreams to realize that there were consequences. For every favor she was given, it meant something was taken from someone else.

For every dance that Atwater asked of her, it was one less that was asked of Cass. She hadn't understood how passionately Cass had wanted the union. She had never realized that Cass had set her sights on Atwater and no other. She had not known that Cass had no desire at all for men and could not contemplate a union with one except with the dearest of childhood friends.

It had all been a delightful game to Louise, rife with innocent teasing and flirting. But she hadn't known the stakes until the very end.

"We did laugh a lot." Cass's face was contemplative as she sipped her brandy. "You and Atwater were very amusing companions."

"You were a delightful friend."

The other debutantes had never liked her and had never understood why Louise wanted to spend any time with her. Cass had been abrasive and impulsive. She had a habit of giving her opinion where it was little wanted, especially if it was about their clothes or the insipidity of the events or the silliness of having to pretend to be sweet innocent flowers for the gentlemen's perusal. The other girls found her annoying at best and threatening at worst—for if they were around her, they feared the gentlemen would think that they were the same as her, when they wished for every insipidity that they could grasp.

Louise had found Cass strange at first, and almost uncomfortable with her frank observations. But she had grown fascinated by her and then looked forward to spending time with her. And they spent a considerable amount of time together, given that Cass was determined to be the future Countess of Atwater.

They spent hours at the same balls, searching for the very best places to be noticed. They lent each other pins and lip salve in the retiring rooms where Cass once allowed Louise to pinch her cheeks to give her color, giggling all the while.

And one afternoon at a picnic, Cass beckoned to Louise to linger with her in the gardens where they had shared their first kiss in the shrubbery instead of picking strawberries with the other young ladies.

"I was more than a friend." Cass stared at her with intensity in her eyes. "I loved you."

"I should have found a way to tell you that Atwater proposed to me." She swallowed. "I only learned that he visited my father on the very day that you discovered that your father had lost that game of cards. I would never have persuaded Atwater to turn away from you in the way that you thought I did. I encouraged him, and I made it clear that a proposal would be welcomed, but I did not know of your sudden change in circumstances or the fact that my father had already accepted Atwater's suit. I am so sorry that you found out the way you did later that night. It should have never been something you experienced in public."

"Those other girls were vicious." There was little enough heat in her voice. Cass sounded more tired than hurt.

"I thought he might prefer you." Louise hesitated, but she needed to confess it all. "I was consumed by jealousy. You and I had already argued that week when you asked me to run away with you, and I had refused. I thought we would never see each other again after that night. I never dreamed that you would still be interested in marrying Atwater, after you told me that you loved me. I thought that the field was clear, and I told him that you would not have him." She felt the pain of it deep inside. "I regret that now. I should have let you speak for yourself, and you should have had the opportunity to tell him how you felt. But I did not think you would have accepted his hand in marriage if he had asked for it."

Cass's face was inscrutable. "I had pinned all my hopes and all my dreams on that proposal."

"And I wish to God I had known it. Maybe things would have been different. I am so sorry that I took that opportunity away from you."

Cass shook her head. "There is no changing the past."

"I changed my life after the wedding because of that night," Louise said quietly. "Darling befriended me and taught me that there was far greater value in being kind and supportive than being judgmental and vapid. I stopped seeing the friends that I had surrounded myself with.

I realized that I did not share their values, and I was ashamed at my own behavior when I was with them. I studied philosophy and attended lectures at the museums and soothed myself with the logic and strategy of card play, and tried not to think too far into the future."

Cass blew out a breath. "There are plenty of times that I do not care to think about it either." She rose and pulled Louise up from her chair. "Times like now."

She grasped her face in her hands and kissed her, and Louise clung to her to prevent herself from toppling over in shock. Whatever she had expected, it has not been this. But then it felt so right to have Cass in her arms, the woman who had been there for some of the most important parts of her life.

The kiss was long and tumultuous.

"There was a lot lost between us," Cass said to her, still cradling her face. "Mistakes were made. People were hurt. But there was love through it all, wasn't there?"

"Yes," Louise whispered. "Above all, there was love." Between herself, Cass, and Atwater, there had always been the undercurrents of love. Perhaps not always romantic in nature, but it had plenty of strength nonetheless.

Cass captured her lips again.

"Perhaps I may seduce you yet," Cass said, the look in her eyes half-serious.

"There is no harm in a kiss, but I will go no further with you."

There was too much at risk. She had lost her heart fifteen years ago and was terrified at the idea of succumbing once more.

"Why is the lady so reticent to be pleasured?"

Louise was flustered and remained silent.

Cass pulled away. "I would never beg. If you love games so much, then the next move, dear heart, is *yours*."

CHAPTER SIXTEEN

C ass refused to approach Louise for the remainder of the week. Her eyes met Louise's more often than usual through the lens of her quizzing glass, which was practically fixed to her eye with how often she peered through it. Each time she looked at Louise, she had a dare in her eyes and a smile on her lips that spoke of untold pleasures.

Louise was left with a pounding heart and weakened knees, to the point where she thought perhaps she ought to consult her doctor. To be in such a constant condition was far from normal.

Even when Louise accompanied Darling to Queenie's, Cass left her alone. It appeared that after their conversation about their past, Cass was willing to leave their future for Louise to decide. She could not deny that she still yearned for Cass's touch. Why was she denying them both the pleasure that they had enjoyed before?

Louise didn't think anything between them had been laid to rest despite the conversation that they had. She ached with renewed regret over how she had behaved in the past. At the time, she had felt that her only option was to accept Atwater's hand in marriage after he and her father had arranged everything between them to their satisfaction.

She had been an obedient girl and had never gone against her father's mandates.

But their wishes for her life had now outlived them both. In light of it, Louise wondered now what would have happened if she had chosen another man to marry. She hadn't told Cass, but she had received three other offers before Atwater had asked her. Each time, her father had counseled her away from them, confident that she would snare a more prestigious title. He had been delighted when a proposal had come from an earl's heir.

If she had insisted on saying yes to one of those other men, her life would have been different indeed. Why, if Cass had then married Atwater, perhaps she and Louise would have found a way to continue their affair.

But perhaps not. It would have been impossible to experience such passion in the shadows without anyone becoming the wiser.

As it was now, Louise was alone, and increasingly lonely.

If she could not kiss Cass, she would need to kiss *someone*.

But if she wished for such a thing again with another woman, was it not prudent to seek out the other woman who knew of her desires, and who shared them? Engaging in pleasures with Cass meant that no one new would know of Louise's preferences in the bedroom. When Louise thought of the situation from that angle, it was clear that Cass was a prudent choice for such a liaison.

After all, Cass had made herself clear from the beginning. She was not opposed to a sexual relationship, but she would never revisit the feelings from the past. She would never trust her heart again with Louise.

There was no danger of anything beyond the indulgence of physical desires.

Oh, how Louise wished to indulge.

Her emotions in turmoil, she turned her thoughts to Mr. Belvedere, who was talking with Her Majesty. She had things she wished to learn about him, and this was a good opportunity while Darling was across the room trouncing his friends at a causal game of whist.

Louise walked up to him. "Good evening, Mr. Belvedere."

He nodded to her, then jerked his head toward Her Majesty. "Could I interest a countess in a drink?"

"You may indeed."

"Champagne punch for the lady."

Her Majesty tossed a lemon into a cup and poured from an open bottle of champagne. Louise was delighted with the drink when he had finished with it and after she had a sip. "Much more potent than at Vauxhall."

"That would be the gin," Her Majesty said. "I've been accused of having a rough hand."

"A heavy hand," Victor corrected him with a wink.

He grinned. "You'd know all about both of 'em, sir."

Louise frowned into her drink as Mr. Belvedere guided her to a table. "I will not hold with you having any amount of heaviness in your hand with my Darling," she said severely. "Not one finger."

He cleared his throat. "Her Majesty was not speaking of anything that would cause one undue harm. I think perhaps your education has been somewhat lacking in some areas? Not too surprising. I was much the same in my youth."

She blinked at him. "How could you consider yourself to be ill-educated? You cannot be speaking of Eton?"

"I did not have the good fortune to attend such a school. I had a tutor." His tone was short, and his eyes, the same honey-brown as Cass's, held a warning.

"Forgive me for prying, but this is my best friend that we are discussing. It merits some uncomfortable discourse to ensure that she is happy after you become the happiest of men."

Mr. Belvedere sat ramrod straight, one knee crossed, a frown on his face. "What do you mean?"

"Well, if Darling is to have a good life with you, then I think I should know more about the measure of the man."

"If you want my measure, you may speak to my tailor. Lady Darling wishes for diversion. She has not mentioned anything further."

"Oh, she doesn't have to speak such things aloud with me. She is my longstanding whist partner. I daresay we are quite in accord with one another, to the point where we can often tell what is in each other's heads." He appeared discomfited, and Louise surmised it was due to his hand being so plainly shown. "Please understand that Darling's well-being is my cherished goal."

"You have made that clear. I myself wish nothing but the best for her." He took another drink and then leaned forward with his elbows on the table. "What about your interest in my cousin, if we are asking questions about happiness? What is your interest there?"

"I have no interest," Louise lied. She was beyond mere interest. She was *fascinated*. "She has asked me to wear your gloves. They are beautiful, by the way. I hope you both make a fortune."

No matter what happened between herself and Cass, the Belvederes deserved all the business they could get.

"I thank you for your well wishes. We aren't interested so much in a fortune, however. Cass wants the glovers to be happy."

"The glovers?"

"All Cass has done since she failed to marry well is try to restore the gloving industry and to ensure a livelihood for our people back home. She wants *them* to be successful—that's more important to her than making money for herself."

Her heart was squeezed as tight as Her Majesty's lemons to learn of Cass's altruism. It made sense that she was so devoted to success if it meant improving the lives of others. That was exactly like the Cass she had known.

Maybe she had the perfect opportunity to revisit the best parts of their past. She and Cass had enjoyed a great deal of fun together once upon a time, until they had ruined everything by falling in love. Maybe they could re-create the pleasures of that long-ago summer without the worry of heartache. They could have their friendship again.

As long as she was cautious.

After her marriage and the restructure of her life, discipline had taught her peace, and brought her steadiness and satisfaction. Caution had become her best friend.

There would be nothing easier.

Louise looked over at Cass as she finished her champagne punch. Perhaps happiness had been before her all Season, and all she had to do was reach out and touch it before it dissolved in the rain.

"I haven't seen you in three days," Cass said to Victor.

After a week of burning for Louise from afar, combined with the stress of not knowing where Victor was from one moment to the next, Cass was on edge and short-tempered.

Victor slumped across the table in the parlor, one hand buried deep in his tousled hair. "My clothing is rumpled beyond repair. My cravat is an utter disaster. I am not fit to be seen," he ground out.

"That much is self evident. Dammit, Victor, I'm tired of this. You promised you would finish the samples."

Victor started to laugh, his shoulders heaving. When his eyes met Cass's, they were filled with disdain. "Don't worry," he said with a sneer. "My hands will be in working order tomorrow. I'll finish the fucking samples. And they'll be more magnificent than you have yet dreamed. We'll get the orders."

"Not if we already missed the opportunities!"

"Is all you worry about is work?" Victor asked. "Is your heart so hard that it is made of pieces of silver? You will note that I do not accuse you of having a heart of gold, for if you are so hardened then there is no soft metal to prove your mettle. It's all wasted on farthings and pennies."

"That's not fair. I was worried about you, Victor. If Her Majesty hadn't sent me a note after the first night that you were staying with him above the tavern, I would have torn London apart looking for you. What is wrong with you?"

His shoulders shook, but Cass didn't think it was from laughter anymore. He looked away.

She sighed. "I care for you. You're my favorite cousin. But you are destroying yourself, and I cannot bear it."

"I cannot be with her!" Victor exploded. "Is that so difficult to understand?" His eyes were red and wild.

"Who? Lady Darling?"

"Of course. Who did you think I was speaking of? Your countess told me what Lady Darling is expecting, and it's a good deal more than I bargained for."

Her countess. Her heart skipped a beat, but it was not the time to think of Louise. "What is the lady looking for?"

"The way the countess was talking, it sounded like *marriage.*" He spat out the word. "How the fuck am I supposed to marry someone, Cass?"

"Does she know anything about your past?"

"Nothing at all. I thought we were enjoying a dalliance, nothing more. She appreciates my gallantry, and she laughs at my witticisms. But she's a society woman. How could I think she might understand?"

"What are your feelings for her?"

"I am besotted," he said flatly. "But what else is new? I have fallen in love half a dozen times over the years, with a variety of unsuitable men and women. My modus operandi is to pine from afar, and then to fuck whoever is nearest and least interested."

"How has that served you?"

"Clearly not very well."

"Then maybe you ought to try something new. Maybe she would understand you."

"If I dared to speak of it. But if I do, would I jeopardize our business? Would she keep my secret? Or would the *ton* know that the Belvedere glovers are steeped in sin?"

"There is no sin in this," Cass said quietly.

"I know that, and you know that. You know who else knows that in these circles? Very possibly no one. I cannot trust her to understand."

Cass sighed and sat down beside him. "Maybe Lady Darling isn't worth the heartache. If the thought of telling her has upset you to this degree, then maybe she is not the one for you."

"I could say the same of you."

She stared at him. "What do you mean?"

"I see the way you look at the countess. Like she is the finest thing you ever saw in your life and you would grovel for the chance to touch the toe of her slipper."

"I don't look like that," she snapped.

"Anyone with eyes can see it. The only one more oblivious than you is her. But I daresay I could light a dozen candles by the heat of your eyes when you are near her."

"Falderol. You're still drunk, Victor."

"That I am," he said, surprising her. His eyes were troubled. "And that's one of the problems. I'm not good enough for her. Lady Darling deserves better than a Belvedere."

"Are we such sorry specimens that we do not deserve to find love?"

"Are we not? I should tell her who I am, but I cannot. Even if I did—even if she understood—even if she *accepted*—she deserves more than a man of uncertain income who is too often buried in drink."

Cass touched his arm. "You could change. God above, Victor, *we* could change."

He shrugged her hand away and laughed. "I told you as soon as we arrived in London that those such as we do not change our nature. I am a man of the dark and the shadows. Strolling in Hyde Park and pretending like I could possibly pay court to a society woman was the aberration, a mere dream. I belong to nights with the lads and enough wine to make me forget that the light even exists."

"Those with our nature deserve whatever we can find for ourselves," she said hotly. "I will never believe otherwise. We may not be free to speak of our desires so casually to others, but where is the harm in it? Where is the trespass against our fellow man? I belong to every minute of every hour of the daytime, just as much if not more than I deserve to shine in the moonlight."

He rose to his feet. "I'm off to bed."

"It's half ten in the morning," she pointed out.

"I shall rise again at dusk to start all this over again," he said, waving his hand in a circle. "Around and around and around we go."

The ouroboros, Cass thought. The snake eating its own tail. That glove had been a message to them both.

She didn't want that to be her anymore. She was not whole unto herself, much as she pretended to be. She wanted to cleave to another.

She wanted Louise, she realized with the certainty of a lightning bolt. Oh, God help her. She wanted so much more than kisses at Queenie's, or the possibility of a tumble in the dead of night.

She wanted the fucking sunshine.

She couldn't seduce Louise. Not when she felt like this. Not when she wanted to...*court* her?

CHAPTER SEVENTEEN

The next time that Cass saw Louise, she was engaged in conversation at Queenie's with Her Majesty and a handful of Victor's friends. Mr. Daruwalla and Mr. Murkute were a devoted pair of lovers, near fifty years of age, and had a long career together as accountants after they moved to England from India. Mr. Yates was a student of law who often looked at Victor as if he hung the moon. Their heads were lowered as they studied the cards on the bar in front of them, Louise evidentially having taken the time to engage in her favorite pastime with whoever would agree to play with her.

Louise was enchanting in a yellow silk sarsnet frock, the neckline framed by thin braiding. A delicate posy of violets nestled between her breasts. The sleeves were long and tight against her arms except for the dramatic ruched puff at the shoulder, which was inset with strips of black lace. Cass's eye was caught by her hands as she dealt the cards. She held one cream Limerick glove but wore the other one, perhaps to prevent as little damage to them as she could by not removing them unless necessary.

Limericks were made of leather so thin that they were often worn one time before they were discarded. Cass wondered if Louise had dozens of wrist-length pairs in her wardrobe, kept folded up as they were sold in their tiny walnut-shell cases, and if it had been convenience to choose to wear them tonight. After all, they were an easy choice, given that they went with almost any style of dress and were always fashionable.

Or did she keep limited pairs, and had she marked the evening as special enough to waste one in order to look her best tonight?

Maybe Cass was making too much of it, but she hoped it was the latter.

She watched her for a time, as comfortable with these men as if they were her own brothers, not even pausing in her explanation of the cards when Mr. Daruwalla and Mr. Murkute shared a casual kiss.

It warmed Cass's heart to see her lack of pretension. Louise had been a stickler for propriety, blushing to see any exchange of stolen passion, and blushing even more when she and Cass had engaged in them together. She had associated with the most proper debutantes and had been courted by the highest of noblemen, but here she was giving pointers at cards with professional men, and mollies at that.

Did she understand that she belonged here amid the cigarillo smoke and the strong scent of gin and rum, as much as she belonged to the glittering and rarified world of the *ton*?

Louise must have sensed Cass's gaze, for she swept her head up and scanned the room. Her eyes widened when she saw her, and a wide smile broke across her face.

"Cass!" she cried, scrambling down from the stool.

She was at Cass's side in a heartbeat and touched her forearm with her ungloved hand. The heat of her touch went straight through Cass's fine gauze sleeve as if it were a scalding hot iron, for all her heart leapt into her throat as if it she had been burned.

"Has the rum taken a liking to you again tonight, Diana?"

Louise laughed. "Your friends are generous in their attentions, as I have been presented by all manner of beverages tonight from all manner of men."

Cass knew they were intrigued by the sudden appearance this past month by two bejeweled and beribboned ladies whose frocks cost more than a month's salary. The fact that Lady Darling and Louise had appeared regularly since then and minded their own business and paid up their bills had gone a long way toward them being tolerated and then welcomed.

"If you are feeling the ill effects of such generosity, would you like to be escorted home?"

"Oh." Louise blinked, then leaned against her and smiled. "My answer depends on what would happen after the escorting."

Cass had meant nothing more than to offer to arrange a hackney to bring Louise back to Mayfair, but she lost herself in those light blue eyes. "What would you wish to happen?"

"Any manner of interesting things," she admitted, then she laughed. "I feel so young again, reckless and wild."

Her head was thrown back, her neck exposed. Cass wanted to kiss the pulse that throbbed in the base of her neck. She wanted to trace her lips across her collarbone to the sharp point of her shoulder.

More than anything, Cass wanted to give this moment to her, to be the reason for the shine in her eyes.

"Seduce me," Louise whispered, and Cass was powerless under her gaze.

Cass swept Louise into her arms, loving the little gasp she made as she was pressed tight against her. "I have wanted you since the moment I saw you again," she growled against her neck. "I have wanted this."

It was true and yet there was an ache in her heart. She did want this. She wanted the physical sensation, she wanted Louise's scent in her nose, her body under her hands.

But her foolish, foolish heart wanted even more. Her heart could not be satisfied with the physical. No, it cried out and hammered in her ears for want of words of love.

Her heart might want, but it would go unsatisfied tonight.

Whatever Cass was offered, she must be content. And to have this woman in her bed tonight was no meagre offering. The opportunity to touch her thighs and kiss her breasts was worth a prince's ransom.

If this was what she wanted—then Cass wanted to give it to her.

Lucky for her, she thoroughly intended to enjoy it.

Darling had been more than amenable to being left at the Queen and Sceptre with Mr. Belvedere, who promised to see her home after Louise left the tavern with Cass. It felt altogether odd to wave good night to her friend and wonder if they were each to be accompanied tonight by a lover to their beds, after so many years of widowhood.

The trip back to her Mayfair townhouse was short and tense, as she and Cass said nothing to one another. Cass sprawled across from her on the padded seat in a most unladylike manner, one arm across the back of the padded bench, and one knee crossed over the other. She watched Louise intently, as if she were afraid that Louise might fling the hackney door open at any moment and flee into the night.

Her dress felt tighter, or perhaps it was that her breathing had become shallow. The sound of the carriage wheels on the cobblestones was louder than usual, but not in a way that was deafening. It was like everything around her was shouting with joy.

It was exhilarating to be wanted like this. To know that every one of Cass's thoughts was about her, and to be aware that she was only waiting for enough privacy before she reached out and touched her.

It had been years since Louise had been touched intimately.

Her carnal relations with Atwater had been pleasant enough, but there had been nothing like the flames that burned between her and Cass even when they were clothed and sitting across from one another. If Mayfair were much farther, she thought that smoke would start to curl from the leather seats amid the risk of catching fire.

Even when they entered Louise's house and walked up two flights of stairs to Louise's bedchamber at the back of the hallway, they said nothing to one another.

Louise lit the candles on the mantle and turned to face Cass.

She was magnificent, her burnt orange dress airy and voluminous as it fell from where it was gathered beneath her bosom. Louise could see glimpses of her white petticoat beneath the sheer gauze fabric, and from where it peeked out from beneath the hem of the full skirt. She wore a white shawl with gold embroidery and tassles at the fringe of it, and as she stood there staring at Louise with hunger in her eyes, the silk shawl slipped from one shoulder to rest against the crook of her elbow.

"I admit to having dreamed of this moment," Cass said, her voice low. "But I did not have all the details correct in my mind."

"Oh?"

She didn't reach out so much as a finger, but her eyes wandered over every inch of Louise in a manner that felt more intimate than a touch.

"You were wearing less clothing."

Louise sucked in a breath and discarded her gloves.

"Your hair was loose from all its pins."

Trembling, she began to slide the hairpins from her curls.

"My name was on your lips."

"Cass," she whispered, her lips throbbing from where they ached to be kissed.

She strode over to her. "And I was touching you like this."

Cass brought one hand to the nape of Louise's neck and the other to the small of her back, and then with one quick movement they were pressed together as tight as pages in a book. Cass's lips moved against hers with ferocity in an open kiss that tasted startlingly sweet, like honey and lemons and the faintest hint of gin. Louise arched her back to bring herself closer, Cass's hands holding her steady as she moved against her heat, yearning to feel her skin against her own. Cass's lips trailed across her cheek to nip at her earlobe, and her head would have fallen back if not for Cass's hand still at her neck, keeping her secure. Her fingers moved from Louise's neck and into her hair, cradling her head as she kissed her lips again, her tongue moving against her own with the heat of the inferno that had always blazed between them.

But for all of her passion, Cass was gentle when she let go and stepped away, and Louise was disappointed at the loss of her.

Cass stripped off her gloves and shrugged off her shawl, then folded it neatly and set it on a chair by the window. She pulled her orange dress over her head and folded that too, until she was in her stays with her bosom pushed high. Her white cotton petticoat was so thin that Louise could see her ankles through the fabric.

Louise was dizzied by the sight of her in the candlelight, in her bedchamber. Soon to be in her bed.

They had never shared a bed before.

Louise could remember each and every intimacy they had shared, having long ago committed them to memory when she realized she would never experience such a thing again. There had been dozens of stolen kisses at various garden parties, ballroom terraces, and once in the retiring room at the theater. There had been the time that Cass had put her hand under her skirts on a stormy afternoon when Louise had received no other visitors. They had taken their pleasure in hurried secrecy, once in a garden maze at an earl's estate, once in the mews behind Louise's father's house, and once in a parlor while waiting for a chaperone to walk with them to the circulating library.

There would be no such hurry tonight.

Would Cass still do that scandalous thing she had done that one time with her mouth?

Would those old feelings still explode across her belly like fireworks at Vauxhall?

There was only one way to discover such things, so Louise went to Cass and unlaced her stays. "I want to see you," she said. "Do you realize I've never seen you? Not all of you. Not as I would have wished."

"There had been no time for that." Cass helped ease the stays off her body and tossed them on top of her dress. "There will be time now."

Louise untied the strings of Cass's petticoat, letting it drop to the floor around her feet, and then brought her shift over her head to reveal the body that had haunted her dreams for years.

Cass's breasts were small and lovely, her hips angular. Her arms and legs were sleekly muscled, and so were her buttocks when Louise saw them as Cass bent to pick up her shift and petticoat. "I am not careless with my clothes," she explained with a half shrug, folding them with quick precision.

"I would not wish you to be careless at all tonight," Louise said softly, swallowing.

Cass grinned at her. "Then I shall unwrap you with all the delicacy that I would show to the finest china."

She did just that, her movements slow and reverent, uncovering each part of Louise with a kiss pressed against the skin that she had bared. When they were both unclothed, Louise took Cass's hand and pulled her to the bed. She flung her arms around Cass's back as Cass moved on top of her, delighting in the weight of her body pressing her into the mattress, and the feel of her hands on her hips and her thighs.

There had been nothing in her life quite like this before or since that summer, and Louise ached with the recognition of it. They had only enjoyed a handful of encounters across a few weeks of their lives, but embracing Cass felt like returning home after years of absence.

Louise kissed Cass's neck and shoulders, reaching for anywhere she could find with her mouth as she writhed beneath Cass's body, her hips straining upward against her.

"Tell me what you want," Cass murmured.

"I want to be touched."

"I have no greater desire than that."

Cass's hands moved with certainty over her body as if there was nothing more natural in the world than a woman giving another woman pleasure, and Louise could well believe it in this moment. But for all that Louise yearned to be touched, she also wanted to remember how Cass felt, so she moved her hands across Cass's strong back and down to her firm bottom and then up to cup her breasts. Louise kissed each of them, and then she wriggled from beneath Cass so that she could prop herself up and look down at her.

Cass's hair was in disarray across the pillows, and her eyes were wide and earnest as she stared up at her. Cass never had any talent for disingenuousness, which Louise had always appreciated about her. Cass might not tell her everything, but she would never hide how she felt.

Louise kissed her and moved her hand between their bodies to lay against Cass's center. Cass sucked in a breath and her hips jerked against her hand, so Louise pressed deeper and slipped a finger inside her.

Oh, how she had wanted this moment again.

She kissed Cass's neck and eased a second finger inside and rocked herself against Cass in a way that met with satisfaction, given the cries of pleasure that sounded in her ears. Cass shifted beneath her until her hand was free to move between them, and she began to stroke Louise at the same time. The pleasure was almost blinding, this push and pull of desire and release and yearning and fulfillment, and soon they were both gasping and shuddering against each other.

Louise pillowed her head against Cass's shoulder after she caught her breath but felt unaccountably vulnerable.

That had been an extraordinary experience.

She could only hope that she was not alone in thinking so.

CHAPTER EIGHTEEN

After her breathing had slowed, Cass rose from Louise's bed. She was more than ready to leave Mayfair, wanting to leave the newly minted memories amid the sheets instead of carrying them close to her heart. The kind of quiet that had settled over them was the kind that might inspire confessions and confidences, and she could ill afford either of them. Emotions that she didn't want to name threatened to spill out of her at the merest provocation, and then where would she be? It would do no good to dwell again on their shared past and would do a good deal worse to think much about what happened tonight.

"I don't suppose it would be too much trouble to ask for your coachman to bring me home?" she asked. "I don't fancy strolling alone past midnight."

"I don't keep a carriage," Louise said, surprising her.

"Don't be coy. Of course you do."

"Truly I don't. I go most places with Darling. We are invited to so many of the same functions."

"Am I meant to believe that this entire household functions without the use of a carriage? You cannot run every errand using your friend's carriage and horses."

She invested some effort to sound disdainful at the very idea, when the reality was that she was touched at the thought that perhaps Louise was trying to convince her to stay. But she couldn't really want Cass, could she? Was tonight more than a dalliance to her? Those dratted emotions welled up in her throat, wanting to form into words, and she swallowed hard.

Louise pushed her hair behind her ear. "Of course I employ grooms and a coachman. But I don't keep a *nice* carriage—not anything that I would be caught being seen in. Atwater has an array of conveyances that he is more than happy to trot out at a moment's notice for me. The family has always been kind to me."

"Do not think me so proud that I would be saddened to be seen in a run-down carriage unfit for the housekeeper," Cass said, amused despite herself. "I daresay no one would remark upon it."

"Oh, stay the night, won't you?" Louise asked, sitting up and clutching the sheets to her breasts. Her eyes were wide and guileless, but could Cass trust her? Could there be some other motive for keeping Cass here, beyond the promise of pleasure in each other's arms?

"What will your maid say in the morning when she finds both of us abed?"

"She is well paid to be discreet."

"I gather this is not the first assignation you've had, then?" It didn't surprise her. She herself had not been chaste all these years.

"Actually, it is," Louise said. "You and Atwater were my only lovers."

Cass absorbed the news, then nodded.

"But I trust my maid not to say anything to the rest of the household."

Cass gave up and grabbed her shift, then pulled it on. It was too vulnerable to be naked here in Louise's room while she beamed up at her from the bed. It was altogether too sweet a vignette. She shouldn't be here overnight, with the pretense that she belonged in this room with her.

She wanted to belong. She wanted nothing more than to slide into the sheets beside Louise, hold her in her arms. But the reality of being with her was terrifying.

She knew Louise was looking for a careless fling. It had been clear from their conversation about the past that she hadn't changed her mind since they were eighteen. While Cass had burned in love for her, Louise had been shocked at the very idea that they could have more than a handful of passionate encounters.

Still, it was easier to stay the night than to rouse the household. And if there was more pleasure to be had, who was she to deny them both what they wanted?

Cass would be sure to keep her heart better guarded this time around.

"Would you have any interest in a game of cards?" Louise asked.

Perhaps that wouldn't prove too difficult a task, as this was far from a romantic offer.

"Very little."

Louise pulled out a well-worn deck of cards from the night table beside the bed, the paint too faded for Cass to make out the motif printed on them. A cloud of white silk was pulled along with them and her cheeks turned scarlet.

"What are those?" Cass asked, intrigued.

"Nothing," she muttered, balling them up and fumbling with the drawer.

Cass lunged forward and grabbed a fistful of fabric. "Stockings," she said, bewildered. She shook them out and studied them. They were gossamer thin, edged with lace, with pinpricked hearts embroidered up the backs. "*Sensual* stockings."

"They were a gift."

"Gloves might be a common enough gift between lovers, but stockings like these…well." She wiggled her brows. "At the very least, you had an admirer if not a lover. And why not, when there is so very much about you to admire?"

"They were from Nell," she clarified with a laugh. "Sometimes she fancies herself to be shocking, which is more wishful thinking than anything. She gave each of us a deck of cards and a pair of stockings last year—myself, Darling, and Isadore. I think she was grateful to find friends when she started playing cards with us."

"Have you ever put them on?"

"Only once to try them."

Cass studied them. Beautiful silk, smooth, neat stitching. Soft as breath. Those little hearts winked at her as she considered how the silk would stretch across Louise's long legs. "How about now?"

"Cass, they're silly!"

"They are decidedly *not* silly."

She grabbed her heel and Louise giggled, losing balance and falling on her back as Cass brought her legs over her lap. She eased one stocking over her toes and the arch of her foot, smoothing the silk up her leg, working it over her knee and tying it around her thigh. Then she did the same to her other leg, taking her time to caress each inch and feeling most gratified when Louise's laughter turned to little sighs of pleasure.

"There," she said. Louise's legs were now encased in delicate finery, while the rest of her wore not a single stitch. It was erotic beyond measure. "Not silly at all."

"I suppose you would say that. Do you ever think clothing is silly?"

"Of course not. Clothes always have meaning, and therefore power. They allow us to tell the world that we have changed, or to warn that we have remained the same." She gestured to the dress she had removed earlier, and which she had folded and placed on a chair instead of allowing it to crumple on the floor. "I was never happier than when I was permitted to spend my father's coin on clothing that suited me, instead of wearing the costume that I was given when I was expected to behave as a biddable girl."

"You always did like hidden meanings. I remember you used to imbue your gifts to me with coded messages when we were young. You never had to say how you felt when I could see it clear as day in your gifts."

"You noticed?" The thought pleased her.

"Of course I noticed. I loved them." She choked on the word, and Cass's heart leapt. "I know the gloves you have given me this Season are not a lover's gift and have not the same implications, but I appreciate their meaning nonetheless. They represent opportunity."

She ran her hands over Louise's stockinged legs. "You are well deserving of adornment." *And adoration*, she wanted to add, but didn't. If Louise wished to hold her words and speak of code, then she would follow her lead.

Louise crossed her stockinged legs across Cass's lap and settled herself against the headboard. She began to shuffle the deck.

"Am I not interesting enough to hold your attention?" Cass asked, trying to keep the bite from her tone as she watched.

"Shuffling soothes me. I mean nothing by it. It has been an eventful evening, and I wish to calm my nerves."

Cass liked thinking that she had stirred her up. "I don't remember you being so devoted to cards," she said, stroking her ankle.

"I always liked to play, but it was only after my marriage that I began to practice in earnest. I find it very peaceful."

"What was *that*?" Cass asked, startled. A black shadow moved, slow and deliberate, and pounced on the bed. It was a thin black cat, sleek and orange-eyed, blinking imperiously at her before it turned and began to groom itself.

"That's Socrates," Louise said, a smile on her face. "Do you not remember him? You should. You saved him."

Her mouth fell open. "The scrap of fur from the horse track?"

They had been watching the races at Royal Ascot, and Atwater had a lot of money riding on a certain horse. Both she and Louise had pretended to be impressed, but Cass remembered spending more time staring at the lace on Louise's bodice than at the horseflesh that Atwater pointed out to them. She had kissed Louise the afternoon before—the most thrilling event of her life—and had tumbled into love as easily as breathing.

Then Cass had seen a tiny kitten darting about the horses' hooves, and she had leapt to save it, knowing that sensitive Louise would be devastated to witness any harm to the animal.

Atwater had been annoyed, but Louise had beamed at her, and Cass had tipped the mewling thing into Louise's reticule and had not given it one more thought in the interim.

"Socrates?" She frowned down at him as he yawned and stretched, ignoring her. His claws snagged the silk pillowcase which still held the imprint of Louise's head, and then he curled into a perfect sphere on her pillow. "Is a cat of much use as a philosopher?"

"He's very wise," she insisted. "I learned a lot from having him with me these fifteen years. He has taught me patience, and love. There is nothing like the affection of a cat to get one through the difficult times in life."

"He's ancient."

"He's *darling*."

"I don't know how he could possibly live up to his name, but he is smart enough to steal the warmth of your bed."

Louise scooped up the pillow and set it and the sleeping cat on a chair by the window. "He's very partial to my pillows."

"And now you must go without?"

"Well...I thought we could share."

Cass grinned and held out her arms.

❖

When Louise awoke, she was surprised that she was still so reluctant for Cass to leave her. She had understood the impulse well enough last night, giddy and enthralled by the most sensual experience she had ever had, but it was difficult for her to reconcile with the fact that she wanted to spend more time with her in the light of day. That would impart too much meaning to what had transpired between the sheets.

Although it made little enough sense to her, Louise wanted more than passion. What was the harm in taking the time this Season to explore what she wanted for herself?

"Do you wish to venture forth into the world with me today?" Louise asked, feigning indifference. Her heart refused to stop racing as she waited for the reply.

"You wish for company to entertain you at a tedious Venetian breakfast?" Cass asked, her eyes still closed as she drew Louise close. "Not my style, dear heart."

"Don't call me that," she said, though the phrase didn't sting as it had when Cass had first resurfaced in her life. She was almost coming to like it now that it had been stripped of its initial mockery, but the realization made her uneasy.

"Of course. Lou."

Louise thwapped her with a pillow. "*Louise*, if you please."

"Oh—you definitely please." Cass opened her eyes and grinned at her.

"I have a few errands I wish to accomplish today and thought perhaps you would like to come with me." Why did this feel like a more intimate invitation than lovemaking? Louise wasn't sure what she wanted Cass to say.

"I have no clothes suitable for daytime," Cass pointed out. "And I don't wish to borrow yours," she said as Louise looked at her overfilled wardrobe and opened her mouth to protest. "Your frocks are most fetching on you, but I find myself unwilling to wear another's dress when my own suit me so well. I like to cut a dashing figure where I can."

Her arrogance was charming.

Cass stretched and sat up, the sheet falling around her waist. "However, I do have another proposition. I could return home to change my dress, and then would be ready to sally forth as your escort."

Louise raised a brow. "My footmen are more than capable of providing escort."

"We won't need a footman. I shall drive us."

"*Drive?*"

"I have something vastly superior than a stodgy housekeeper's third-best carriage," Cass announced with satisfaction. "I have the sleekest little curricle you ever saw."

"You keep a *curricle?*" Louise fell back among the pillows, earning a yowl from Socrates before he moved to a new spot in the blankets. "Will you never cease to surprise me?"

"Victor bought it when he first moved to London years ago. He had fallen in with a fast group of friends and was partial to raising hell and rash decisions when he was younger. It's an expense to keep the horses, but he does love it." Her face softened. "I endeavor to support what brings him joy. He has not had an easy life."

"And you know how to drive a curricle?"

"I am a proficient enough whip." She winked. "You'll see."

When Cass returned an hour and a half later, Louise was in awe. She cut the most dashing figure that she had ever seen. She wore a smart green riding habit with braid trim that marched down the font of the bodice and which had a neat line of ornamental Spanish buttons at the sides. Her black beaver hat was set at a jaunty angle, and the fluffy ostrich feathers fastened into the hat band waved as she moved. The curricle was glossy yellow and black, and pulled by two spirited mares. She handled the horses with precision and confidence, her face serious as she touched the whip to bring them to a halt in front of the townhouse.

It was most unconventional, but what did Cass ever do that did adhere to convention?

To Louise's surprise, although the curricle was most decidedly in fashion, the horses were not.

"Was it too expensive to find a matched pair?" she asked, eyeing the piebald mares. They were similar size, but their black-and-white markings were as unalike as could be.

Cass smiled. "Victor cares not one whit for how the horses look, as long as they are willing to fly down the road. At one time he had the most beautiful pair of matched bays, but he is far more concerned these days with good performance over impressing others."

She leapt from the curricle and insisted on helping Louise take her seat.

Seated beside her, they were snug. The heat from Cass's body warmed Louise in a most delightful manner. She had admired Cass's muscular arms in bed last night, but it was delightful to see how her biceps tightened beneath the sleeves of her spencer as she handled the whip with precision.

They sped across the cobblestones, and Louise gripped the side panel. Oh, it was glorious to feel the wind on her cheeks as she was escorted through London in Cass's care.

"You're so powerful," she said, and couldn't help the admiration that seeped into her voice.

"Leather work takes a lot of strength if you wish to do it right," Cass said, glancing at her. "Some of the scissors that I need to wield are heavy, but I have also done my share of dressing and tanning."

"When did you learn to make gloves?"

"I insisted on taking my apprenticeship at thirteen, to the dismay of my mother and the amusement of my father and had studied enough to become proficient by the time we met."

She was surprised. "You never spoke of it."

Cass laughed. "My parents forbade me from mentioning it for fear of deterring both friendship and courtship."

"On the contrary, it's fascinating. Whyever did you want to learn a trade? I have never even heard a whisper of a gentlewoman doing such a thing."

"I am not most gentlewomen," Cass admitted with a sidelong look. "My father always spoke so highly of the business and the glovers. He was very involved in managing the business himself, as the Belvederes have been handing the sale of the finished gloves to the London wholesalers for generations. At the time, he sold the hides to the fellmongers who prepared the leather before selling it to the glovers. I grew up listening to my father and uncles talk about gloving, and I was enamored. Of course, my father never thought I would spend more than a day as an apprentice. He thought it a lark, and had always been indulgent of my unladylike habits, but he was upset when I continued and insisted I never mention it outside of our home."

"You have a great deal of courage to apprentice."

"According to most, what I am is stubborn and headstrong." Cass's tone was dry as she steered them around a tight corner, and Louise wished for more courage of her own as they hurtled forward. "But I like compliments, so am happy to accept it."

"What are you purchasing today?" Cass asked Louise after they arrived at the shops, flipping a coin to a boy who eagerly agreed to watch over the horses.

"I commissioned a new whist marker last month, and it should be ready."

Louise spoke with the merchant, and he went to the back room to fetch her marker. When he brought it out, she was delighted. The oakwood gleamed beneath thick lacquer, its sheen brilliant in the sunlight that streamed through the open window. It was the size of a small novel, and slender enough to tuck into her reticule if she wished. There were five tabs that could be popped open to keep track of each trick, and three narrower tabs to tally up the rubber. She picked it up, marveling at how lovely it was. The wood was inlaid with a design of wildflowers and animals, and it was even lovelier than what she had requested when she had explained what she had wished.

Cass peered over her shoulder and with one finger flicked open one of the flaps. "Cat and mouse? How fitting."

Louise smiled. The little mice were peeking through the bluebells, and the cats snaked around the flaps with malice in their eyes. "I thought so."

"You are more cutthroat than most would guess." Cass's voice held an edge to it.

"Only in whist."

Cass made a small sound in her throat and moved away to look at the other items for sale. "Does anything else interest you here?"

The shelves displayed ornate chess boards and intricately carved bishops and queens and pawns. There were scarlet and black backgammon boards, with counters made of leather or enamel. Dice of all shapes and sizes were displayed in enamel dishes, boxes of spillikins were stacked on a table.

"I think I have everything I need."

Cass gazed at her. "Do you not wish to peruse in case there is something that catches your eye?"

"I am afraid I am too practical for such things," she said, half-apologetically. "I try my best to visit the shops with Nell because it pleases her, but she is annoyed each time when my coin remains in my reticule instead of my custom being scattered across town. She is keen on buying anything that catches her eye."

"And you are not?"

She shrugged. "What need do I have of new counters or dice? I have what I want already and replace what I need. I only purchased a new whist marker because mine is worn and scratched, and I thought…"

She hesitated.

"You thought what?" Cass asked.

"It's silly. Even more so than those stockings of mine." She shook her head but decided to say it anyway. "I thought if I bought something nice enough to be seen in a ducal establishment, then somehow it might help will an invitation to the tourney into existence. I am embarrassed to even say it aloud."

"A ducal tourney?" Cass looked interested. "I think it's a fine reason. But do you never buy something because you like it? Because it pleases you?"

"I have what I need."

"I am not speaking of needing. I'm speaking of wanting."

"I think you speak of more than markers and counters." She put a hint of warning into her voice.

"It's all one and the same," Cass said with a shrug. "I like having things in my life that bring me nothing more than the pleasure of enjoying them. It's nice to look, but it's nicer to *have*. I like to hold on to life through things that bring me happy memories. Remember that wine we drank in the maze? Remember the feel of your bonnet strings against your neck when I pushed it off your head to kiss you? Things are imbued with memory and take on a form and function of their own, separate from the thing itself. Now every time that you put on a bonnet, do your fingers linger on the strings, and do you think of me?"

Louise was flustered.

"It so happens that there are two glove shops on this very same street, so you might as well come with me to take a look at the paltry display that they have to offer. You can tell me how much nicer the Belvedere variety is." She winked, and Louise laughed, relieved that the odd mood was broken.

CHAPTER NINETEEN

It felt as natural as anything for Cass to bring over a carpet bag with a change of clothing and to spend another night in Mayfair. Louise thought she would feel hesitant at extending the invitation, but she found herself wanting to keep Cass to herself for as long as she could. It had been years since she had slept so well through the night, and she would never have guessed that Cass would ever be the cause of a peaceful rest. She slipped into her life with ease, which was shocking considering the nature of their arrangement.

"Victor will be cross with me for keeping the curricle," Cass said cheerfully. "But it serves him right for all the nights he spent at Queenie's without me. At least I left him a note with my whereabouts, which is a greater courtesy than he tends to extend to me."

"You have a close friendship. I admire it. I am not close with any of my family."

"You never spoke much of them when we were young."

"I was glad enough to enter society and be free of my sisters," Louise admitted. "I was no longer simply the youngest Sheffield girl."

"You were never the least of them. I'm sure that wasn't true."

"It felt true enough. But with the least amount of attention from the other debutantes, I was swept up in my own ambition and delighted with my popularity. If I had not let it feel like the most important thing in the world, I should have never let you down."

Cass took her hand. "Maybe I expected too much."

Louise stared at her. Cass had never admitted it before. "I didn't think we could have had any kind of future. I had never even dreamed there was anyone else *like* us. Maybe if I had known of such a place as

Queenie's…but even if I had, I would have been too terrified to choose anything but marriage. I had been told all my life that I would one day be a nobleman's bride, and any other future was unthinkable."

Cass's eyes were troubled. "I dislike to admit when I am wrong, but I don't think we had much of a future." It looked like it pained her to admit it.

"You were so optimistic."

"It was entirely misplaced." She gestured at the marble mantle above the fireplace and the fine inlaid table between them. "I couldn't have given you even a fraction of such a life when I begged you to run away with me."

"If I had listened to my heart, I would have gone. I loved you, Cass." She bit her lip. "But it would have been a hard life."

She laughed, and it was a hollow sound. "I suppose it had been a wild wish for the moon and all the stars, but you're right, you know. We would have had no income, and no family to help support us. Why would you have gone with me into the depths of uncertainty, when you could marry and be the mistress of your own home? What kind of choice was I giving you?"

"It was never a rejection of *you*," Louise said. "I went to call on you the day after my engagement party, but you had already left London."

It had been a terrible shock to know that she would never have the chance to explain. She had been torn between the joy of winning Atwater and the sorrow of losing Cass.

"My father decided there was little enough reason to stay after he lost everything. He knew that no one but Atwater would have been kind enough to ask for my hand. There was little point in staying once you were betrothed to him."

"I would have liked to have said farewell to you."

"I know that now. So would I."

The maid entered with Darling in tow, with as little pomp and circumstance as usual for their nighttime visits. When she saw that Louise had company, Darling stopped short.

"I beg of you to forgive the longstanding habit of old friends," Darling said, eying Cass with curiosity. "I came by for a rubber of whist, nothing more."

"However are we to decide who is de trop here?" Cass asked, her eyes half-lidded. "Is it I, interrupting what is clearly a longstanding habit?"

Darling tapped a finger on her chin. "Or is it I, interrupting such a cozy tête-a-tête?"

Louise laughed. "I suppose both of you are, so I do hope that you both choose to stay."

There was something wonderful about this. Her lover, casually embedded into her life, and her dearest friend, coming by for a game of cards and bit of gossip.

How could something so simple fill her heart?

But what was this thought of her *heart*? It was merely pleasure. After all, happiness was the natural companion of pleasure and could do no harm. She could not afford to risk more than that.

The maid had drawn her own conclusions that no one would be leaving, for she returned a quarter hour later with a cup of Darling's preferred green tea and enough lemon biscuits for all of them. Socrates emerged from Louise's bedchamber upon hearing Darling's voice. He stretched in the doorway, then leapt onto Darling's lap and settled in with the comfort of long routine.

"I suppose as we are three and not four that I should forfeit the usual cards and proceed with gossip?" Darling smiled. "Is there any opposition?"

"Of course not," Cass said. "I would wish you to feel as comfortable as if I am not even here."

"That would be most displeasing, because what I wish to speak of is your cousin." Darling's face turned dreamy. "I think most highly of him."

Cass's face was guarded. "Victor has many admirers."

Darling paused. "Is that so?"

"He is something of a charmer."

"Hmmmm." Darling sipped her tea. "How intriguing. He has not mentioned any such admirers to me."

She shrugged. "A gentleman wouldn't."

Darling stroked Socrates, who began to purr. "I shall endeavor to discover more the next time I see him. I am very keen to see him again, you know."

Cass said nothing, and the smile on Darling's face dropped before she turned her attention to Louise.

A half hour more was spent discussing the various goings-on in Darling's family, in particular Samson's plans to retire to the country sooner than was fashionable so that Katherine might spend her confinement at their estate. She took her leave soon after.

Louise glared at Cass. "Did you not think you could have been more encouraging?"

"Maybe there is nothing to encourage."

She scoffed. "You have seen how they act when they are at Queenie's together. Mr. Belvedere is so clever and so charming, and delights in making Darling laugh. And Darling has the sort of elegance of manner he seems to admire. His heart is in his eyes whenever he looks at her."

Cass's eyes were shadowed. "Not everything that feels like it belongs truly does, Lou."

Louise stilled. Was she still speaking of Darling and Mr. Belvedere? Or was she speaking of herself?

Cass nibbled on the last crumb of a lemon biscuit and pushed Socrates off her lap after he jumped up to investigate the treat. "When shall I have earned the privilege to be served my preferred drink when I arrive?"

Her tone was light, and Louise knew she was striving to ease the tension.

"Whatever do you mean?"

"Lady Darling was very well provided for by your maid when she came to your bedchamber. I wonder if someday I might garner the same reaction from your staff. Thus far, they have viewed me as a curiosity."

Louise stilled. This affair was temporary. It was true that they had spent the better part of three days together, and it had felt as natural as breathing air. But that didn't mean Cass could establish her own habits and her own routine in her home.

Enjoying the easy companionship of tonight did not naturally lead to wanting a hundred such nights. And yet the very idea of a hundred nights, or a thousand, had her almost gasping with longing. It was as seductive as it was frightening.

Her breathing came faster. She couldn't. Not with Cass, of all people.

She would have suggested that Cass spend the night at her own home, but although she did have a third-best carriage in the stables, she was loath to disrupt her servants to summon it.

They did not speak much for the rest of the night. Their lovemaking was swift and fierce, and Louise was worried at the urgency of it.

But she reminded herself that this was a romantic interlude. Cass had offered seduction, nothing more. They couldn't have what Darling and Mr. Belvedere could. It was no more possible now than it had been when they were eighteen.

But it didn't stop her from weeping into her pillow when Cass took her leave early the next morning.

Cass was cross from the moment she arrived back at her townhouse. The rain pounding against the windowpanes gave her a headache, and a chill air seeped into the parlor. She liked nothing better than to work in the early morning light, but the slate gray skies were of little help to her.

Two hot cups of tea were needed to warm her before she could even begin to think of leather work, and she set a third steaming cup on the Wedgwood table beside the hide that she had selected for the next pair of gloves.

It wasn't entirely the rain that had soured her mood.

The last two days with Louise had been wonderful. She had never thought that she might like to have someone who was simply *there* in her life. Someone to be next to her when she awoke, and who was available to visit the shops at a passing fancy, and who included her in their daily routine as easily as anything. Wasn't companionship meant to be something grander than these small things?

Yet it was perfect in its simplicity, and to her surprise she found it was all she could possibly want now.

It was everything that they could have never had fifteen years ago.

Cass had always felt that Louise's actions had been a choice between love and betrayal. But Louise had been right to refuse her offer, much as it hurt to acknowledge the truth of it. She had not chosen riches and comfort so much as she had chosen the only life that she had been capable of imagining. How could Cass have faulted her for choosing survival?

She hadn't wanted to think of the reality, as lost in love as she had been.

Cass picked up the white doeskin and began to stretch it against the edge of the table. She would cut a pair of long mittens for Louise. After all, she would need something to wear on the night that she won the whist tourney.

Louise was every inch as popular and lovely now as she had ever been, and Cass had been impressed by her dedication to playing whist at every opportunity. She had every expectation that Louise would be invited wherever she wished.

It had been intriguing to learn that the tourney was hosted by a duke. Wherever a duke crooked his finger, wealth followed. It would be an exceptional opportunity for the Belvederes if Louise wore their gloves to play cards, as all eyes would be on the players' hands. What better solution than to ask Louise to don a pair of mittens for the game? As they were fitted up the arm and over the hand to the base of the knuckles, but had no fingers, Louise would not need to remove them to play. The tourney might be some hours long, and the mittens would prove to be an excellent advertisement for their skills.

They were easy enough to cut, and Cass finished them quickly. She set the panels aside for Victor to embroider.

Her tea was cold, but she sat in an armchair across from the work desk and drank it anyway. She was still feeling out of sorts about the past few days. Louise could not have made it clearer that if she had a need, she went and satisfied it. She had needed a new whist marker, and she promptly arranged to get one, but she hadn't cared to look at anything that wasn't already in her plans.

Cass existed outside of Louise's plans just as much now as she always had.

What more was their affair than filling a simple sexual need?

What if Louise had been chasing the memories of what they once had together, instead of wishing to build anything new?

Unlike Louise, Cass was willing to be distracted. She was curious about what she could discover if she looked around her. She wanted to plumb the depths of what could be, even if it felt impossible. Even if the future was as cloudy as the rain clouds today.

Cass had tried to erect walls around her heart, but they had fallen at the first threat. Now she was in dire jeopardy.

At least their affair was easier as adults. When they had been young, it had been a terrifying ordeal to sneak kisses where they ought not, and the few glorious times that they had made love had been rushed and frantic. She had thrived on the trifecta of youth—hope and optimism and bravado.

But was she no wiser now? Hope still pounded painfully against her breastbone with every heartbeat. She might be older and more experienced, but she still *wanted*. She still *yearned*.

A spinster and a widow generated little gossip if they were respectable enough in public. Although it was easier in terms of circumstance, it was far more fraught emotionally. When she had been young, she had believed in the strength of Louise's affections with more conviction than she had believed anything.

But now...she was far from certain what Louise wanted, or what she felt.

Maybe staying away from Louise was wise.

If only she didn't wish to be reckless, heedless of anything but the time and space created for them in this moment.

She had wasted enough years with regret as her companion, had she not? Couldn't she change the trajectory through her own wants and needs? Maybe with time she could convince Louise that there was more to their affair than mere seduction.

But Cass would also have to convince herself that she could offer Louise enough this time. After all, Louise could still have her choice of men if she ever wanted another husband. How would it be possible that this time, Cass could be enough for her?

Cass returned to the worktable and chose a soft lemon-dyed hide. She prepared the leather and cut a pair of gloves for the daytime, for another stroll in Hyde Park, perhaps. She scored the leather and cut, then stretched and cut again, and was left with a neat pile of leather ready to assemble.

She drew out the embroidery skeins from Victor's sewing box. This pair she would embroider herself. She was not a genius of the craft like Victor was, but her skills were fine enough to do the gloves credit.

Emotion was twisted in the linen yarns threaded through the needle and into every stitch. Cheerful white daisies, like the ones she had picked for Louise at a long-ago picnic. Thin green vines, connecting their past with their future.

Victor entered the parlor, clutching a cup of tea. His hair was in disarray, and there were deep shadows under his eyes. "Already hard at work? You always did insist on rising with the dawn."

"It is almost noon." She added another stitch to the daisy she was working on. "I have been busy since dawn."

"Of course you have." He looked at her work. "Are you taking on my share now?" His voice had an edge to it.

"I would not dream of it. This pair is an exception."

He gazed down at the gloves thoughtfully as he sipped his tea, then threw himself down on the Chesterfield and drew his sewing box close to him. He studied the pair of mittens. "Those are new."

"Those need to be the best work we have ever done." She explained that she wanted Louise to wear them to the ducal tourney, and he looked interested.

"Would a card motif be too on the nose?" he asked, smoothing the leather against his knee. "Hearts and spades, perhaps?" He wrinkled his nose and drank more of his tea. "Saying it aloud convinces me it would come across as too eager by half. Maybe more florals. But no, that is too dull for a duke's table."

"Whatever you do will be marvelous."

"She wants to win, does she not? Perhaps a peacock feather. A symbol of good luck and pride."

He picked up a piece of foolscap and drew a design on it, then began to select his threads. When he was satisfied, he placed the foolscap on top of the leather and pricked through it with a sharp awl to give himself guidelines on the leather for his embroidery needle, then he fixed the wood hoop in place.

"Have you been to bed yet?" Cass asked.

"I don't wish to talk further," he said, scowling into his tea. "My head aches too much. I wish to stitch."

They sat in silence for half an hour, the rain pounding and the wind rattling the windows. They didn't often work together. It was nice to have his company. It reminded her of how it used to be at home, before they had come to London and everything had become so complicated.

"What do you think of love?" Cass asked, frowning down at the glossy leaves that she was piercing into the leather.

"What do either of us even know of it?" There was a hint of laughter around his mouth.

She slowed her needle. "It may well be that I am currently in such a sorry state."

"If you have fallen, then I cannot help you up. I have been victim to love's poison many times and never once found the antidote."

"What does such an antidote entail?"

"To be loved in return, I fear. Very difficult to arrange. The timing of such a thing has proven simply wretched."

"I think your time has come," she said quietly. "With Lady Darling."

"I beg you not to speak to me of her. I have told you before—I am not meant for one such as her." He stared down at his yarns. "Given that you brought up the bloody subject—are you enamored with your countess?"

"I wish I wasn't. What do I have to offer her?"

Victor shrugged. "Exactly right. We Belvederes have the means for dalliance, but that's all we can have with proper ladies."

Dalliance.

Cass was in the midst of sewing the most romantic pair of gloves she had ever made, and she wasn't even sure if she would ever give them to the intended wearer. If Louise saw them, she would guess right away the meaning of them.

She would know that this was love.

Cass could not bear to risk her heart. Not now, and perhaps not ever—so she went to her bedroom and tucked the gloves deep in her drawer, next to the neatly pressed handkerchief that she had never told anyone that she kept close at hand.

CHAPTER TWENTY

Cass watched as Louise and Lady Darling arrived at Queenie's. It had been a few days since she had seen either of them, as she had busied herself with glove making. In truth, she had been worried about seeing Louise again and stirring up feelings that were far better left in the past. Louise held her skirts to one side as she moved around a crowd at one of the tables, and Cass caught a glimpse of white silk with a blood red heart.

She remembered those sheer stockings and the sight of Louise wearing naught else as she sprawled across Cass's lap.

There was comfort in the lust roaring to life, driving away emotion and replacing it with desire.

"We have business to attend," she said to Louise without preamble.

Louise lifted her eyes to meet hers. "We do?"

"Upstairs."

Louise's eyes widened, and then she smiled. "I would love to discuss business with you."

Cass turned and strode to the staircase, knowing that Louise would follow.

The first room at the top of the stairs was empty, and Cass ushered Louise inside and closed the door behind them.

"What is the meaning of this?" Cass grasped a handful of silk skirt and lifted it up to reveal Louise's legs.

She pointed one foot and admired her own leg. "I had hoped you would remember."

"Of course I remember. I thought those were for *us*."

"They are." Louise lifted her chin. "I hoped this might happen."

Cass dropped her skirts. "You hoped that I would make love to you in a tavern, with our friends downstairs?"

"Yes," she breathed. "I want to feel like we used to, when we were young and daring."

Cass grinned. "As the lady wishes."

It banished any doubt she might have still had that Louise belonged here—and with her. A tiny seed of hope nestled against her heart. This was not behavior she would have expected of Louise, but maybe it meant she was willing to risk more than interruption. Maybe she was willing to take a risk on Cass.

When they had made love last week, it had been gentle. Tonight felt different. There was a fervent energy in the air between them, almost frantic. Louise threaded her fingers through Cass's hair and kissed her hard.

Cass tugged her velvet spencer off and removed her linen dress, then pressed a firm kiss against the swell of her bosom above her stays.

Louise's eyes were dark with desire and her full pink lips were damp and slightly parted, and her body was half-exposed as she stood there with one hand on her hip as if daring Cass to continue to disrobe her.

Her legs were visible in an almost transparent muslin shift, her waist and breasts were bound tight in her stays, and her arms were bare from shoulder to fingertip in contrast to her legs barely covered by the saucy clocked stockings.

"I didn't know you liked to be looked at like this."

"I didn't either. Do you not enjoy this? I don't have so much experience, you know."

For a moment, she lost the flirtatious look in her eyes, and Cass gathered her in her arms and kissed her temple. "You have plenty enough for me. We don't have to do anything you don't want to."

Louise pulled back. "But I do want to. When I was with you, I had always felt like the very best version of myself. I felt…free. I don't feel like that anymore, and I think—I think I would like to feel that way again."

"I want to make you feel better than you have ever felt in your entire life." Cass pushed her hand beneath Louise's shift and ran her fingers up the outside of her thigh, flirting with the strings that tied her stockings high above her knee. "You certainly feel better than anything I have ever experienced before."

Louise sighed, a smile on her face as she closed her eyes.

Cass eyed the bed and decided it was unlikely to be the best of environments for lovemaking. She doubted the ropes beneath the mattress were tightened often, and she had no desire for a sore back or to press her face against a sour coverlet.

Instead, she spread her petticoat over the armchair by the bed and sat on the clean cotton, then pulled Louise down onto her lap, facing away from her. Louise's pert bottom nestled into Cass's loins, and when Louise shifted, a spark of pleasure ran through her.

She loosened Louise's stays enough to lift her breasts above the garment, exposing them to her touch. Cass ran her hands over Louise's thighs, enjoying the slide of silk against her legs, then moved her fingers over her hips. She settled one hand against Louise's full breast, with her fingers splayed over her nipple, and pressed her other hand between her legs and beyond her soft curls to her center. Louise was slick and ready, and the faster and harder that Cass pressed against her, the more she rocked her bottom against Cass, driving her wild with desire.

Louise looked down at her from over her shoulder, a crease between her brows. "Would you do what you once did with your mouth?"

"What did I do?"

"You remember." Louise's cheeks flushed scarlet. "In the garden maze."

Oh, the garden maze. Memory flooded back to her, of Louise sneaking a bottle of claret between the folds of her skirt when they had been meant to be touring the grand house on an earl's estate. Cass had fled to the maze to be alone, upset because the other debutantes had been taunting her about her manners. Her heart had almost stopped when she had seen the beautiful smile on Louise's face, framed by a straw bonnet with a silly amount of ribbons and gewgaws on its brim, and her hand shyly presenting the bottle from around her skirts.

They had sat on a carved iron bench, drinking from the bottle and giggling, and in a moment of youthful bravery, Cass had knelt on the gravel and lifted Louise's skirts and tasted her with her claret-drunk mouth.

It had been the headiest moment of her entire life.

"I wonder if I still remember how to do it?" Cass mused now, tapping her lip.

Louise's mouth fell open. "You have not done such a thing in all this time?"

She leaned forward and pressed a kiss between Louise's shoulder blades. "I am teasing. I have done it dozens of times and loved each and every one. But never more so than the very first time with you, with the sun beating down on my shoulders and rocks digging into my knees and my name spilling out of your mouth."

Cass tipped Louise off her lap and rose up, then pushed Louise onto the chair. She was beautiful in her disarray, her nipples puckered and her breasts thrust upward from where her loosened stays still kept them in place, her shift pooling around her hips, the gossamer silk of her stockings teasing her eye. Gently, she nudged Louise's thighs open with her knee, then dropped to the floor before her.

Even if Cass had truly never done such a thing since that summer day, she still would have known exactly what to do, for this moment had lived within her heart her whole life. The sight of Louise's trembling legs and beautiful quim was as gorgeous now as it had ever been, and Cass inhaled deeply as she nuzzled Louise's upper thigh with her mouth. She stroked her fingers against Louise's calves and kissed the inside of each knee, then traced her lips up her thighs up to the crease of her center.

The scent of her desire was lovelier than any perfume.

The taste of her was better than any drink that Her Majesty could conjure up, and Cass didn't think she could ever have her fill of it. Cass moaned as she moved her mouth and tongue against Louise, her sex swollen against her lips. Cass flicked her tongue against her most sensitive spot and was rewarded when Louise gasped and thrust her fingers in Cass's hair, dislodging her pins and sending them clattering to the scarred hardwood floor. She kissed her, stroking her tongue inside her, encouraged by the keening sighs that Louise let out with each breath. Louise moaned and raised her knees, settling her legs over Cass's shoulders and opening herself more to her ministrations.

Cass slid a finger inside her, then a second, curving her fingers upward as she thrust inside and continued to lick and stroke Louise with her mouth, increasing the pressure and the rhythm until Louise stiffened beneath her and cried out, frantically raising her hips against Cass's mouth until she shuddered and sighed.

Louise fell back against the armchair and her legs slid from Cass's shoulders. Cass eased herself up and looked down at her, the very image of a satisfied woman, a dazed look in her eyes.

Cass dropped to one side of Louise's lap with her legs pulled up to her chest and cradled her in her arms until she could feel Louise's frantic heartbeat slow. She kissed the top of her head. "Was it as good as you remembered?"

Louise laughed. "You outdid yourself, and you know it."

"I always aim to excel."

Louise ran her hands over Cass's hips. "Perhaps you would enjoy a reward for your hard work."

Cass grinned and shifted so that she straddled Louise. "I could be enticed."

She captured Louise's lips as Louise slid her fingers against her, then inside her, finding the pace she needed. Louise kissed her breasts, pressing her face between them, and then sucked on her nipple to feed the fire that burned inside her. It felt extraordinary, the feel of this woman beneath her, working to pleasure her, and it didn't take long for her to find her release, as aroused as she had been when under Louise's skirts. She bucked her hips hard against Louise and moaned against her shoulder as pleasure coursed through her body, until she could bear no more and she slumped against her.

"You are amazing," Cass murmured, her eyes heavy.

"I believe that would be you."

Louise held her in her arms, and for a moment everything was perfect.

❖

Louise was in charity with her life and the world. How could anything be nicer than this? She had hesitated only a moment that evening before pulling on the heart-embroidered stockings, knowing they would make Cass wild to see them. She had been unable to keep the smile from her face as she finished her toilette, even after her maid had remarked upon it.

The anticipation of seeing Cass's face when she saw her in the stockings was almost as delightful as the reality of it. It was lovely to know that she was as attuned to Cass as she had ever been. There was a joy to knowing someone with such precision.

She smiled as she took Cass's arm. "Perhaps next time, I shall bring Nell round. She would enjoy it here, I think."

Cass stopped halfway down the stairs and stared at her. "You bloody well will not."

She was surprised at her vehemence. "The Queen and Scepter is a public tavern, is it not?"

"Yes, but it's *our* tavern!"

"Are you in business now with Her Majesty?"

"You know well enough what I mean. It's for people like us. Not for onlookers and gawkers to be entertained of an evening." There was an unfamiliar look on Cass's face, and Louise dropped her arm. "You cannot simply invite who you like here."

"My friends are like family to me. Why are you so unwilling to share what we have with others? I thought you would want more people to know about us."

Cass's eyes narrowed. "Were you truly thinking to share with your friends that you are having an affair with another woman?"

"I—I suppose I had not thought of telling Nell about *us*," she admitted, and felt heat rise in her cheeks. The notion of bringing Nell here had been a whim not well enough examined. Although she was terrified for anyone knowing the truth of her liaison with Cass, part of her ached for those closest to her to know her. To understand her. "Would it be so unwise?"

As soon as she said it, she regretted it. This was something they could never have. There was little point to telling anyone, after all. The affair wouldn't last longer than the Season, when Cass would return to the Cotswolds.

Why did the idea fill her with sadness?

"It is often unwise, yes. I know it is difficult. My own family knows nothing of my romantic pursuits, and I dislike the pretense of it."

"Mr. Belvedere knows who you are."

"Yes. He is one of the most important people in my life."

Louise grasped her hand. "Then why are you so unsupportive of his marriage to Darling?"

"As far as I am aware, Victor has not proposed."

"I am certain that he wishes to do so at the earliest opportunity, and if you give him some encouragement about how Darling feels—"

"Victor has a perfectly capable head and can do as he bloody well feels like without me cracking the whip to guide him on a path that you would like to see him on."

"I am doing no such thing!"

"Besides, we aren't talking about my family. We're talking about you wanting to bring your friends to a molly house."

"I trust my closest friends with my life."

"I don't have the same assurance. How can I trust Mrs. Fenhurst?"

"Why did you trust me enough to bring me here?" Louise held her breath. *Did* Cass trust her?

"Because I already knew from being beneath your skirts enough times that you understood what kind of goings-on could be had in such a place as this!" Cass looked exasperated.

"You didn't know who I was bringing with me when I asked for invitations."

"Very true, and now I think it was beyond foolish of me to have ever invited either of you." She rubbed a hand over her face. "If anything were to happen, the threat to Queenie's would be my fault." Her voice was hollow.

"You are worried for nothing. Nothing shall come to pass. Nell has been unhappy these days, and I thought to cheer her up."

"She won't find happiness here. And what kind of man is her husband? What hell will he wreak if he knows his wife is here amongst mollies? Just because some people don costumes doesn't mean that this is theater, Louise. This is real life."

"I know." She hadn't meant to imply otherwise.

"Do you know? Because if there is a raid because Mrs. Fenhurst's husband has enough power to call upon to shut down this establishment, people could be arrested and put to death," Cass snapped. "You and I would be safe enough. The law isn't concerned about women. But the law is highly interested in people like my cousin—Her Majesty—my friends. We are from different worlds, you and I."

"We are not so different." She shook her head. "I will not invite her. I promise. I had not given it enough thought, and I understand it better now. I understand your point—and I would never want to bring harm to the people here."

"The sad truth is that you cannot trust everyone that you are friendly with. For someone like you who is so popular with so many people, maybe that is a difficult concept."

Louise continued down the stairs. "I do not appreciate that assessment of my character."

"Have you even changed at all, Louise?"

"What happened to *dear heart*?"

Cass's eyes were guarded. "I may have lost sight of her. Or perhaps I am seeing her for who she truly is."

Gripping her elbow, Cass escorted her to Darling, and then left her without so much as a bow.

Louise sat beside Darling, who pushed a cup of punch toward her. "You have the appearance of someone in need of comfort." Louise explained what happened, and Darling frowned at her. "Cass had every right to chastise you. Nell is one of my dearest friends too, but I would never dream of bringing her here. You and I barely belong here."

"It was naïve of me." Louise hated to admit that she was wrong.

She had believed herself so changed from her younger self. But was she so steeped in her own circumstances that she did not think clearly about the needs and concerns of others? It was sobering.

Darling frowned into her cup. "In fact, perhaps we don't belong here." She was quiet. "Mr. Belvedere is not in attendance tonight."

"Maybe he is not the right man for you."

"Maybe you do not need to dispense quite so much advice."

Louise was stung. "I want the best for you!"

"The best advice is not often given by pontificating."

They returned to Mayfair together in chill silence.

Had she lost her lover and her friend tonight? Louise stared into the night sky through the carriage window. She had been so upset with herself at what had happened between herself and Cass and Atwater fifteen years ago that she had tried to spend the rest of her life preventing others from making her mistakes. But had she ever helped anyone through the years by her earnest attempts to guide them?

Cass and Darling were right. She could not dictate how others acted and had spent more time lecturing others to try to ensure their happiness instead of improving her own self. Through her affair with Cass and her evenings at Queenie's, she was seeing a new life for herself emerge, and it was both freeing and terrifying.

She needed to learn to embrace it, but it meant letting go of the past and accepting that the changes in her life might well lead to mistakes made along the way. If she was too afraid to make them, she might have earned nothing but the empty life she already had created for herself.

CHAPTER TWENTY-ONE

A twater!" Louise said brightly. "How very good of you to call."
"I always have time for my favorite aunt," he said, and brushed a quick kiss to her cheek. "Of course I answered your summons."

She laughed. "An invitation to luncheon is hardly a summons."

He grinned at her. "I suppose it is not, and your cook is a compelling enough reason to attend upon you."

Atwater was a slender man with bright blond hair and a cheerful countenance. At six-and-twenty, he had taken all the responsibilities of the earldom smoothly after her husband's death. He had a young man's attraction to a dashing type of style. There were no shirt points high enough to please him and no horse fast enough to satisfy him, so he would have been admired by his friends even without the benefit of his title.

They spoke of a few repairs he wished to do to the estate and some improvements to the fences around their sheep farms. With an abashed smile, he then mentioned a house party that he was considering to host at the end of the Season, and a few of the women he was planning to invite upon the urging of his mother. "I would like you to attend too, Aunt Louise. That is, if you have no other plans. You know how much I value your opinions, and you know everyone in society. Mama and I know we can count on your judgment."

"Marriage is a significant undertaking. Of course I will try to be of help to you. I would be more than happy to host a dinner party here in London with guests of your choosing before you settle on the invitation list, if you would like to spend more time with anyone in particular without arousing any suspicion from the young ladies—or their mamas."

"I knew I could count on you."

They had retired to the drawing room and were partaking of tea when Louise broached the subject that had been her reason for inviting him to luncheon.

"I had the great pleasure of receiving a pair of gloves as a gift from an old friend," she said. "The Belvedere family. I am sure you remember that they had a thriving glove business once upon a time? Their land abuts yours, to the east."

Louise had given much thought about how best to support Cass. She had been humbled to realize that she might not have changed as much as she thought she had over the years, and she wanted to do something for Cass. She yearned to help her, and this was the best way she could think of to do it.

The Belvedere gloves were magnificent, and they did deserve to be first in fashion. It was time that Louise used her personal connections to make such a thing happen. She could hardly believe that she hadn't thought of asking Atwater to patronize the gloves before.

He frowned into his tea. "Yes, they are good enough people. I pay a call upon Sir John Belvedere and Lady Belvedere each time that I visit my estate."

"Their daughter Miss Cassandra is in town for the Season. We were debutantes together, though she has not been to London since."

She was surprised when his frown deepened. "I have met Miss Cassandra. She has often been in residence with her parents. A mannish sort of woman."

Louise sipped her tea. "I consider her dashing."

"Dashing? I always assumed her to be rather fast."

"She isn't in the least fast. She's completely respectable."

"Then we have different definitions of the word, for I do not consider unladylike manners to be respectable. You are my uncle's widow, and I have an obligation to warn you that Mr. Pierce has not had kind things to say about her."

Mr. Pierce. She had wondered if he would gossip about Cass after their brief altercation but had hoped it had been a minor enough transgression to be of little interest to him.

"What manner of unkind things has he said?"

"Oh. Well, it was discussed at the club, you know. And—well—he wrote a wager in the betting book." Atwater reddened. "I will not repeat the details in front of a lady, let alone my aunt."

"What a miserable excuse for a man, hiding behind the secrecy of a gentleman's club where a woman has no recourse to repair her good name. Mr. Pierce is a boor."

He looked startled. "He is not. He is a fine shot and cracking with a curricle."

"There is more to a man than his expertise with a whip."

"Aunt Louise, I am looking out for you and your good name."

"I appreciate it," she said shortly. "Whatever your opinions are of the lady, I meant to speak only of her family's gloves. As you are acquainted with them, then you are aware of the exceptional gloves the Belvederes make."

"I was under the impression that they did not make gloves any longer."

"They have undertaken to revive the business." She drew out a pair of lavender riding gloves that Cass had given her, with decorative dark purple stitching on the backs of the hand and a scalloped edge at the wrist. They were scented with almond and wondrously soft. "You are a man of fashion. Would you not be interested in having gloves as fine as these? It would be good of us to support business from the Cotswolds, would it not?"

He blew out a sigh. "They are fine." He drew the pair into his lap. "Very fine. I may well consider it, out of respect for the longstanding friendship of my uncle with her father, but temper yourself around her, will you? I would appreciate it if your names were not linked as friends."

Louise's first instinct was to say no.

Atwater had always been good to her. Louise had a comfortable jointure, but she still owed much to his generosity. He had not taken possession of the Mayfair townhouse where she had lived with her husband, though it was part of the estate and he had every right to demand that she find other accommodations. He indulged her preference for not keeping a carriage and lent his own to her whenever she needed it. He consulted her opinion as often as he did his own mother.

It was a little enough thing that he was asking of her now.

With a start, Louise realized that Atwater was speaking again of his house party, and had been for some minutes. He had taken it for granted that she had already acquiesced to his demands and agreed not to seek friendship with Cass.

For all his regard for her, he had assumed that she would follow his decree with no further discussion.

Louise's temper simmered, but she didn't say anything. She was being dealt the same hand as Darling, relegated to the position of matriarch, useful in relation to what benefit she could bring to the family. Once Atwater married, she would become the dowager countess, and her position would be at the edge of the family's sphere of influence instead of close to its center. It didn't mean that there was no love from her nephew, but she had not realized what it would feel like.

She had the right to her own thoughts, so she chose not to share them with him. Her decision was easy to make. She had hated herself once for betraying Cassandra Belvedere and not standing up for her when it was important, and she would never make the same mistake again.

Even if it meant losing the good opinion of her nephew.

Was this love? The desire to choose uncertainty instead of security? What cruel circumstance was this, to force her hand when she didn't even know if Cass would have her?

❖

The invitation to dance at the Duchess of Melsonby's ballroom came as a surprise to Cass and Victor. Cass thought she had nodded to her once several months ago, and Victor was quite sure he must have kissed her hand at a rout last week. The ball was to be held only three nights hence, so Cass decided that they must have been selected as replacements for more notable guests who had declined at the eleventh hour.

It was no matter, as they were glad to accept any invitation that graced their path. Although Cass had proclaimed herself tired of the excessive décor and vanity displayed at many of London's ballrooms this Season, she was awed when she and Victor were announced by the butler and stepped into the room.

This was pomp and circumstance the likes of which she had rarely seen. The ballroom itself was cavernous and filled with a crush of guests, almost none of whom Cass recognized. Half a dozen chandeliers, each boasting four magnificent candlelit tiers, glittered with crystals from the ceiling, which itself was a marvel painted with angels and cherubs. The pine wood floor had been painstakingly chalked with the duke's coat of arms. The beautiful image was ephemeral, for by the end of the first minuet, the chalk would be displaced by shoes and hems and slyly dropped fans from women who hoped their beaux would be gallant enough to pick them up.

The invitation seemed a distinct mark of favor. It must have been orchestrated by Louise somehow. Cass picked up her quizzing glass but could not find her.

"Is that the duke by the doorway?" Victor asked with interest, craning his neck.

She swung her glass over to look. "It is indeed." Cass felt a rush of excitement. "A wealth of opportunity awaits."

"Opportunity for wealth is always welcome," he murmured.

Lady Darling caught sight of them and walked over to greet them.

"I hope the evening finds you well?" she asked. "The Duchess of Melsonby is an old friend of mine and was kind enough to send an invitation to you both at my request. She is a dear woman."

An unwelcome feeling stole over Cass. She had assumed this had been arranged for her sake, a show of Louise's feelings after they had left Queenie's on uncertain terms.

But instead, it was a mark of Lady Darling's affections for Victor. Perhaps Cass did not mean as much to Louise as she hoped.

He brushed a kiss against the back of Lady Darling's hand. "I appreciate the favor, my lady." His tone was as cool as the expression in his eyes.

She dropped her hand. "I went to some lengths to arrange this. I thought it would be helpful to your endeavors."

He gazed at her with half-lidded eyes. "I am gratified."

Cass wished to kick him in the shins, much as she had when they were children and he was being unreasonable. "We are truly appreciative," she said to Lady Darling. "This means a great deal to us both, and I am honored that you thought of us."

Lady Darling nodded at her, mollified, and took her leave of them once Victor showed no signs of engaging further in conversation.

"You are behaving like a cad," Cass told him.

"I have no right to any claim on her time when I will not offer what she wants. She is better off finding another admirer." There was pain in every word, and his mouth was tight.

"Talk to her, Victor. Please. If you have any regard for her feelings and for your own, it would be wise to talk to her and explain. Even if you cannot tell her everything."

"It is a risk I am unwilling to take. My heart has been torn apart too many times by lovers who could not accept me as I am. How can I expect this time to be any different?"

"I wish it was not so difficult," Cass said quietly. "But you love her."

"I do."

"Then the regret may haunt you the rest of your life."

"I accept its spectre with open arms."

Louise appeared in Cass's line of sight, standing with a group of women that she did not recognize, laughing as if there was nothing more entertaining in the whole world than this very moment. This was the effect that Louise so often had, that knack of engaging with others that made them comfortable around her. Cass appreciated her genuine interest in other people, and the way that she accepted them. It was as apparent here as it was at Queenie's.

Who was Cass to preach at Victor of love and regret when she had been so afraid to talk to Louise about her own feelings? It was time to tell her that she loved her. There would be no better time than tonight, after the ball.

She had been upset the last time that they had talked, but it could not erase the love that had grown deep inside her.

As she looked again at Louise, she thought there was something familiar about one of the women near her after all. Cass settled the quizzing glass against her cheek and felt temper simmering in her belly.

Miss Emily Price.

CHAPTER TWENTY-TWO

Miss Emily Price could not be her name now, of course. If desperation was any measure of success on the Marriage Mart, she had in all likelihood snared a title as long as an opera glove in the interim. Cass remembered her well. It turned her stomach to see her laughing with Louise, like she had in the old days, as if nothing had changed.

Was it possible that Louise hadn't changed at all?

But that was an uncharitable thought. Louise was being polite to Miss Emily. Yet if that were the case, she was being *awfully* polite, given that she had now spent over a quarter hour with the group.

It tore open the patch that Cass had sewn over the old wounds. She never had been as neat at stitching as Victor.

Louise floated away from the group, and Cass let the quizzing glass drop. It was past time for champagne. Nothing could hold a candle to Her Majesty's rum punch at a moment like this when nerves wanted steadying, but wine was a very welcome prospect.

First, she scanned the room for Lady Ingalls. Spying her with her cronies and no refreshment in hand, Cass brought her a cordial.

"Always appreciated, my dear Miss Cassandra!" Lady Ingalls beamed at her. "You are such an attentive miss. Much more so than my own relatives."

Cass bowed her head. "I am accustomed to arranging strangers into family. It's a talent I've had all my life."

She thought of the glovers and a warmth spread through her heart. They would be proud of her. Here she was, at one of the most exclusive events in all of London. Even if she never sold another pair of gloves, they would be so bloody proud of her anyway for trying.

She returned to the refreshment table, needing time to collect her thoughts. This was the most important social event she had been invited to, and she and Victor should focus on strengthening their acquaintanceship with anyone who they were lucky enough to be introduced to. There were a small number of people who could help her, Lady Ingalls and Louise and Lady Darling amongst them, but she had other friends now too that she could count on.

Louise had been right to caution her against speaking too freely of business on such occasions, and she vowed to take her advice to heart.

Cass took a sip of champagne and turned to face the room again.

She would not fail the glovers.

But there she was in front of her—Miss Emily, her eyes glittering and her teeth bared in a smile.

Cass eyed her over her champagne flute. "And who, pray tell, might you be?"

It was petty of her to pretend ignorance. Her mouth was dry, so she took another sip. Seeing Miss Emily dragged her back to that time and place so long ago when she had been young and defenceless.

But Cass wouldn't flee tonight.

The night that Atwater had rejected her had been the scene of her nightmares for years. He had been kind enough, the sympathy clear on his face even in memory, but the other debutantes that he had courted had been merciless, and they had supposed Louise to be their young queen. She could almost hear the laughter of the girls around them, and could almost see Louise's face, shadowed and cold.

Where was Louise now? Was she watching them? Cass refused to look, for it would be unbearable to see her now if she looked anything like she did then.

Miss Emily had been the one to spill a glass of red wine on Cass's white muslin after Atwater had told her that he was engaged to Louise. Her dress stained beyond repair, Cass had been unable to join the soiree. She had already lost her chance at Atwater, but she had always thought that attending that evening would have helped improve the standing of her family after her father's disgrace.

But maybe that had been her foolish optimism at play.

Miss Emily had been friends with Louise during that Season and had sneered at Cass behind her back at every chance. She had delighted in mocking her and gloated in her downfall that night.

And Louise had stood there in silence while it happened.

Miss Emily bristled. "You don't recognize me, Miss Cassandra Belvedere? I am the Marchioness of Welton. You might remember me as Miss Emily Price."

"Ah, yes. Miss Emily. I hope time has treated you well."

"Very well indeed, as I am a *miss* no longer. Unlike yourself."

"There is no shame in being unmarried," Cass said. "There are distinct advantages to not being constrained by a husband. One may consort with whom one wishes, for instance."

"I daresay I don't know what you could mean. I am a chaste and respectable woman." Lady Welton looked at Cass, her gaze lingering on her pale blue lambskin gloves.

"I said nothing of your chastity, but please draw whatever conclusions you wish. It is of no import to me."

She sniffed. "I have heard that the only thing of import to you is your droll talk of commerce. How *very* like you, Miss Cassandra!"

"How flattering. I was unaware that my reputation had preceded me."

"One only needs to look at you to see that you are so *very* unusual." She laughed. "Oh, don't mind me! I mean no offense. It is simply a different kind of woman who would bare their arms as you do, with such unseemly arms as you have! I cannot even imagine how you came to have such a physique."

Cass had dreaded the interaction but found with some surprise that it was much easier than she had thought it would be. Had she truly been anxious to face such tame opposition? The marchioness had fire in her eyes and malice in her mouth, but what did Cass care for her opinion? She was proud of herself, of her appearance, of her business. What shame could she feel?

Cass sipped her champagne. "I daresay many things are outside the realm of your imagination. But then perhaps you have not been tasked to use it often, so it is no wonder that your mind is unused to the exertion."

"The Countess of Atwater was right about you. You are...how did she say it? A true Original?" But the way she said it, it wasn't a compliment. "Perhaps you are influencing her, for the dear countess is something of an Original herself these days with her *bold* choice of gloves." She tittered behind her fan.

"What did you say?" Cass asked softly.

"Your association with her has made things interesting. You must admit that you are an unusual choice for Lady Atwater's friendship."

Anger had her clenching her fist around her champagne, not giving a damn if a drop spilled on her gloves. "Lady Atwater's name is not fit to be in your mouth."

Lady Welton raised a brow. "Are you her champion? How *very* amusing! I suppose those muscles are good for something."

Cass thought of tipping her wine all over Lady Welton's pale pink silk dress in a satisfying act of retribution. Through an exertion of will that she didn't know she possessed, she stayed her hand. After all, her actions reflected on others. Victor would be disgraced by association, and Lady Ingalls would find such action shameful. Louise would surely encourage her to remain calm.

Besides, champagne would cause hardly as dramatic a stain as burgundy or claret. It would be little worth the splash.

But then Louise strode up to them, hellfire blazing in her eyes, and Cass was so surprised that she dropped her champagne anyway. The flute shattered against the wood and the wine spattered up Lady Welton's skirts in exactly the most satisfying way she could have imagined.

The candlelight glittered on the shards of glass, and the wine stain bloomed like the love in Cass's heart.

Louise had come to her rescue.

Cass felt as light as the very air.

Louise did not like the idea of the Marchioness of Welton saying one word to Cass. She remembered the last interaction between them fifteen years ago all too well. How had she dared fling her wine on Cass as if it was nothing? As if *she* were nothing? Louise had been shocked into silence, staring into Cass's pale face for what felt like an hour but must have been less than a minute.

Louise had never expected society to have turned their back on Cass so fast for what her father had done. She had not understood until the moment Miss Emily had tossed her wine on Cass's dress that the other girls had celebrated Atwater's proposal to her to as a slight against Cass, a rejection of her oddness and her forthright manner. She had not known that they would cheer her demise in society.

Louise's heart had already broken when she had told Cass that they had no future, but what was left of it crumbled into dust that night upon witnessing the cruel actions of her supposed friends. After her marriage, she had taken pains to distance herself from each and every one who had ever laughed at Cass.

"What an unfortunate incident," Louise said coolly, looking at the wine spilled on Lady Welton's dress.

There was vitriol behind her eyes, though she managed to smile. "Such clumsiness is expected of those who stay in the country and do not venture forth to the capital on occasion. One can only forgive when others know not what they do."

"I know exactly what I am doing," Cass told her. "The misfortune was that this was an accident. I regret that it was not deliberate."

In the middle of the ballroom with half of the richest lords in London looking at them, Louise knew with certainty that she was in love.

How else to explain the surge of emotion as she watched Cass refuse to be cowed? How else to explain the admiration and pride she felt?

"Miss Cassandra is *such* an odd companion for you, Lady Atwater! I do wonder at it. We all wonder at it."

A footman appeared to clean up the glass, forcing the three of them closer to the crowd of people who had gathered with interest once they heard the glass break.

"I don't know if I need your opinion of who I associate with."

Lady Welton was as insufferable now as she had been all their lives, but Louise kept a smile on her face, aware of the onlookers.

"Well, we run in the same circles. With my dear marquess, I must confess I am a half rung above—but that's neither here nor there! Besides, you have always appreciated my feedback. You were saying so, not even half an hour ago."

"Perhaps I never meant it." The truth tumbled out of Louise's mouth, shocking her. Cass whipped her head round to look at her, surprise in her eyes, and Louise grinned at her. If she had not been by her side, she didn't think she would have had the courage to finally say what she meant.

She had distanced herself from these people, but she had never told them how she felt about what they had done and what they had continued to do to those who were weaker and less influential than they were. Louise had thought herself so pious and so changed by removing herself from their society, but it had been cowardly to continue to bear witness to their cruelty.

She should have followed Cass's example and told them plainly.

If it meant garnering a reputation for plain speech, so be it.

Louise was no longer an unmarried miss, uncertain of herself. She was an influential widow, the aunt to an earl, and above all, her own woman with her own reputation. Didn't she have enough of her own power to stand up for what was right?

What use had her popularity been through all these years if it meant leading people to believe she shared their own awful opinions? Was that what it meant to be popular? If so, she was astonished she had ever wished for it.

She had been willing all this time to avoid causing tension with Lady Welton because she had an influential husband. It was not worth it, and had never been worth it.

Lady Welton's eyes narrowed. "I had thought you a woman of too much taste to surround yourself with tawdriness, but I was mistaken."

"There is nothing in the least tawdry about the Belvederes."

"You may well regret this association." She was vibrating with anger.

"I think I am done with regrets," Louise mused, and was at peace when she realized that it was true.

❖

Cass accompanied Louise home after the Duchess of Melsonby's ball. Lady Darling's carriage was spacious, but Cass chose to sit close enough to Louise that their thighs touched with each turn in the road. There was no danger here, after all. Lady Darling was the only friend of Louise's who knew of their relationship.

Lady Darling's face was inscrutable in the shadows. "I had hoped this would prove an opportunity for you and Mr. Belvedere, but I am afraid that the evening did not have the intended effect."

"You had a very kind thought when you arranged for the invitation. Victor understands that it was my fault that we were not a success tonight," Cass said. "I spoke to him before I left. There will be other opportunities."

"There is no fault." Louise took her hand and squeezed it. "Lady Welton is a misery."

"I have never liked her either," Lady Darling said. "The marquess is a true gentleman, and his father the duke is a marvelous wit, but Lady Welton is too full of her own importance to remember to be kind."

Cass's heart was so full of love that she was shocked when Louise turned to her and asked if she would mind to return to her own townhouse tonight. She looked preoccupied.

"Of course," she murmured, and said not another word as the carriage made the detour to Chelsea to release her.

She did not understand why Louise would not wish to celebrate their triumph tonight, but she took her hurt feelings to bed with her and stared at the ceiling until sleep overtook her.

CHAPTER TWENTY-THREE

Nell's sitting room was grander by far than Louise's. Mr. Fenhurst had bought a house in Marylebone that was elegant from the outside and ostentatious almost to the point of gaudiness inside, but Nell didn't seem to mind. Louise only cared if their parlor offered a card deck and a bottle of wine.

Last night had changed everything.

Louise shuffled before dealing, flicking the cards onto the table in front of her friends as if they were darts.

"Patience," Darling murmured.

"I've none left," Louise snapped.

There was an uneasy silence. She knew why. She had always kept her temper so well guarded that Nell and Isadore had likely never even seen a hint of it before.

Defeat shrouded her like a cloak, heavy and itchy and all-encompassing. She wished to shrug it off, to laugh and shake out her silks like nothing bothered her. But her temper seethed and boiled, refusing to be soothed ever since it had been roused last night.

How could she expect it to ease, when everything she had worked toward this Season had been ruined? She didn't regret her actions for one minute. The Marchioness of Welton had behaved terribly—both fifteen years ago and last night—but in doing right by Cass, Louise had dashed all hopes for herself.

Atwater had already sent her a missive today expressing his disappointment and concern, citing Cass as a poor influence on her. Louise had read the note, then tossed it in the fireplace.

"Why are we doing this again?" Isadore frowned.

"To cheer up Louise," Nell snapped. "Anyone can see she's as mad as a soaked cat." She thrust a plate toward them. "I asked Cook to make the very best cheesecake she could. Please do enjoy."

"Society's mind will wander to something else soon enough," Darling said. "I know you are disappointed, but this will not last."

"Have I missed something?" Isadore demanded, putting her cake down. "Is there some scandal?" Her face was pinched with worry.

Louise scowled and bit into her piece of cake. "There is no scandal," she said. "All that happened is that I lost out on an opportunity. I shall not be invited to the whist tourney."

"Oh." Isadore's face softened. "You did speak of it with such enthusiasm. But there is always next year."

"I shall not be invited next year, nor any other year." She looked at her cards, annoyed that she had a poor hand with nothing higher than a seven of any suit. "I was upset with Lady Welton last night, before all of her friends. She will not forget it."

It was the Marquess and Marchioness of Welton who hosted the whist tourney at the end of every Season, at the residence of her husband's father, the Duke of Leverton.

"Lady Welton?" Isadore frowned. "She is very powerful. Was that wise?"

"Some things are more important than wisdom," Louise said. "But regardless, the die is now cast. There was never any love lost between us. Any amicableness was on the surface."

Louise had strived for years to be correct in her word and her behavior. It was difficult to reckon that society would think ill of her when she had finally done right by someone she cared about, rather than saying the right thing that people wanted to hear. Louise was well-liked, but Lady Welton had the power to change everything with the snap of her finger. She might have already done so.

It had been worth every moment, come what may.

Cass deserved Louise's support in society, and it did not matter what effect that support had on Louise's plans. She had not been able to bring herself to explain the depths of Lady Welton's influence or what it had cost her to speak against her, so she had given Cass's hand a fervent squeeze, and then promptly returned her home in Darling's carriage.

She loved Cass, and she had wanted to tell her last night—but she wanted that moment to be shared with joy and happiness, and not under the shadows of the bitter memory of the marchioness. Her confession of love could wait another day. She needed the companionship tonight of her friends.

"Perhaps an invitation would have never been forthcoming," she muttered, glaring down at her cards. She wondered now if Lady Welton had never wanted her to forget that although Louise had been the most popular debutante in their Season, she had been the one to snare the highest title with her marriage to the Duke of Leverton's heir apparent. Lady Welton held the most power of all of them by the end of that summer. "Are hearts trumps?" It was unlike her not to remember, and Isadore stared at her in concern.

"No talking in whist," Nell admonished her.

Isadore rapped her knuckles with her own set of cards. "Surely there can be talking tonight."

"Louise asked me to put together a night of cards, and I have endeavored to please," Nell said archly. "It is my house, after all."

"And she's our friend," Isadore said. "Tell me, which comes first for you?"

Nell frowned, then reached out and patted Louise's shoulder. "We are here to listen, of course," she said, her brow creased. "What do you need? Shall I ring for Cook? Or do you wish a footman to fetch delicacies from Fortnum and Mason? It's after hours, but I've enough money to make miracles happen if you wish for caviar."

Louise laughed. "That is very kind of you, but this is far beyond Fortnum's capabilities."

"It isn't the worst thing that could happen," Darling said briskly, staring down at her cards and selecting one with triumph. She took the trick. "There are other tourneys. What you have gained this Season far outstrips what you have lost." She gave Louise a pointed look.

"Yes, I know." She struggled to find words to explain. "*This* tourney was my chance to play amongst the very best the *ton* has to offer. I do not care for Lady Welton or the prestige of the house party. This was my opportunity to be recognized for my ability, among a group whose talents equal or exceed my own. The duke is a renowned player, as are his friends. I love this game. I love to play, I love to win, and I would love to play among the very best. I love it for the strategy, the skill, the tension, the adrenaline." She sighed. "I learned to love myself while playing." That was hard for her to admit. Darling knew of her feelings, but she had never voiced it aloud to her other friends. "I disliked myself for a very long time when I was young, and I found comfort in divorcing myself from my emotions and temper and embracing the logic and strategy of cards."

Darling had encouraged it early in their friendship, and it had also helped her foster new relationships with an older crowd to replace the friends she had lost after her marriage. Cards and friendship had always gone hand in hand.

Nell's lashes covered her eyes. "Is it so necessary to love oneself when one has money to purchase the affections of others?" Louise recognized it for the self-deprecation that it was, and her heart ached for a moment for her friend. She hoped someday Nell would find the love that she so clearly wanted in her life.

Isadore tossed her cards to the side. "Money is not everything, Nell. Louise, you will always have cards. You may not have the tourney, but you will always have us to play with."

"This is the best hand of cards I shall ever be invited to," she said, and as she gazed at her friends and saw the concern in their eyes, she knew it was true.

Louise knew every detail of their card play. Isadore's hesitation to use low value cards, Nell's reckless use of face cards, Darling's stoic and measured play of each suit. Knowing them so well didn't diminish the pleasure of sitting down with them. And it never would, for even more than she knew their gameplay, she knew her friends.

Darling's staunch support of her after she had been widowed, showing up night after night in her townhouse for green tea.

Nell's constant efforts to distract her from her problems with shopping and dinners and gossip curated to make her laugh.

Isadore's thoughtful observations and earnest intellectual discourse during their suppers at the balls.

These women were so very dear to her.

"Thank you," she whispered, staring down at the queens and kings that blurred in front of her through her tears.

There was still a throbbing ache in her skull that no amount of headache powder would cure, and no amount of wine could ease. But her friends would never abandon her, and the ache in her heart began to subside.

"Perhaps we should leave off cards for the evening?" Nell asked, tossing her hand to the table.

Darling nodded. "I think that's a good idea."

"Tell us about your beau," Isadore said, nudging Darling's knee after they abandoned the card table for the more comfortable armchairs near the fireplace. "Let us talk of love."

Love. That twisted her heart further, but neither Nell nor Isadore knew anything of her feelings for Cass, and they hadn't meant to make anything painful for her.

She wished she could say everything she wanted to them. But she had not yet even told Darling of the strength of her feelings, preferring to wait until she revealed them to Cass first.

"Mr. Belvedere is a treasure," Darling said, but her face was pinched. "I think I shall invite him to my son's dinner party next week."

"Did we not already dine with him at Samson's?" Louise asked.

"We did," she acknowledged. "But my Alexander has yet to meet him. And of course it would be an ideal opportunity for him to show his gloves to people who I know would listen. I have already told my son all about him." Her face was shining. "I am so proud of his accomplishments. All the Belvederes need is a little encouragement in society, and they shall have all the business they wish. Nothing could be easier."

Louise sat in silence with a second untouched piece of cake before her, as her friends laughed and talked of Mr. Belvedere and teased Darling about the potential in her future.

What of Louise's future? She could never enjoy this kind of moment with her friends about her own relationship. Her love affair with Cass would forever be hidden, something they did in the shadows. As long as he came up to scratch, Mr. Belvedere could keep his secret evenings at Queenie's, and their friends would be none the wiser and would celebrate their marriage with joy.

Louise hadn't been able to even conceive of such a thing as a true relationship between women, so she had never yearned for it when they had been young. She had such a limited understanding of the world—

all she had known of her future was that she was meant to marry, and naturally that meant that she would be wedded to a man.

But now she realized what Cass must have felt. Maybe there had been situations they could have had together, in lieu of marriage. For the first time, she understood the depth of Cass's rage and pain when she had chosen Atwater so long ago, and her heart broke all over again for her.

Louise thought of her friends and family toasting her and Atwater on their wedding day. Such a thing was impossible for her and Cass. But there was something special in keeping their relationship private, intimate for the two of them. All she could do was treasure the woman in front of her and to guard her heart from now on as carefully as her own.

Louise wanted to show Cass for the rest of their lives that they were meant to be together.

❖

Cass fretted all the way to Mr. Darling's house the next evening. She had been pleased at the invitation, but far less pleased that Victor had begged off at the very last minute. She did not relish the expression on Lady Darling's face when she had to explain to her that Victor was honored but could not attend.

Of course, that was not how he had phrased it.

"I'm not going," he had snarled at her, eyes bloodshot and cravat loose around his neck. "I'm not fit to be seen."

The sneer on his face broke Cass's heart. Victor had so much love in him to give but was turning his back on a chance at happiness. He had sauntered out the door to Queenie's, and Cass was powerless to stop him.

Why now, when they were so close to success? He was running away from what they had worked so hard to achieve.

But she had no answers tonight, so when she arrived, she kept her regrets on his behalf to a minimum and averted her eyes from Lady Darling's crestfallen face.

Her reprieve lasted as long as the wine was passed around the parlor, but Lady Darling sought her out before dinner was announced.

"Where is he?"

Cass knew the look of a scorned woman, and it was writ as large as life on her face. Lady Darling was smiling and her hands were folded in front of her, but her eyes were flinty and her tone was hard.

"Victor was indisposed." She couldn't imagine Victor had felt in the peak of health as he had stumbled out the door.

She was quiet for a minute, her lips pressed tight. Finally, she nodded. "Do tell Mr. Belvedere that he is welcome to call on me to explain in person."

"I apologize on his behalf, Lady Darling." Cass struggled with what to say. "He is a good man. But I understand that he is more complex than perhaps one might gather from first acquaintanceship."

"Complex. I suppose that is as good a word as any." She shook her head. "As are you, Miss Cassandra."

She frowned. "Everyone has their share of complexity."

Lady Darling leaned close. "You hold the happiness of my best friend in your hand," she said, her voice hardly above a whisper, and as cold as ice. "If you dare to trifle with her as your cousin is trifling with me, you shall regret it."

Cass stepped back. "No one is being trifled with."

"Louise has sacrificed for you, you know."

"Whatever do you mean?"

"The Marchioness of Welton and her husband host the whist tourney. Louise shall never be invited now."

Cass felt a crushing weight in her chest.

"Make sure you appreciate her. Be certain that you're the one who will give her everything that she deserves."

More than anything, Cass wanted to be that person. Would Louise be willing to accept such a thing from her? Her feelings must be deep if she had jeopardized her chances at the tourney. Emotions whirled inside her during dinner, and she was quiet all the way through the soup course and the meat and the fish and the sweets.

As soon as dinner ended, she sought out Louise.

Louise beamed at her. "I was looking forward all evening to speaking with you."

"Why didn't you tell me?" Cass asked.

"Tell you what?"

"About the Marchioness of Welton and the tourney."

Louise flicked her eyes away. "I suppose Darling spoke to you."

"I would have preferred hearing it from you, but I'm glad that she told me. I never realized that I would be the one to interfere with your chances at an invitation." She felt wretched.

Louise looked her in the eye. "I did what I ought to have done fifteen years ago."

"I appreciate it more than I can ever say. But to give up your dream!"

"There will be other dreams." She didn't sound convinced.

"I swear I will make it right for you. I don't know how, but I will repay this sacrifice."

No matter what it took, she was resolved to get Louise to that tourney. It didn't matter if she had to tear society apart to find someone—anyone—who might help her. She would find a way.

She would do anything for Louise.

She only wanted Louise to understand how much she meant to her.

"What talk is there of repayment?" Louise looked upset. "My affection for you is not based on trading favors."

"I know." She grabbed her hand. "But I want to make sure you understand how much I appreciate you."

Her eyes were soft. "I could be convinced of such a thing."

"I would be delighted to make the effort. Tonight? Will you do me the honor of coming home with me to Chelsea?"

"I would like nothing better." Louise smiled at her, then turned to join Lady Darling's son and his wife.

There was a roar of laughter in the hallway as a group of men came in from the garden, the scent of cigar smoke clinging to their clothes, and Cass was shocked to see Victor among them.

Cass stared at him, then looked around for Lady Darling. She did not need her quizzing glass to see the fury that emanated from her.

Victor came over to Cass. "These fine gentlemen know worth when they see it," he said, pride evident in every word. "Our luck has turned. I've made some sales tonight."

"Do *you* know worth when you see it?" Cass snapped at him.

"I beg your pardon?"

"Lady Darling is glaring daggers at you from across the room. She was most upset when I told her that you were indisposed. And now here you are, ignoring her and making a liar out of me."

"I thought you would be gratified that I managed to sell our gloves." He looked down his nose at her. "Is nothing I do good enough for you?"

"I wonder if any of it is enough for you."

"I did try to apologize to her when I arrived, but she wanted nothing to do with it."

"You should be ashamed at the way you are treating her. I think she loves you, Victor. Have a heart."

"How can I explain that I am doing this for her sake?" His face was resolute. "I cannot offer her a life with no money, Cass! If I can make sure that we have a good livelihood, then maybe—maybe I could talk to her. I could give her what she deserves. But first I need to make these sales. We may have limited opportunities now after last week's ball."

Lady Darling strode toward them, her eyes hard. "I would like a word with you, Mr. Belvedere, if you would be so kind. In the garden."

Victor pulled Cass along with him. She almost tripped over her skirts as she tried to stay behind, but the look that he gave her over his shoulder was so filled with pain that she knew she must go with him if it would help him in any way.

There was no one on the terrace, and Victor wasted no time to plead his case. He faced Darling. "I know I have been inconstant, Lady Darling, and I can only apologize again and again for my behavior." He swallowed. "The truth is that I have the greatest esteem for you and have been too afraid of these feelings to share them with you. But I swear that if you give me a chance, I'll do better. Let Cass be my witness—she'll know if I transgress. If I step one foot off the straight and narrow, she has my blessing to tell you. Believe me."

"This is too intimate for me," Cass murmured, and stepped aside. If he had wished her to bear witness, she had done her duty, but further conversation should be held between them in confidence. "Do let me leave you to work this out between yourselves."

"Stay." Victor held her gaze. "Please."

"Your pretty words are for naught. I trust you not at all," Lady

Darling said. "You came straight from that tavern to my son's doorstep tonight, have you not? You have embarrassed me in front of my family."

He looked aghast. "I came here to increase my fortunes, so that I may have more to offer you. I would not dream of embarrassing you. Not for the world would I have done such a thing."

"Unless I am very much mistaken, you are filled to the brim with Dutch courage. I am afraid I do not appreciate the odor, nor the limpness of your cravat or the pink in your eyes."

Victor was a wreck of a man before her. "I admit that I have long relied on whatever I could in order to get through the nights. But I can see that there is so much more to life, if I embrace the days for what they are instead of hiding from them. Darling, there is so much I need to tell you, but I need your discretion."

"You could have had everything from me," she said softly. "But my patience ran thin."

A couple came onto the terrace, laughing, and Cass sighed. "This is not the right place for this conversation. Lady Darling, perhaps we could invite you to come to our house tomorrow to continue this discourse?"

"Yes." Victor seized on the idea. "Please do, and I will explain everything."

"Words are one thing, Mr. Belvedere, but I am afraid I need more than explanations."

"Then I will show you." His jaw was set, and his eyes were fierce. "Give me one month. I promise you that it shall be worth it, for I will make myself worthy of you."

CHAPTER TWENTY-FOUR

After they left the carriage and were in the privacy of Cass's bedchamber, Cass took Louise in her arms and kissed her.

"I have never even visited before," Louise said, looking around Cass's bedchamber with interest. "It seems most odd that we have spent so much time together, and yet none of it here where you live."

The townhouse that Cass leased with Victor was fashionable enough but snug. The paint was fresh and the furnishings were modern, but Cass smiled when Louise's eyes lingered the longest on the sizeable bed.

"Its charm lies in its location," Cass told her. "Victor insisted on staying as close to the Queen and Scepter as we could manage, and it is but a walk of ten minutes."

"That is a very good reason." She leaned against Cass and rested her head on her shoulder. "Queenie's has changed my life. I can only imagine the good that it has done him through the years."

Cass tipped her chin up and kissed her. "I am glad to have brought something good into your life, as you have done for me. I never told you how much it meant that you defended me against Lady Welton. I am unaccustomed to someone rescuing me, but am grateful that it was you."

"To be fair, you were holding your own against her. You didn't need me."

"But I did need you. I needed to see that you are nothing like her, once and for all." She paused. "It worried me to see you talking with her."

"She will be a duchess someday, so I have been polite for far too long. But no longer, given that I have now mortally offended her."

Cass grinned. "You *did* offend her. The shade of red that she turned was most unflattering with that pink dress."

"I should have done such a thing a long time ago." Louise looked up at her and held her tight around her waist. "I did it for you. And I did it because I was inspired by you. I love how you do not hesitate to say what you mean."

The last ill-stitched patch around Cass's memories of that summer was smoothed and settled like silk, covering the hurt like a balm. Louise was magnificent in temper, and that temper had been roused on her behalf. She had changed.

There was a chance for them after all. It was never too late to hope for love.

"Those words are the greatest gift you could have given me." Cass took a deep breath. "But I must know—what is our relationship to you? Pleasure? Sexual desire? Are you looking to lose yourself in the memories of youth and lost opportunity? Because I have far too much pride to be sought after for memory alone."

"You must know it's more than that. It's *love*, Cass. I love you."

Cass made a sound deep in her throat and she leapt at Louise, toppling her to the bed. "I love you, dear heart," she said fiercely, her voice muffled in between Louise's shoulder and the mess of hair that tumbled from its pins. "I love you."

"I wish I had said it fifteen years ago," Louise said, cupping Cass's face and gazing into her eyes. "I felt it then. I was terrified beyond measure, but I felt it. I wish you had known it."

"I think I always had," Cass said. "It would never have hurt so much if I hadn't thought that you cared. But I'm glad you said it now." She traced a finger down Louise's cheek, past her neck, and settled on her breast over her heart. "Perhaps I ought to show you how glad I am."

She kissed Louise with all the love she felt for her, hoping that her emotion was conveyed in her lips and her tongue and the touch of her hands, because she felt more alive than she ever had when Louise was in her arms.

Cass didn't care where her clothing ended up but needed it to be off her body in as little time as possible, so in between deep, lascivious kisses, she wrenched her spencer from her arms and tugged her dress over her head, and with one hand fumbled behind her back for the laces of her stays. It took some effort and some help from Louise, but soon they were both naked and in each other's arms in the bed.

Louise kept holding her face and kissing her, her mouth moving across her lips and pressing her tongue against hers, and then dropping kisses against her cheeks and her eyelids and her forehead.

Cass wanted nothing more than to be adored by this woman.

"I love you," Louise breathed, kissing her neck. "I love you."

"I love you."

Louise's eyes were shining, and there was the sweetest smile on her lips as she looked into Cass's eyes. Holding her gaze, Louise shifted on top of her. Bracing herself against the mattress on her forearms, she slid her thigh between Cass's legs until she had pressed herself tight against Cass's center. Soon she had angled herself so that with each gentle thrust, her own slick center connected with hers.

She brushed a strand of hair from Cass's forehead and kissed her, her breasts brushing against Cass's own and causing the sweetest of friction as she continued to thrust against her. They were gentle with each other tonight, tender in their movements, willing to savor each moment for as long as they could until they shattered in each other's arms.

❖

"Do you have any cards?" Louise asked afterward, snuggling close to Cass.

"There must be a deck somewhere. In the parlor, I think."

"Will you fetch them?"

Cass stared at her. "Now?"

"I can only know you if we play together."

"You do not think we know each other now? My understanding is that we could not be more intimate."

"All of my relationships are improved from seeing how one plays cards. Please indulge me?"

Cass sighed but agreed. In a quarter hour's time, she rounded up a deck of cards, a bottle of Madeira, and an assortment of cheese.

"This is lovely," Louise said, cutting a neat slice of brie. "It is as if we are at a fine supper after the very best sort of entertainment that I could imagine."

"I am happy to please."

Cass fell back into an armchair and pulled the wine bottle close to her. "I warn you now, I do not have a great deal of patience at cards, and I like whist not at all."

"The rules are simple—"

"Lou, even children play whist. I know the rules."

"Well, then. Shall we play a rubber and then see if we wish to make it more interesting?"

Cass waved a hand. "As you wish."

They played much slower than Louise was accustomed to. Cass did know the rules, but she dithered over each choice, scowling at the hand she was dealt as if it would change the circumstances that she found herself in. She kept little track of how many cards Louise played, and although took her time in contemplation, had a reckless style of tossing down face cards with no thought to whether she had a short or long suit.

After a few hands, Louise thought she knew enough of her play. "What are you willing to bet?" she asked.

"You know I dislike gambling." Cass pushed the pile of discarded tricks away, and Louise gathered them up to shuffle.

"You do not have to bet more than you are willing to lose, you know. It does not have to be all or nothing."

Cass shook her head. "Would you be content with penny stakes?"

"No, I would not."

"My limited fortune is tied up in gloves. I would have thought you had enough pairs from me that you would be little enough interested in another."

"I love your gloves," Louise said, and she meant it sincerely. "I would be happy with a new pair of riding gloves, if you would like to bet them."

Cass went to rummage through a box on her dresser and returned with a pair of buttery soft lilac doeskin gloves with a thin white leather bow sewn at the wrist.

"Those are delightful! But they do not look like riding gloves."

"Take them or leave them, Lou." Her voice held enough irritation that Louise decided to stop teasing. "What will you be betting, if you insist on something other than money?"

"Oh, I shall have to give you my vowels," Louise said, and scribbled something on a piece of paper. She folded it and placed it next to the gloves.

Now that she understood Cass's strategy—or her decided lack of it—Louise kept careful track of each trick and each hand and was able to adjust her own play accordingly. By the end of three hands, she was able to ensure that she lost.

"I am not sure that this was fair play." Cass eyed her. "Even I can see that you have far more skill than that. But I am glad enough that it is over, and I hope you were happy enough with the evening's entertainment even though I am a poor partner."

"You have a good deal of potential," Louise told her. "You also have enough beginner's luck to have won."

Cass leaned over and picked up the piece of paper that Louise had written on, and Louise held her breath as Cass opened it and stared at it.

"This was what you wanted when you sought marriage with Atwater." Louise was nervous. Cass was blinking down at the paper, but she was not smiling. "Now you can have it."

"The sheep? How is this possible?"

"I seem to have lost them to you in a card game." She shrugged. "It can happen to the best of people."

"But it isn't your farm to lose. It's Atwater's." She began to crumple the paper, but Louise stilled her hand.

"Not quite. He does have a farm, of course, and it is as prosperous now as it had been when you wanted to marry him. But these sheep are mine."

"I do not understand."

"Part of my dowry was a quantity of sheep to add to Atwater's holdings. Now that I am widowed, the dowry has been returned to me. I may sell it or gamble it or gift it as I see fit."

Cass's eyes were uncertain. "And what does it mean that you are willing to give part of your dowry to me?"

Louise had thought that this would be the most difficult part of all, but found the words were easily spoken now that she had already confessed her love for Cass. She took her hand in her own and met her eyes. "It is my commitment to you."

Cass inhaled sharply. "Commitment."

"It will be nothing like marriage," Louise acknowledged. "We can never have that together, of course. But if we both moved back to the Cotswolds, we would be neighbors, would we not? Our family's estates touch one another. And now you would have the farm, so it would raise no brows for you to spend a significant amount of time on my side of the pastures."

"I had not thought of such a thing." She nodded slowly. "I very much like the idea. After all, a walk of two miles is nothing when there is love to spur one's heels. But, Lou, this is too generous. This is a significant financial investment."

"It is one I want to make for you. And with you." She swallowed. "And because I think maybe Atwater would have liked for this to happen, in the end. He liked you. He almost chose you. I think there were times that he regretted that he had to choose at all."

"He was a good man. And you are a good woman."

Cass kissed her, and Louise's heart was full. She knew there were many things to talk about regarding the practicalities of their future, but they would find a way as long as they could do it together.

❖

"I don't wish to go to the ball tonight."

"We are not cowards. We belong in society if we want to be, and you already accepted the invitation a week ago. Would it be easier for you if we arrived together?" Cass tried to make light of it though it sent warmth all through her body to think of spending as much time with Louise as she could, wherever she pleased to be. "Would you like me to drive us in the curricle?"

She hoped it would make Louise laugh, but instead she sank further into the pillows. Socrates leapt up to the bed and pawed at the pillow until she moved enough for him to curl up beside her head.

"Where is his wisdom tonight?" Cass asked, stroking his head as he purred.

"He is showing me that the correct course of action is to stay right here. I don't know what could be wiser than that."

"That isn't wisdom. It's fear." She tried to say it as gently as she could.

Louise scowled. "I do not wish to see the Marchioness of Welton or her smug face."

"If you see her, so be it. You cannot hide forever."

"You ran away for fifteen years rather than face society's censure," Louise pointed out.

"Is that why you think I left London?" Cass was surprised. "Lou, there was nothing left for me here. Yes, my father was ostracized for losing so much of our fortune at cards. Yes, I wanted time to lick my wounds and heal my broken heart. But I stayed out of London because my priority was never the social whirl. I had business to take care of after my father lost his heart for it. I wanted to protect the glovers and the industry as best I could." She shrugged. "The opinions of wealthy lords and ladies who fawn over each other in a select few drawing rooms didn't matter much to me then, and not to me now. I want their money, not their approval, and I don't need to like them to sell gloves to them."

"Perhaps their opinions ought not matter, but my reputation reflects on Atwater, and our family. I have tried for years to make a sterling reputation for myself. It is a reflection of who I am—who I have strived to become."

Cass kissed her forehead. "You are making too much of this. Your actions were barely a ripple."

But when they arrived at the ball, Cass understood what Louise meant.

No one gave her the cut direct, of course, but it was a far cry from the constant stream of affection and greetings that followed in Louise's wake at every other event where she had been courted and sought after.

This was the first evening that Louise spent more time by Cass's side than not. Although Cass appreciated her company, she could see Louise wilting under the pressure, and her heart broke for her.

Louise gripped Cass's hand, and Cass looked down at their joined hands in surprise. "I love nothing more than to hold you, dear heart, but this will cause more talk than anything else you might have done."

"People will not guess at the nature of our relationship."

"I doubt that they would, but I meant that it must be odd to see the

Countess of Atwater clinging to a nobody's hand instead of talking and dancing all night with the somebodies of high society."

Louise squeezed her hand before letting go. "You are not a nobody."

"I never had any illusions to what these people thought of me."

She was quiet for a moment. "It is one thing to have ruined my own opportunity for a whist tourney, but it's quite another to have people frown at me all night like this. Atwater will not be happy."

"You are worth more than what your nephew thinks of your behavior."

Louise's face was pinched, and it sent a sharp pain through Cass. It was her own association with Louise that had caused society's censure. Maybe she should return to the Cotswolds early. Maybe it would help restore Louise's reputation if Cass was nowhere to be seen.

But she loved her, and could not bring herself to ever let her go. If Louise would have her, then Cass would stay by her side. There must be a way to bring the light back into her eyes.

Cass vowed to find it.

CHAPTER TWENTY-FIVE

Two weeks passed, with Louise refusing each and every opportunity to see anyone in society. She decided against going to the theater or the opera, and she even eschewed walking in the less fashionable parks lest she be seen. She dreaded the potential of speaking with anyone.

She told herself that it was not so very different from her life in London when the Season was over and everyone of note retired to the country, except that she could not bring herself to even shuffle a deck of cards, let alone entertain a game. She asked Cook for more cake in a week than she normally consumed, and the only guests that came to her table were Cass and her closest friends.

Shopping with Nell was the most she had been willing to do outside of her home, and she had even made a handful of purchases that she had not planned for. A small jade statue of a tree, which rested on her writing desk in her drawing room until she found a more suitable place for it. A silk velvet hat that did not match anything in her wardrobe but was a very fetching color. A book of poetry, which she was devouring every night with Socrates curled up on her lap for company. Nell had encouraged her to try a new scent, so she now had a glass vial on her wardrobe that filled the room with the aroma of lavender each time she unstoppered it.

"You must rejoin society at some point," Darling pointed out one evening over a cup of green tea.

Cass nodded in encouragement. "If you will not listen to me, then please do listen to Darling. You have always said that she has never once given you poor advice."

"I shan't give up society outright. Don't be absurd. I simply don't wish to see the inside of a ballroom anytime soon. The Season is almost over, and there is nothing unusual in not attending as many engagements these days. My absence will not be noticed."

"You cannot stay in your townhouse forever with Socrates. A change of air will do you good." Darling's face was concerned.

Louise sighed. "I did promise Atwater that I would make the acquaintanceship of a few ladies he is thinking of paying court to. I will need to host a dinner party." It was less daunting to invite people to her home than to think of going out.

"Will he still want you to do such a thing if you have not given up our relationship?" Cass asked gently.

Louise had told her about Atwater's censure of what he thought was a friendship between them. If he knew there was even a hint of anything more, he would be shocked to his core.

"If I invite him at the same time that I invite everyone else, he will have little choice but to dine with me. I have a duty toward my family that I will fulfill, whether or not he likes the way I go about things. This is the right time in Atwater's life to find a bride and have an heir, and I want to help him and the earldom."

"Family can have high expectations of one's behavior," Darling said. "I hope you do not relegate your life to fulfilling your duty. You must give yourself permission to seek joy."

"I love him as much as you love your sons," she said. "Atwater's family became my own when I said my marriage vows, and I want to see my nephew well settled, and happy. Love is neither a debt nor an obligation, but it requires us to think of others and to be selfless on their behalf, does it not?"

Darling had once accused her of pontificating when giving advice. She resolved to ensure that Atwater would be the one to make up his own mind on who he wanted to invite to his house party, and he would choose among them for his bride without undue input from her. He didn't need his aunt to make his decision for him, but she did want to offer him the choice of the kindest women she could find.

"Society will move on to something else besides you." Cass sipped her tea. "This is not a scandal that anyone can sink their teeth into."

"That is because it isn't scandal at all. That is what makes it harder. There is nothing to latch on to and thus nothing to move on from. There will always be the perception that I am rude and callous, or that I am disingenuous. That I say one thing and mean another. It will never be interesting enough to make the scandal sheets, but Nell has given me all the details of what people are saying about me, and it is not kind."

"The Marchioness of Welton was always jealous of you," Darling said. "She may well never let go of this opportunity to flaunt your supposed faults to whomever she can get to listen to her."

"Not everyone will listen to her," Cass said.

"Enough will." Louise sighed and leaned her head against the back of the armchair. "And the impact of it will affect Atwater."

Cass took a deep breath. "For too many years, I allowed my father's actions to dictate how I lived my life. I thought he had failed the glovers, and so therefore I must work to save them. But the rise or fall of our fortunes should not have been my burden. My family should have worked together and combined our strengths. We could have lived in greater harmony instead of the discontent that has been sowed between us for years."

"That is different. Your father took a risk that could have been well avoided, and he should have been the one to take action to correct the situation instead of letting it fall onto your shoulders. You were so young, Cass."

"His choices impacted mine. But I have been bullheaded too. I could not have succeeded here without Victor to help sell the gloves, and it took me a damn sight too long to realize it."

"How is Mr. Belvedere faring?" Darling asked. "I have not seen him since my son's dinner party." She leaned forward and perched on the edge of her chair, but her face held a look of studied indifference that did not fool Louise for one moment.

"Victor is doing well." Cass hesitated. "I cannot speak for him, so I do not wish to say anything that may increase your hopes—but he looks better than he has in a long while."

"I am happy for him."

"He has been instrumental in interesting people in the gloves. Victor has been most diligent about soliciting business. He conducted half a dozen meetings last Thursday, showing off our work, and gained us an order worth several hundred pounds." Cass's pride was clear as she spoke of him, her voice warm. "He has done an excellent job."

Darling's smile flickered. "I hope his fortunes continue to rise, if this has been the missing key to his happiness. And your own, of course. I wish you both well in your endeavors before the Season ends."

"As do I," Louise said. "I know you had counted on my standing in society to help get your gloves the recognition they deserve. I am sorry if I have impacted your business."

"You have been an enormous help, and I appreciate it more than I can ever say. But I never meant for you to be the ambassador of my gloves forever. Both of you have been very kind in securing invitations for us, and have given Victor and myself the opportunities we needed. There is now some interest in the Belvedere gloving, and I will be forever grateful. If that interest dwindles from the actions of the other night, then so be it. The past is fixed and we must leave it behind and forge a new path forward. Again, and again, and again—no matter how long it takes us, because our journey is never done until we are beneath the ground."

❖

In an effort to occupy herself, Louise insisted on helping Cass to organize her glove samples. She spent hours in the parlor with Cass, and sometimes with Mr. Belvedere when he decided to sit and embroider while they worked, and it was altogether pleasant.

Was this what she could look forward to in a sort of domestic companionship with Cass? It was perfectly lovely. Cass was solicitous of her every desire, whether it was for lovemaking in the afternoon, or whether she expressed a whim for poultry in aspic for dinner.

"You are terrifyingly efficient at this," Cass told her as Louise catalogued each pair of gloves by color, size, function, and pattern. She folded each one into a shallow paper box with a sachet of dried violets and stuck a note on each box to detail what was inside.

"I have a good eye for details, and I like to sort things into order. It's what makes me a good whist player." She saw the frown on Cass's face when she mentioned whist and blew out a sigh. "If I have moved on from my disappointment about the tourney, then you should, too."

"I wish for you to have everything that you want. It pains me that you do not have this."

Louise picked up another pair of gloves and wrote a description of it in the catalogue. "I wanted to prove myself to be the best. But why should I need accolades from strangers?" She knew she did not sound convincing, because she was struggling to believe it herself. She did want to feel singled out and lauded for her efforts, rewarded for the long hours and months and years of practice. Cards had both soothed her and had helped her feel like a better person, and recognition of her mastery over them would feel like receiving recognition that the person she had become had been worth all that effort.

"It is not wrong to want something for yourself," Cass said softly. "Neither is it wrong to want to succeed at something that you are passionate about, and to be counted among the best of them."

"I will be delighted to help you succeed at your passion instead."

"You are a wonderful help, and I appreciate all of your efforts. But I cannot help but feel that what you are doing is hiding from your life by sitting here with me instead of taking your place in society where I know you belong."

Mr. Belvedere entered the parlor, clean and bright as a new penny. "Hiding isn't living," he said to Louise, dropping a perfunctory kiss to her hand. "I know that better than anyone."

Louise pursed her lips. "Then why haven't you pursued Darling yet?"

"I told you I needed time to get myself straightened out, and that's what I've done," he said proudly. "I plan to pay a visit to her very soon."

Cass squeezed his hand. "I think Lady Darling will be delighted to see you again."

"I should hope so. I have not had a drop to drink in the past week, and I don't plan to drink to excess again. I have finished all the gloves that I set out to make. I have gone to Queenie's—I shall never give it up, and she will have to understand that—those people are my family and my dearest friends. But I don't need to stay out until all hours of the morning carousing with them. I have been too afraid to try a different sort of routine, but I must confess that it is one that I have longed for all my life."

He left, and Louise frowned down at the gloves in her hand. "Darling will indeed be delighted that he's doing so well, but I don't know what her answer will be."

"He will understand it if she can't accept him after the way he has behaved, but it will break his heart."

"She has played her cards close to the chest when speaking of him recently."

Louise knew Darling had been hurt by Mr. Belvedere, and she was not sure how much she would be willing to forgive.

Mr. Belvedere was right about one thing. Louise needed to be brave enough to grasp onto a new way of living. It might be different from what she was used to, but she had made her choice and she was never going to return to the past. Memory was all well and good, but she was finished chasing the way things had been, holding on to her routines and habits because they had once given her comfort.

It might be difficult, but it would be worth every minute to embrace something new.

To embrace a life with Cass.

CHAPTER TWENTY-SIX

Although Louise refused to attend a single rout or soiree, Cass continued to go with Victor to anything that they were invited to. She was determined to see the Season through to the very end to win as many orders as she could for the glovers. Victor had been building on the success that he had experienced at Mr. Darling's, where he had finally secured a handful of sales, and Cass was impressed that they had started to see a steady trickle of clients who came in for their hands to be measured and to peruse the leathers and samples in their townhouse.

Lady Isadore came to greet Cass soon after her arrival at the soiree that night. Cass was heartened by her loyalty to Louise in that she insisted on maintaining a friendship with her.

"When will we see Louise again?" Lady Isadore asked, frowning at her. "I thought where you might be these days, she would follow."

"Louise makes her own choices where to go. She follows no one."

"I had hoped she was feeling better. Nell and I are concerned about her."

"I shall relay your message to her when next I see her."

"You are as gallant as you are dashing." Her eyes lingered on Cass's dress.

"What I am is flattered," Cass said. "You are in fine looks yourself tonight, though you must know that you always are."

"You are proficient at flattery yourself."

"I am also observant. You seem to be at a great many balls this Season for someone who does not seem to wish to dance very often."

Cass had spent enough time with her quizzing glass looking for Louise across various ballrooms to be well enough acquainted with the routines of her friends. Mrs. Fenhurst and Lady Isadore flocked with Louise to the card room and the supper room and spent a good deal of time laughing together near the refreshment tables. But despite a surfeit of potential partners, Lady Isadore only ever danced once or twice of an evening, even if the musicians were to play ten sets of the most rousing country dances.

"You do enjoy plain speaking! The truth is that I have been a spinster forever and have no plans to change my circumstances. I am comfortable living with my cousins and doing as I like. Why should I change my life to suit a husband when I am enjoying myself as I am?"

"That is very wise from one so young."

"Five-and-twenty is not so young as that."

Cass noticed Lady Ingalls across the room. "I see a good friend of mine who I must go greet. Please do excuse me."

Lady Isadore glanced over. "Oh, you know the dowager duchess?"

Cass paused. "Duchess?"

"Yes, the dowager Duchess of Leverton."

"I think you are looking at someone else."

Lacy Isadore plucked Cass's quizzing glass from around her neck and peered through it herself. "That lady with the gray curls and the green silk hat and the yellow muslin? That is most definitely the dowager."

Cass was most definitely not sure about that.

"Ah! I was looking for you." Lady Ingalls beamed at her when Cass approached.

She didn't feel like grinning. "Waiting for a glass of champagne, ma'am? I would be happy to fetch one for you."

"I would indeed."

Cass hesitated. "I must confess to having heard a rumor about you."

"I love a piece of gossip. Do tell me all about it."

"Someone has told me that you are not a countess at all, and nor is your name Lady Ingalls—but you are duchess? The dowager Duchess of Leverton, in fact?"

She laughed, peals of laughter rippling out. "I wondered how long it would take you to cotton on to it! I knew you didn't recognize me when we met!" Instead of affronted, she seemed delighted.

Cass shook her head. "I do apologize, Your Grace. I thought I had

recognized you from my debutante year when I first saw you in May."
Embarrassment had her heart pounding as if she were a schoolgirl again.
"I meant no disrespect to you by having mistaken you for someone
else."

"I have enjoyed being incognito. My name really is Elvie, by the
way, and you are one of the few who are welcome to use it." Lady
Leverton patted Cass's hand. "It has been a delight to have someone so
solicitous of me on the strength of acquaintanceship and not because
I am a duchess. Even with the title, there are those in my family who
pay me as little heed as they can get away with." She snorted. "Without
my money, they would be absolutely nothing, and at least they have the
sense to acknowledge that."

"They do themselves no credit by dishonoring you."

"I heard an interesting piece of gossip myself recently. About you
and your friend."

"My friend?"

"The Countess of Atwater." Lady Leverton shook her head with
impatience. "I say, is it possible that you are you confused by *everyone*
you thought you knew?"

Cass was surprised. She didn't think the dowager had ever paid
attention to Cass's goings-on. "My friend is a woman of sterling
character."

"That may be, but I heard she is rude."

Cass was indignant. "That is far from the truth. She encountered
some snide behavior from an utter snob, if that is the source of your
gossip, and yes, she returned like for like in a way that was most
deserving."

"You seem to care a good deal about this."

"I am disappointed on her behalf. Unfortunately, the countess has
wanted nothing more than to be invited to some infamous whist tourney
but the lady in possession of the snide behavior is the hostess, and so
my friend will never get her chance to play despite being most skilled."

Lady Leverton tilted her head. "Who might this snob be?"

"I knew her once as Miss Emily Price," Cass said, with some heat
in her voice. It was petty of her not to use her title.

"Ah, that makes sense." She nodded and unfurled her fan, then
waved it in front of her face. "My grandson's wife has a viper's heart. I
didn't support the union, you know."

Cass reeled. There seemed no end to the surprises tonight. "You are *related* to her? Your Grace, my sympathies."

"She married into the family fifteen years ago. I have made my peace with it, but I don't care much for her. Emily is all simpers to one's face, and spitting fire when one is out of the room. I like to linger within earshot," she said peaceably. "I like to know what people are saying about me."

"I hope you hear delightful things. I must admit that you brighten my evening every time you cross my path."

"You, my dear, have a heart of pure gold."

"I wish I did," she said, staring down at her gloves. "But I have much to learn in life."

"We all do. Even at this age of mine, there is much to learn. It makes the journey all the more interesting, don't you think? If we never learned anything past the age of twenty, how very dull the rest of our lives would be!"

Cass laughed. "You are very right, Your Grace."

"I knew you were a good one, ever since that first night when you made sure I was comfortable. Now, I think I know how to cheer up your friend. I hate to see people suffering in the doldrums."

"Oh?" Cass had been caught off guard through the entirety of the conversation and could not fathom what else the dowager had in mind.

"I hereby invite you both to the house party at which the tourney is being held." She smiled when Cass gasped. "Yes, it's a very prestigious invitation, you know. Lady Atwater was right to yearn for it. We invite only two dozen people, and the tourney includes the prime minister and several dukes. It's an opportunity for you, too." She nodded at Cass's gloves. "These people have a lot of money, and I know your interest in business. My son is a man of some enterprise."

She hardly knew what to think. If the Belvedere glovers could earn the patronage of a duke, their fortunes would be assured. "How could I ever repay you?"

"What is this talk of repaying? People are allowed to do things to make others happy. You have made an old lady happy all Season. Perhaps it is I who is repaying you."

❖

Cass was so anxious to give Louise the news of the dowager Duchess of Leverton's invitation that she checked to see if the curricle was available, but Victor was not home and neither were the horses. Too impatient to walk, she flagged down a hackney instead, and was so giddy that she almost forgot to breathe on the quick journey to Mayfair.

She tossed a coin to the driver and exited the cab. To her great surprise she saw Victor hurtling down the same street in the curricle, the horses' hooves clattering on the cobblestones. The well-trained mares stopped at the brush of his whip, but the curricle was so light that it swayed. One wheel must have hit the curb at an awkward angle, for the curricle tipped and Victor tumbled out from the high perch of the seat. He let loose a strangled cry as he hit the ground.

"Victor!"

Cass ran across the street to him and knelt at his side, not caring about the dust that settled in the folds of her skirt. "Are you hurt?"

His eyes were already open and he was struggling to sit up, bracing himself on his elbows. "Nothing but a scratch, I am sure."

"What on earth are you doing here at Louise's house?"

"Louise? Why would I be here to see her? I am here to see Darling."

Of course. Cass remembered now that she only lived three houses down the street from Louise.

"Are you drunk?" Lady Darling cried out.

Startled, Cass looked around. The crash had brought people out from their homes, and Lady Darling was among them.

Cass's heart sank. *Had* he been at Queenie's?

Victor stumbled to his feet, brushing away Cass's hand as she tried to help him. "Not at all. I have given up excessive drink in the past month. I have embraced a different sort of life altogether. I had to visit my sister in Islington to fetch something from her and was impatient to bring it here."

Cass sucked in a breath. Though Victor's sister did not live far from them, they never spoke to each other. It must have been an errand of utmost importance.

Louise came out of her house with a pair of footmen in tow and stopped short when she saw them. "Cass? Mr. Belvedere?"

Cass waved her over. Louise directed her servants to help with the curricle and then joined Cass's side.

A thin trickle of blood seeped from a cut on Victor's forehead, and his knee was buckling, but Lady Darling stood there like a Valkyrie and glared at him. He pulled out a box from his suit and opened it to reveal a glittering ring.

"This was my mother's, given to her by my father on their wedding day. My sister was in possession of it, but I am the eldest. I know she wished for me to have it to give to my bride-to-be. I thought that day would never come, until now."

Lady Darling gasped.

"I am not the easiest person," Victor said, but his head was high and his back was straight. "I can admit to that. I know my flaws. Arrogance is one that I have been accused of many times. My inclination toward strong drink is another. I am stubborn and I have an iron grip on my grudges. We have a great deal else to talk about before I can ask anything of you, and before you agree to anything, I beg of you to listen to what I have to say with an open heart. But I wish to make my intentions clear. I want to marry you, Darling, if you will have me."

"Even the best of diamonds needs a little polish before it is set in its band." Lady Darling hesitated. "I do, too. I can be impatient with people, and I have a tendency toward stoicism that has not always helped me in my life. But if you can be honest with me, then I shall be honest with you. I find myself wanting to be everything that I am with you, with fears and no secrets. Maybe we could spend the rest of our lives growing more polished with the years."

He strode up to her and kissed her, one hand cradling the back of her head and the other at her waist, in plain sight of Cass and Louise and the servants tending to the curricle and the horses, before all the passersby who whooped as they crossed their path and before the footmen from other houses who had come out to see the commotion.

"I have so much more to tell you," Victor said, gazing down at Lady Darling. "But this is the perfect end to our imperfect courtship."

CHAPTER TWENTY-SEVEN

Cass's heart was full as she watched Victor follow Lady Darling into her house. Louise squeezed her arm, then took her hand and led her inside her own home, not stopping until she reached her bedchamber.

"That was wonderful to witness," Louise declared. "I am so happy for Darling."

"I am happy for them both. I know you once thought I opposed the match, but that was never the truth of it. I had wanted Lady Darling to be cautious because I was unsure if Victor would ever offer his hand in marriage, and I did not want to see her hurt."

"They will be good for each other."

"I think so, too."

"Fears of our future drove us apart before," Louise said. "I am still afraid to think of it. I am happy with what we have right now together, and I can think ahead by a few months or perhaps a year or two. But the idea of living in secrecy forever is daunting."

"We might not ever know what will come, but we can't be afraid forever. I don't like to let life happen. I vastly prefer choosing to live it instead."

"What if we make a mistake?"

"I have made my share of them. But when I look back on my choices, I see a life well lived. Above all, I want the chance to make mistakes by your side."

"I want what Mr. Belvedere and Darling have found together," Louise said. "I think we have found the same thing."

She kissed Cass, her lips expressing the depths of her feelings. They made love on the bed, and it was a slow sensual experience that

Cass would not soon forget. The afternoon passed in pleasure as they moved against each other, seeking comfort in their lips and tongues and fingers, exploring each other's bodies and experiencing ways of love that felt new each time they lay down together.

"Now I have a surprise for you." Cass pulled her shift on and rose from the bed after some time had passed, unable to keep still as excitement coursed through her. "I forgot once I saw Victor, but I came here to tell you something."

"This is turning into a surprising sort of day." Louise propped herself onto her elbow and watched Cass dress herself. "What is it that you have?"

"An invitation to the duke's tourney."

Her eyes widened and she sat upright, clutching the sheet to her breasts. "What? How?"

"Our mistake is that we thought that the marchioness was the person with the most power, but I made an unexpected friend a few months ago. My friend happens to be the dowager Duchess of Leverton, and the marquess is her grandson. We have been invited to the house party where the tourney is held."

"I cannot believe it! You are sure about this?"

"I have never been more certain of anything."

"How very unexpected." Socrates leapt into Louise's lap and began to knead his paws in the sheets. She lifted him onto the pillow, where he stretched and yawned before curling into a ball. "I appreciate this." She stroked the cat's head and he began to purr. She met Cass's eyes. "But the house party itself is not the tourney."

"You will have a seat at the table. The dowager promised it, and I trust her word." She pulled her dress on over her petticoat and began to lace it up. Long accustomed as she was at doing for herself, she fumbled with the strings. Louise's reaction was not what she had expected. "Why are you not excited? I thought you wanted this?"

"I do. I am grateful. I thought this chance was lost to me forever."

"And yet?" Cass didn't like the sight of the furrow on her brow. "You cannot mean to turn the invitation down because of what happened with Lady Welton? I know she will be in attendance, but this is the perfect opportunity to show her how little you care for her censure. If the duke deigns to pay attention to you, then the opinion of his daughter-in-law will mean much less to anyone."

"I would not dream of refusing the invitation! I would never waste the opportunity." She hesitated. "But this is not the same as being invited for my skill."

"It doesn't matter. You will show them your skill."

"But if I'm not good enough, I will waste their time."

"If you sat to play with someone below your level, but who was still very good—would you consider it a waste?"

She considered. "No. A good game is reward enough." She straightened her back. "Besides, I *am* good enough. I have believed it all Season—I must continue to believe it now, when it is most important."

"That's the spirit, dear heart. You can do anything."

"We can do anything," Louise corrected her with a kiss. "I suppose I will need to borrow Atwater's carriage. We cannot arrive at a duke's estate in my third-best carriage with its faded paint. Though I am not sure Atwater is enough in charity with me these days."

"The dowager told me that the estate is less than ten miles from London." Cass grinned at her. "I shall take the curricle."

"The curricle! On a journey of ten miles across country roads! You may do as you wish but I will not set foot in it. Your cousin came a cropper just now on a well-maintained city street. We shall never make it beyond the Thames without falling into some disaster."

"Let us be adventurous. I am an excellent driver."

"What about our maids?"

"I reckon a dukedom can spare a maid to share between us," she said cheerfully.

"And our luggage?"

"Do we need much? As long as we have a few presentable items, and as long as I have the showiest pair of gloves in our collection for you to wear to the tourney, we should be more than fine with a carpet bag tucked at our feet. Where is your spirit of adventure? There are always other options, but why not choose the one that will give us the most *fun*?"

"Is not a carriage more fun, in that we can be covered from the elements and have space to take what we need? I need more than a carpet bag if I am to visit a duke." Louise crossed her arms over her chest. "I am quite firm on this."

"Fine. If you think Atwater will refuse, I will ask round at

Queenie's if anyone has a conveyance that they could spare for a few days."

"That sounds perfect."

"Anything to please you."

❖

Driving around London with Cass in the curricle was dashing enough, but taking them to Leverton Manor in a borrowed barouche was an exhilaration that Louise knew she would never forget.

How utterly romantic it was. The sun was shining and the sky was a beautiful shade of blue, and she agreed against her better judgment to keep the hood down for the journey. The wind whipped at her hair and sent her bonnet ribbons dancing, and she could not keep herself from laughing with joy.

Cass's body was tense as she expertly controlled the horses as they flew down the dirt-packed lane away from London and set off on their grand adventure. She looked like an angel, handsome and bold and dashing.

Louise could trust Cass to get them to the manor.

There was no one she would trust more.

It was a notion that would have shocked her a few months ago. She would have never dared dream of traveling with no groom and no maid. It was not wise, and in fact it courted danger in a myriad of ways.

But being with Cass never felt dangerous. Louise had never felt safer in her life than when she was beside her.

It was a short journey, but Cass had insisted that they stop for a picnic luncheon along the way. Sitting beside the road in an open field with the sun on their bonnets, Louise felt as if there was nothing that could go wrong.

"Are you nervous?" Cass packed up the remnants of their hamper. She stood up, shook the grass from her skirts, and stretched.

"Ever since the twist of fate that provided us the opportunity to attend the house party, everything has gone right." Louise remained sitting and tipped her head up to feel the sunlight on her cheeks. She wanted this moment to last forever.

"Everything?" Cass's smile was teasing.

Louise counted off her fingers, admiring the stitching on the York tan gloves that Cass had given her the day before. "Mr. Belvedere and Darling are now engaged. I have won every hand of cards that I have sat down to play with Nell, Isadore, and Darling in the past few days. I am astonished that they have been as patient as they have been, but they have been so marvelously happy for me. Darling's daughter-in-law, Katherine, has been safely delivered of a daughter. There is no more room for bad luck these days."

"That is encouraging, as we did encounter more than our share of it already."

Louise looked up at Cass, who was pressing her hands against the small of her back and rolling her shoulders in preparation for the next leg of their journey. The journey that Cass had undertaken on Louise's behalf. The one that she had orchestrated without even knowing it, through her kindness and thoughtfulness to the dowager. This woman was extraordinary.

"Perhaps everything went right ever since the night that I insulted Lady Welton," Louise said slowly.

"That is a curious statement if I ever heard one. Are you feeling the effects of too much sun? Or was there a hidden bottle of wine in the hamper that you did not share with me?"

Choosing Cass was like choosing a whole new life. One that felt freer and easier, even though there were things she found difficult. The secrecy of their union would always be hard for her, but the moments that they shared together were worth more than anything.

"That moment led to this one and will soon have us at a duke's doorstep, won't it? I would be grateful for that fact alone. But more importantly, that wretched night brought us together. I have loved these past few weeks with you, where we have spent so much time in each other's pockets. I have learned a great deal about myself, and I feel so much more capable of love than I ever thought I could be." She took a deep breath. "I was always so afraid of losing my temper, and I had not realized how often I avoided any situation that would result in such a thing from happening. I was so tightly wound around my routine and my cards and my schedule of events that I have not even gone back to the estate since Atwater died—I have spent all my time doing all the same things in the same way in London. Until I met you again, Cass. You've changed my life."

Cass reached out her hand and pulled Louise up. "You changed your own life." She cupped her face in her hands and kissed her. "It was you who said yes to these opportunities. You could have turned me down when I asked you to wear the gloves. You could have turned tail as soon as you walked into Queenie's that first night. You made all the choices, dear heart. It is your strength that has led you to wisdom now."

"How I would have regretted it had I never experienced any of these things! And worse, if I had never stepped foot in Queenie's, I would never have realized how very much of life there could be to regret."

Louise hugged Cass tightly before they set off again for Leverton Manor.

The prospect of the tourney should have been among the greatest stresses of her life, but instead of fear and worry, she felt at peace.

With Cass by her side, she could accomplish anything.

Whether Louise won or whether she was the first to be ousted, she had now made it almost to the table. There was not much that she could change at this point, whether she fretted or not.

It was an attitude that she would be forever grateful to Cass for helping her to find.

It was satisfying beyond measure to arrive at the ducal manor east of London. It took over a quarter hour to drive the barouche up the path that wound its way across the grounds. The house was visible from every turn of the path, growing larger until Cass stopped the horses at the front steps and could see that in fact it was nothing short of palatial. It soared four storeys high, with two wings that sprawled in either direction across the manicured lawns studded with precisely planted trees. A marble fountain gurgled from the middle of a glassy lake that looked like it would never dare to ripple in the presence of such nobility.

Cass marveled that she was here as an esteemed guest.

She was grateful that Louise had insisted on taking a larger carriage than the curricle. As grand as she would have felt tearing up the path and roaring the horses to a halt, she was glad that the barouche had enough space for a small trunk of clothing. A duke's business was something to be courted, and she could not bear to approach him in a sadly wrinkled dress that she would be forced to wear multiple times in the week.

"Is that Lady Atwater and Miss Cassandra?" a voice called out as Cass and Louise were following a footman to their bedchamber.

Cass walked to the open door of the parlor where the dowager was taking tea with the duke. "Indeed it is, Your Grace. We are most gratified to be here."

"We are most pleased you could accept our invitation," the Duke of Leverton said.

They were dismissed when Leverton returned his attentions to his mother, and Cass and Louise curtsied and left their presence.

"He has always been cordial," Louise said to her as they resumed their walk to their bedchamber behind the footman who carried their trunk on his shoulder. "It is very kind of him to greet us. I have never been invited to any of the balls that his wife has thrown in London, but I have seen him many times through the years at different events. Atwater had a passing acquaintanceship with him—he belonged to the same club."

After the footman left, Cass sat on the edge of the bed. "I think this is a feather mattress—how very grand! I must say that the ducal accommodations are a sight above what I am accustomed to. Can you believe that we shall consider this to be our home for the next few days?"

It was happenstance that they were sharing a bed tonight, though it was far from unusual to share a bedchamber with a friend or another guest when accommodations were tight. The room was not large, but beautifully furnished with a Hepplewhite side table and a cheval mirror set into an elaborate mahogany frame.

"Our home," Louise repeated, warmth in her eyes. "I like the sound of it."

It was a sort of play-acting, Cass supposed. As if they were married. As if such a thing were as possible for them as it was for Victor and Lady Darling.

It would always pull at her heart that she could not publicly claim Louise as her own, not even in front of her friends. And yet, perhaps they could have more than she had dreamt.

There could be other opportunities like this one, after all. There was no reason that they could not go to and from the same events together. Louise and Lady Darling had done so for years, sharing a carriage and attending most of the same engagements with no one thinking anything of it.

Why could she not have a similar relationship with Louise? Society would soon accept that where one went, the other would not be far behind. Lady Isadore had seemed to expect no less of them at the soiree the other night, and Cass doubted that she had even an inkling of their true relationship.

It might not be as much as she wanted deep in her heart, but it would be something. If all she could do was grasp at straws, she would try her best to gather enough to make a house of dreams where they could live.

CHAPTER TWENTY-EIGHT

Cass stared into the trunk, both hands grasping the edge as she put her face so close to it that she was almost inside it. "I do not believe this. They're gone."

Louise paused in the middle of arranging her brush and lotions on the dresser. A maid had been assigned for them to share, as they were also sharing a room, but they had dismissed her after she had finished putting away their clothes. "What is gone?"

"The mittens." Her eyes were wild. She wrenched herself away from the trunk and tore at the carpet bag that she had brought along with their trunk. "They aren't here."

"The ones that I am to wear at the tourney? But it is tonight!"

Cass overturned the carpet bag onto the bed and shook it, but nothing came loose from its depths. "I don't know what could have happened."

"There was that one point in the journey when the barouche rounded the corner so sharply—could the box have been flung out of your bag?" She hadn't seen such a thing happen, but she didn't understand how else it could have been dislodged.

"If that is the case, how could I have been so careless!" Cass's face was white, her eyes round.

"It was not carelessness. It is happenstance."

"What if I have left them in London? Perhaps they are still in the parlor with the other gloves that we catalogued." She slumped into a chair and held her head in her hands.

It was a monumental disappointment for Cass. She had been so excited to display the best of her gloves at the tourney. Louise was sure that she would have packed them as carefully in the carpet bag as if they had been made of gold.

"Perhaps they are in the barouche?" Louise suggested.

Cass brightened and was out of the bedchamber without another word. It was not long before she returned, but Louise knew from her hunched shoulders and the slowness of her pace that although she was clutching the mittens, she did not have good news to share.

"I did find them." Defeat was heavy in her voice. "But they are ruined."

She tossed them to the bed, and Louise picked one up. The white lambskin was dirty, and the embroidery had snagged. The design was beautiful—a peacock feather, studded with tiny crystals and pearls. But she could see where there were jewels missing, and there was a rip near the palm.

"Victor worked his fingers to the bone with the gold and silver embroidery. The crystals would have glittered in the candlelight, and I am certain that people would have remarked upon them."

Cass was more upset than Louise had ever seen her.

"They are beautiful."

Louise was touched that Cass and Mr. Belvedere had worked so hard on what she was to wear tonight. She knew the opportunity was as important to Cass as it was to her, but she also knew that Cass had put a great deal of thought into the design. She had thought of *her*.

"They were beautiful," Cass corrected her. "Now they are but scraps. I reckon they fell out of my carpet bag and onto the floor of the barouche. A groom showed me to the stables and the gloves were half-hidden in the hay near the horses. I think one must have stepped on them. Although I might be able to remove the dirt with enough time, there is no amount of brushing that can remove scuffs and scratches from leather like this." She paced the room. "I have time enough to drive to London and return with another pair, but it would mean missing dinner tonight. I think it would look most odd if I were to deposit you here and leave immediately."

"Do not worry about how it would appear to others," Louise said. "You have not cared a whit about such things all Season, and you should not start now. I want you to have the best opportunity that you can to show the gloves that you want."

Cass bit her lip. "I do not wish to cause offense to the dowager. I cannot disrespect her after she has been so kind. We would not be here if it were not for her."

"I would have loved to wear a pair of Belvedere gloves tonight. I will have to make do with white kidskin, or perhaps a pair of Limericks if it looks like it might be less formal. But all is not lost. After all, you will be wearing your own gloves sewn by your own hand, and you will be able to talk of them to whoever will listen. There will be plenty of other opportunities at this house party to speak of business."

"I do have one other pair." Cass hesitated. "But I hadn't meant for them to be displayed."

Louise's interest was piqued. "A second pair? That was clever of you. Excellent thinking."

"You are the strategist between us. I confess I didn't give a moment's thought to ever needing another pair! No, this was meant to be a gift." She sighed. "I was going to wait and present them to you after you won the tourney."

Louise burst into laughter. "There is no guarantee that I will win! Oh, Cass. How sweet you are!"

The tips of her ears reddened. "I don't know about sweet. But I wanted you to have a keepsake."

Cass went to the drawer where her belongings were stored and rummaged through it until she found a slender white box. She held it close to her chest as if loath to hand it to Louise. "It seems portentous to give you this now. I do believe you will win, Lou. I didn't think of you wearing these gloves at the tourney, but maybe it makes sense that these should be yours now."

She thrust the box at Louise. "Open it."

Louise eased the lid away and lifted the white silk that protected the gloves inside. What she drew out had her gasping. "Oh. Oh, Cass."

"They aren't as magnificent, I know that," Cass rushed out. "There's no jewels. Nothing but plain embroidery floss."

"I love them." Louise stared down at them.

The gloves were pale yellow, delicate and soft and perfumed with Louise's own scent of vanilla and honey—how clever Cass had been to include it! But it was the gloves themselves that charmed her. Little daisies were embroidered down the length of the arm and on the back of the glove. She remembered once that Cass had picked her a bouquet, and to her mother's bemusement Louise had insisted on placing them on the table beside her bed so she could look at them every night until she fell asleep.

"They are beautiful."

Delicate, charming, and pretty. They were not showy, but they were cut to perfection, as soft as a dream, and gorgeous in their utter simplicity.

"I embroidered the flowers myself," Cass said. She hesitated, then drew out a scrap of fabric from the pocket of her frock. "I don't know if you remember, but once upon a time, we argued over who Atwater would dance with next. You bet your best handkerchief, and you lost. And—well—I kept it."

"All this time?"

"All this time."

Louise took it in her hands almost reverently. Her first instinct was to dab at the tears running down her face with it, but she restrained herself. She gazed down at the fine linen, the wildflowers that she herself had stitched into all of her favorite handkerchiefs at the age of seventeen, next to the initials *LS* for Louise Sheffield in the center.

It was a tangible reminder of their intertwined lives, their past catching up to their present and defining their future.

"I cannot believe you kept it."

"I loved you, dear heart. I have always loved you."

"I love you, too."

Louise leaned forward and kissed her, everything that she could not express in words passing through her lips, the tears on her face now running down Cass's own cheeks. She sought to put all of herself into this moment, even as memories flooded her of the girls they had been together, and of Atwater. It felt as if she honored his memory by honoring the people that they had once been. For he had liked them both and had always been happy to see them together as friends.

He had never known of their affair, of course, but somehow now that all had been said and done and all this time had passed, she rather thought that he would have found a way to understand it. Oh, how she would have liked to explain to him. She had loved him, too. It was a different kind of love, but did it matter how one loved as long as one *did* love?

She drew back and brushed her tears away from Cass's face. "I didn't mean to get you damp."

"I don't mind," Cass said, her voice as soft as the well-worn handkerchief that they were now clutching between them. "I have done my share of crying over the memories, too."

"I love that you kept this, and I love that you thought to embroider the gloves with the daisies. I would be honored to wear them to the tourney."

"They may not garner much interest in the gloving business," Cass said, looking down at them. "They may be too plain for such a prestigious crowd. But I want you to wear them. I want you to think of my love every time you make a play and look down at the gloves in your lap. I want to give you every ounce of support in my body, and to be as close to you as I can get even though I won't be at the table."

Cass made her feel as if she could do anything.

Louise took a deep breath. "I have a tourney to win."

Excitement rushed through her.

Cass had thought it might be difficult to attend dinner with the Marchioness of Welton, but it appeared as if the presence of her father-in-law had subdued her. She did not so much as glance at Cass or Louise, for which Cass was grateful.

She was surprised to be seated near the middle of the table instead of the very end and knew that the dowager Lady Leverton must have had a hand in arranging the table. Cass had expected haughtiness from everyone she met but was cheered when she discovered that they were refreshingly easy to converse with. The duke had excellent taste in dinner guests.

If all of the society events had been like this, the summer would have been a good deal better.

Throughout the evening, Cass stole glances at Louise, seated farther up. She was so damn proud of her. She knew how much Louise had wanted to be here tonight, and it was wondrous to witness her ease with the other guests as if she had known them for years. Louise held her head high as she spoke with the duke after dinner had ended, most likely thanking him again for the invitation. She was as comfortable conversing with the duke as she was with Her Majesty at the Queen and Scepter.

That was her woman, Cass wanted to proclaim to the people around her. That was her own dear Lou.

It was enough that she knew it in her own heart.

CHAPTER TWENTY-NINE

With four tables drawn up for sixteen guests, the drawing room felt cozy even though it was thrice the size of Louise's. The French doors were open to the garden and the heady scent of freesia wafted in on the summer breeze.

Louise had hardly partaken of the dinner, sumptuous as it had been. She had watched as footmen presented dishes of caviar and platters of duck and salmon and French beans, and although she took a few bites of each course, she was unable to recall how any of it tasted. She had drunk no wine, as her mind whirled enough with excitement and she wished to be as sharp as she could be when they sat down to play.

Now that she was in the drawing room, her belly clenched with nerves.

Her hands began to sweat in the beautiful daisy gloves, and she drew them off to keep them in her lap for the rest of the evening.

It was terrifying, the prospect of playing with these people.

It was also exhilarating.

She looked down at the gloves, then over at Cass standing at the side of the room. She lifted her champagne glass and smiled at her, and Louise felt peace. All would be well. She had made it to the tourney and had a seat at the table. The rest could not be determined, but she was ready to give it her all.

"I win most of the tourneys," the dowager duchess said as she sat beside Louise. "I am pleased you are here as it has made my friend Miss Cassandra happy, but I do play to win."

She was methodical, reminding Louise of Darling, and Louise was impressed when Lady Leverton won the hand even when she felt a keening disappointment as it meant that Louise had lost. She was still able to move forward, but not against the winning players of that hand, and she knew it put her at a disadvantage.

The play was sophisticated, and fast. The baron seated across from her in the second round had a way of running his thumb under his cards when he had a high trump card in his possession. The lady that the baron was paired with had a faint squint when she played from her weakest suit. The other gentleman Louise could not read at all, and as he was her partner, it made for an interesting game.

She was cautiously optimistic when she and her partner won that round, and the opposing pair left their table and new opponents sat down for the next hand.

The evening passed in a whirl, but she would never forget the crisp feel of the cards in her hands, the hush in the room as the play progressed, and the honeyed vanilla scent from the gloves in her lap mixed with the freesia from the garden. For as long as Louise lived, she knew she would be able to recall the cleverness with which her partner in the third round finessed with a queen and then took the last trick with the ace, and the sheer luck that allowed her to win the sixth round with a meagre four of spades, and the certainty that she was playing among her equals in skill and also in temperament.

These people were here due to the love of the game. The duke was part of the draw, but the tourney was not studded with sycophants. These were serious-minded players, who had as much love for the game as she did.

It made the thrill of victory even sweeter during the hands that she won and tempered the sting of disappointment when she lost.

Although she had told herself to keep confidence in herself, it was still a shock to be seated at the last game with the last four players, the other twelve having been eliminated.

The duke had been ousted in the penultimate round, but Lady Leverton had won her way until the end and sat next to Louise and across from a poet. Louise's partner was a member of parliament who played a little more recklessly than she cared for.

Only three more hands were between her and potential victory.

Louise stared at her whist marker with its etching of cats and mice slinking across the tabs. She considered it a good luck talisman as much as a practical accessory to the game. Having it beside her on the table reminded her of purchasing it when she had been with Cass, and it steadied her nerves as much as looking at the gloves on her lap, the daisies bringing to mind memories of their youthful affair. Her old handkerchief was folded in her pocket. What would that girl have thought if she had been told that one day she would be seated at a duke's table? It would have astonished her.

In this moment, before the game began, she had everything. She knew from long experience that the anticipation of the last hand could be almost better than winning. She loved the feeling that all outcomes were still possible. The most wretched loss could come before the most glorious win, because everything came down to this final round, without any importance given to what came before.

It was Louise's turn to shuffle for the last game, and she took it as a symbol of good luck. She always preferred to shuffle, as it helped provide her with much-needed clarity before playing.

Time slowed as her world narrowed to queens and kings and spades and clubs, each card noted and analyzed as each trick was won and swept away and a new trick began. There was a routine to it that Louise loved. Every movement had its purpose, and every trick had its logic. It was orderly and regimented, but that didn't mean that there wasn't drama in each hand.

Finally, the last card was put down, and Louise and her partner had won the tourney.

Everything she had done to arrive at this moment had been worth the effort.

All the work she had poured into herself had been worth it. *She* was worth it.

She wished Darling and Nell and Isadore were there to see her win, but she knew they would love to hear her recount the tale when next she saw them.

The most important thing was that Cass was here to witness her triumph, and that was sweeter than the win itself.

Much later that night, after they had a bit of celebratory supper and champagne and after Louise had talked to everyone she had played with, Louise lay in Cass's arms and allowed herself to relax.

She had made so much of this tourney for months, and it was almost strange to consider that it was now over. The cards had been dealt, she had won, and life was much the same as it had been yesterday.

"You were magnificent," Cass said, and pressed a kiss against her temple. "I am so proud of you."

"You helped me," Louise said. "I drew strength from your presence. With your love, I can do anything."

"It was your skill and your perseverance that rewarded you tonight."

"But it's worth all the more because you were at my side."

The weeks after the Duke of Leverton's whist tourney brought a turn of fortune that Louise found most satisfying. News of the duke's good opinion and of Louise's triumph at the table had spread across London, and though the Season was over and there were far fewer social engagements, Louise had been welcomed and fêted wherever she chose to attend.

Louise was sitting with Cass in her parlor, and she noted a new pair of gloves in the catalogue. Business had been excellent for the Belvederes, because before they left Leverton Manor, the duke had ordered half a dozen pairs of gloves from Cass. He had cited a dire need as the hunting season had started. Louise suspected that the dowager had pressured him to place the order, but there had been no mistaking the genuine appreciation on his face when he had been shown the pair of gloves that Louise had brought to the tourney.

"I must return soon to my house," Louise said, turning the page and making another note. "The dinner I am hosting for Atwater's potential brides is tonight, and he means to send the invitations to his house party next week. I do hope you will be joining me?"

Atwater had accepted Louise's friendship with Cass since their return to London. Now that the duke's family had shown partiality to Cass, she was considered refreshingly forthright and a credit to any entertainment at which she was present. Once word was out that the duke had ordered sheepskin hunting gloves, Atwater had done the very same thing, and it seemed that half the members of his club followed suit.

Atwater had never revealed the details of the awful wager that Mr. Pierce had made about Cass in the betting books, but did confide in Louise that it had been scratched out and that nothing more would be made of such a thing without one of the Belvedere gloves being slapped across Mr. Pierce's face.

Society was fickle. Where one turned against her, they all had turned against her. But where favor was shown by a duke, they were quick to follow.

"Stay another half hour," Cass said. "I wish to consult with you on something."

"Oh?"

"In the bedchamber," Cass clarified with a grin.

Before they were halfway up the stairs, they heard the front door open.

"Is this the house of Mr. Victor Belvedere?" A voice boomed out as boots stomped toward the drawing room.

"Her Majesty!" Louise gasped after she came back downstairs with Cass. It was most odd to see him without his wig towering on his head, or his leather apron on. He looked as plain and unassuming as any gentleman.

He winked at her. "Mr. Harris outside the tavern, if you please. We don't blaspheme outside those walls, too dangerous by far! Doesn't change who I am, now, don't believe nothing different. I'm a man who believes in prudence. I heard you lot needed help with the gloving. I'm here to lend a hand."

Mr. Belvedere entered the parlor halfway through Mr. Harris's speech. "Ah, Mr. Harris. Thank you very much for coming over."

"What do we need help with?" Cass glanced between them with a puzzled frown.

"You're forgetting I was a brick layer by trade, before I bought the Queen and Scepter," he said, dusting his hands together. "I'm here to see about putting on a little shop to the front of the house."

Mr. Belvedere grinned. "We won't lay one brick without talking it over first with you, Cass, but I thought Mr. Harris could help us sort through what we might want to do."

He scratched his beard. "I think we could make do here without too much fuss," he said, looking around the room. "This room here would do well enough with some work on it, but are you sure you want to do business out of a townhouse? If you like the sight of something else, you could rent a little storefront somewhere and I could help fix it up for you."

"I hadn't thought at all about doing business in London," Cass said.

"I don't want to return to the Cotswolds," Victor admitted. "I want to stay in London. But I want to be part of this venture together, Cass. We work well together, and I want to do my part for the family fortunes. I thought maybe we could have a shop here, and I could sell and show people the gloves."

"Not without me," Cass said. She gazed at Mr. Harris. "Do you think we could find a little space in the back for a leather workshop?"

"You can't make all the gloves by yourself in London," Mr. Belvedere said.

"No, I never could. But I've enjoyed working on samples. Maybe we could take the bulk orders and have them made up by the glovers back home, but you and I could do custom work together? What do you think?"

Louise was delighted. She had wanted to stay in London too, and had not thought of the possibility that they could find a way to stay. This was perfect. "What a wonderful idea."

Mr. Belvedere grasped Cass's hand and shook it so hard that Cass complained, laughing.

"To our shared success," he said.

"To making our dreams come true. Each and every one of them."

EPILOGUE

Ten years later

Cass pulled a piece of thin tan leather tight against the sharp edge of the table before rotating it and stretching it in the other direction. The hides from Louise's sheep farm had proven time and again through the years to be a most superior quality, and it had become a hallmark of the Belvedere gloves. They had found a devoted clientele through the years that sustained the village back home with plenty of work.

The Duke of Leverton had proven instrumental in that regard. He had continued to voice a preference for the Belvederes' workmanship every year or two, and each time he did so, the glovers were flooded with almost more orders than they could handle. They had expanded the sheep farm and were considering doing so again next year.

"Remember, you need to make the hide as pliable as you can," she explained to Nancy. "Else you will have a stiff pair of gloves instead of one that fits properly to the hand. Preparing the leather is as important as cutting and sewing it."

Nancy nodded. She was Darling's eldest granddaughter and had been intrigued by Cass's work with leather since she was a young girl. At fifteen years of age now, she had declared that she wished to learn all she could from Cass as an apprentice of sorts.

Cass had liked the idea, and with Darling championing it too, it hadn't taken long for her parents to agree. Nancy had moved in with Cass and Louise to the Chelsea townhouse where she helped with the storefront on the first floor in the mornings to learn all she could about the business and studied the art of glove making with Cass in the afternoons.

Cass ran a blunt tool down the length of a ruler to score a perfect rectangle on the leather before cutting it, and then placed her pattern on top and ran the tool around the paper in the shape of the glove hands and fourchettes. She explained to Nancy every step, the same as she did each time she made gloves, and the same as the old glovers in the Cotswolds had done for her when she had apprenticed. Each piece of leather was different and could have its own inconsistencies in dying, or blemishes to cut around, so each piece that she ever cut felt entirely familiar and yet new at the same time.

She wouldn't give these gloves to Nancy to stitch, though Nancy was excellent at all forms of needlework. This pair was important for Cass to make by herself, so she dismissed Nancy for the day.

Victor interrupted her as she was cutting the last of the fourchettes. The years had been kind to him, gracing him with fine lines near his eyes that added to the dignity of his face.

"What is this you are working on?" Victor peered down at the pieces she had placed on the table. "Very fine work."

"It should be," Cass said. "They're for you."

"For me!"

"I am making you a gift to celebrate your tenth wedding anniversary next week."

After all these years, the pride Victor had in his wife had him puffing out his chest. "Darling is still the greatest gift of all in my life."

"Such a feeling does you great credit, but these gloves will be counted high in the list." She made one final cut and beamed down at her handiwork. "I have cut a pair for you and a pair for Darling from the same hide, so they will be perfectly matched. I thought you might like new riding gloves for your trip to the Lake District later in the summer. They will be magnificent."

He laughed and sat beside her. "Neither of us ever did learn much humility, did we?"

"We try, dear Victor. It is all anyone can expect of us. And we certainly did learn it where it counted, in matters of the heart."

"Your Louise is almost as grand a woman as my Darling."

"We are fortunate to have a well-matched pair of women in our lives."

Louise had moved in with Cass within a year of their love affair. She and Darling had found it inconvenient to live so far apart from one another after having been neighbors for such a long time, so Victor and Darling had decided to purchase a townhouse on the same street in Chelsea. None of them paid the least amount of attention to ceremony and were wont to visit one another at any hours of the day.

"It was the grandest happenstance in all our lives that our wives are the best of the friends," he said.

They could never marry, but Cass and Louise had long considered themselves to be wedded in every way that counted.

"Your wedding was a joy. I am happy to celebrate it each year."

"That is because you were delighted by the party that we held at Queenie's that night."

It had been a night to remember, though the memories were blurred through the vast quantities of rum punch that Her Majesty had poured with a liberal hand. Someone had brought a fiddle, and another a flute, and then some of their friends had clattered up the street with a harpsichord in a wagon. A group of them helped haul it inside and pushed it into the corner where it remained to this very day.

Louise had volunteered to play that evening, and the voices of their friends joined in song to celebrate Victor and Darling had been something marvelous to hear.

Louise and Darling entered the parlor, looking fine as sixpence. "We are on our way to Nell's to play whist," Louise announced. Her love of the game had never dimmed, and she, Nell, Isadore, and Darling held card evenings at their houses each week.

Cass pulled Louise close and kissed her cheek. "Give my love to her." She had become close with all of Louise's friends, and though she enjoyed their company, she had never learned to enjoy cards.

"I will. And I will give you all my love upon my return."

"Like always," Cass said, and kissed her again.

"From now until forever."

About the Author

Jane Walsh is a queer historical romance novelist who loves everything Regency. She is delighted to have the opportunity to put her studies in history and costume design to good use by writing love stories. She owes a great debt of gratitude to the local coffee shop for fueling her novel writing endeavors. Jane's happily ever after is centered on her wife and their cat and their cozy home together in Canada.

Books Available From Bold Strokes Books

All For Her: Forbidden Romance Novellas by Gun Brooke, J.J. Hale & Aurora Rey. Explore the angst and excitement of forbidden love few would dare in this heart-stopping novella collection. (978-1-63679-713-7)

Finding Harmony by CF Frizzell. Rock star Harper Cushing has to rearrange her grandmother's future and sell the family store out from under her, but she reassesses everything because Gram's helper, Frankie, could be offering the harmony her heart has been missing. (978-1-63679-741-0)

Gaze by Kris Bryant. Love at first sight is for dreamers, but the more time Lucky and Brianna spend together, the more they realize the chemistry of a gaze can make anything possible. (978-1-63679-711-3)

Laying of Hands by Patricia Evans. The mysterious new writing instructor at camp makes Grace Waters brave enough to wonder what would happen if she dared to write her own story. (978-1-63679-782-3)

The Naked Truth by Sandy Lowe. How far are Rowan and Genevieve willing to go and how much will they risk to make their most captivating and forbidden fantasies a reality? (978-1-63679-426-6)

The Roommate by Claire Forsythe. Jess Black's boyfriend is handsome and successful. That's why it comes as a shock when she meets a woman on the train who makes her pulse race. (978-1-63679-757-1)

Seducing the Widow by Jane Walsh. Former rival debutantes have a second chance at love after fifteen years apart when a spinster persuades her ex-lover to help save her family business. (978-1-63679-747-2)

Close to Home by Allisa Bahney. Eli Thomas has to decide if avoiding her hometown forever is worth losing the people who used to mean the most to her, especially Aracely Hernandez, the girl who got away. (978-1-63679-661-1)

Innis Harbor by Patricia Evans. When Amir Farzaneh meets and falls in love with Loch, a dark secret lurking in her past reappears, threatening the happiness she'd just started to believe could be hers. (978-1-63679-781-6)

The Blessed by Anne Shade. Layla and Suri are brought together by fate to defeat the darkness threatening to tear their world apart. What they don't expect to discover is a love that might set them free. (978-1-63679-715-1)

The Guardians by Sheri Lewis Wohl. Dogs, devotion, and determination are all that stand between darkness and light. (978-1-63679-681-9)

The Mogul Meets Her Match by Julia Underwood. When CEO Claire Beauchamp goes undercover as a customer of Abby Pita's café to help seal a deal that will solidify her career, she doesn't expect to be so drawn to her. When the truth is revealed, will she break Abby's heart? (978-1-63679-784-7)

Trial Run by Carsen Taite. When Reggie Knoll and Brooke Dawson wind up serving on a jury together, their one task—reaching a unanimous verdict—is derailed by the fiery clash of their personalities, the intensity of their attraction, and a secret that could threaten Brooke's life. (978-1-63555-865-4)

Waterlogged by Nance Sparks. When conservation warden Jordan Pearce discovers a body floating in the flowage, the serenity of the Northwoods is rocked. (978-1-63679-699-4)

Accidentally in Love by Kimberly Cooper Griffin. Nic and Lee have good reasons for keeping their distance. So why does their growing attraction seem more like a love-hate relationship? (978-1-63679-759-5)

Frosted by the Girl Next Door by Aurora Rey and Jaime Clevenger. When heartbroken Casey Stevens opens a sex shop next door to uptight cupcake baker Tara McCoy, things get a little frosty. (978-1-63679-723-6)

Ghost of the Heart by Catherine Friend. Being possessed by a ghost was not on Gwen's bucket list, but she must admit that ghosts might be real, and one is obviously trying to send her a message. (978-1-63555-112-9)

Hot Honey Love by Nan Campbell. When chef Stef Lombardozzi puts her cooking career into the hands of filmmaker Mallory Radowski—the pickiest eater alive—she doesn't anticipate how hard she'll fall for her. (978-1-63679-743-4)